FAERIE REALM

THE CHANGELING CHRONICLES: BOOK THREE

EMMA L. ADAMS

This book was written, produced and edited in the UK, where some spelling, grammar and word usage will vary from US English.

Copyright © 2024 Emma L. Adams
All rights reserved.

No part of this book or cover was created by AI, and no part of this book is permitted to be used in AI training.

I stood ankle-deep in a swamp, the Mage Lord at my side. A circle of iron surrounded us. The blade in my hand was iron, too, as were the swords Vance could grab at a moment's notice and the daggers sheathed at my waist. Considering we were here to meet a faerie who'd tried to kill us once already, we had good reason to be laden with as much protection as possible. Assuming she showed up at all.

I tapped a foot. "She's late to her own appointment."

"Maybe she's hiding." Vance studied the oak tree in the clearing's centre. "Can you see anything unusual?"

I tilted my head but saw no weird shimmering that usually indicated a faerie glamour. "No."

Unlike me, Vance didn't have the Sight. In fact, I didn't know any other humans who had the ability to see through the fae's illusions, as mine had come about as an unintentional side effect of stealing a Sidhe Lord's magic during my escape from captivity in the faerie realm. Not exactly a common human experience, though my accumulated wariness around the fae hadn't stopped me from getting myself ensnared in a bargain with the Lady of the Tree. I owed her a favour in exchange for her offering me information on how to find a pair of missing human children, and while the lead she'd given me had nearly ended in my death in an old station, she'd kept her word in a roundabout way. Therefore, I was bound to hold up my end of the bargain, and typically, she'd decided to call in her favour when Vance and I were making out.

You could always count on faeries to have the worst sense of timing.

"What manner of faerie is she?" he asked. "Not Sidhe?"

"A dryad," I said. "An ancient one. And powerful."

Her roots had nearly skewered me to death during our last encounter, but in Faerie, words were power, and it was the vow I'd sworn to her that had come back to bite me. The Sidhe—the highest class of Faerie, with egos to match—could literally command the world to rearrange itself on a whim. Their promises gained a life of their own. The Lady wasn't quite on that level, I didn't think, but she'd still managed to drag me halfway across the city on the strength of a vague agreement we'd made weeks ago and that I'd almost forgotten about, given the sheer tsunami of crap the universe had thrown at me since then.

Among other things, I'd nearly died twice, and I'd nearly witnessed the end of the world as we knew it. Okay, I'd spared us from near-catastrophe when I'd killed the half-faerie Calder and sealed the magic he'd unleashed, but the Lady of the Tree hadn't given me long to recover before she'd decided to give me an unpleasant reminder that no favour from a faerie came without a knife in the back. Or branch.

"Didn't she claim to be dying?" Vance said.

"We should be so lucky." I scowled at the giant sprawling oak tree. This area, once the Botanical Gardens, had turned into wild forest when the faeries invaded, and it was easy to forget we were in the middle of the city. "Guess it was too much to ask for the universe to give me a break."

Or a proper date with Vance. Standing in the mud waiting for a foul-tempered tree to deign to speak to us didn't count. Recent rain had turned the ground to marsh and while Vance's polished shoes were covered in the usual dirt-repelling spell, I had to balance on top of a raised part of the ground to stop the water leaking into my boots. My ears picked up on every small noise and I kept reaching for the sword strapped to my waist each time a leaf fluttered to the ground. Irene's blade gleamed in the weak sunlight streaming through a gap in the grey cloud cover, and I idly wondered if giving the tree a firm poke would be worth the risk if it brought an end to the monotony.

As I pulled the blade partly from its sheath, the nearest tree root began to stir. *I knew she was here.* I glanced down to check that the iron ring surrounding us remained unbroken.

Then I looked back at the tree and damn near fell *out* of the ring. A face stared back at me. Not the broken old faerie woman I'd seen last time, but a complete stranger. This face was youthful, beautiful as any faerie queen, with high cheek-bones and velvety green eyes. Her full lips curled in a smile. Curly brown hair framed her elegant features, though as before, the rest of her body had merged with the wizened oak tree.

"Ivy Lane," she crooned.

Whoa. This was the Lady of the Tree—but not as I'd seen her before. A young and beautiful stranger, not an ageing crone who'd told me she was dying.

"Did you get a facelift or something?" Shock had obliter-ated my filter. Not that I was usually the epitome of polite-ness, least of all when it came to the fae, but I hadn't thought it was even possible to reverse the effects of being trapped in the mortal realm long-term. Not without going back home.

She smiled, disregarding my rudeness. In the corner of my eye, I saw Vance shift on his feet as though preparing for an attack.

"I have my immortality back," she said, "thanks to the veil opening, and allowing me back into Faerie."

My jaw hung slack. "Uh… what?"

No way. The path to Faerie had opened to the Grey Vale, not Summer or Winter. The Courts existed on another plane entirely to the dark forest where the Sidhe sent outcasts and exiles. The faerie who'd opened the veil—Calder, son of Avalin—hadn't known the difference. Neither did most half-faeries. Probably for the best they didn't. The Grey Vale was a life-sucking death trap, and I'd been lucky to escape on the two occasions I'd ended up in there myself.

"I was able to return to my home," said the Lady of the Tree. "When the veil opened, the layers between the realms thinned enough for me to cross over, but in the process, I learned that something is gravely wrong. The heart of one of the Great Oaks of Summer is missing."

"What… in Summer?" My heart sank when her beautiful face crumpled, and tears streamed from her bright-green eyes. Their brightness told me her magic was at its peak—or as powerful as it could be here in this realm, anyway—yet that only made her expression of utter devastation more pronounced.

Not that there was any guarantee it was genuine. Faeries might not be able to lie with words, but they could deceive in other ways, and it made zero sense for the Lady to have made it to the Summer Court where no other outcasts had ever achieved the same, as far as I knew.

"My home is dying," she whispered. "I am the Lady of the Great Oak. I know when a heart is torn from one of my fellow trees, and I need the help of someone who has ventured beyond this realm to retrieve it."

"You need…" Ah, *shit*. "Look, I've never been to Seelie territory. I physically can't, and I thought you couldn't, either. Isn't there someone else you can ask? Someone actually *in* Faerie?"

"The heart of a Great Oak Tree of Summer was *stolen*." Her vibrant green eyes locked onto mine. "And it was brought into this realm."

"This realm?" I repeated. "How do you know?"

"I know." Her voice rose higher, gaining a grating edge that set my nerves afire. Her story had more holes than my old jeans did, but the dangerous undercurrent to her voice warned me that our bargain remained intact, and that she wasn't the weakened creature she'd been during our first encounter.

"Er… how exactly am *I* supposed to find this missing heart? I'm human."

"You carry the magic of a Sidhe Lord."

Ice slid through my veins. "Who told you that?"

Half the city probably knew by now, but I didn't want my circle of enemies to grow any bigger when it could have filled an auditorium already.

"He told me," she whispered. "Before you killed him."

My spine stiffened. "What… Calder? Or Velkas?"

"The boy came to me for a favour," she said mournfully. "The poor soul was desperate to return home, but that was a gift I couldn't give, and now it's too late for him."

"You do realise he tried to kill everyone in this city, don't you?" Between this and how she'd looked the other way when those children had been taken, there were few people I was less inclined to offer a favour to. *Damn. How to get out of this bargain?* "How long were you working together?"

"I merely offered him a bargain, as I did to you."

"What, you sent him into a creepy train station and nearly

got him killed?" I spat at her. "Yeah, I'm not doing you a favour. You can forget it."

"Our promise is binding," said the Lady of the Tree. "If you fail to bring me what I desire, you will die."

Well. There is that slight issue. "How am I supposed to find this… this oak tree's heart? I don't even know what it looks like."

"You will know it when you set eyes upon it," she said. "That I guarantee."

"And what's stopping *you* from searching for it?" I kept one eye on the root snaking along the ground as I spoke to her. "Sounds like you just want me to do your dirty work for you. There's no reason why you can't find the heart yourself."

"Wrong." The ground trembled underfoot, and I unsheathed my sword, feet braced. "You and I are bound, and you *will* bring me what I desire."

Beside me, Vance hissed out a breath. The roots circled him, close enough to press against the iron barrier where he stood. A jolt of alarm hit me. The Lady might need me, but she didn't need the Mage Lord.

I'll kill your mage first, Calder's voice whispered in my ear.

The ground burst open beneath Vance's feet. He leapt aside, out of the iron circle, as two roots rose upward from where he'd stood.

"Hey!" I yelled. "That's not playing fair."

Vance extended his blade to point at the Lady of the Tree. Anger suffused his expression, manifesting in the form of black scales spreading from his weapon hand down to the hilt of the sword.

The blade disappeared from his hands and rematerialized in midair, slashing at the tree's root. A shrill, furious scream rent the air as a jet of bluish red sprayed out. *Time to go.*

I ran to join Vance and smacked into another tree root. My sword bit into the bark before it could get a grip on me, but the blade didn't cut all the way through. At another diagonal swipe, red-blue blood spurted out of the root, and a shrill scream came from the Lady of the Tree.

"I can't help you if you keep attacking us," I shot at her. "That includes Vance, too."

A root latched around my ankle like a whipcord, hoisting me up into the air. *Not again.* I swiped and slashed, freeing myself and flipping to land on my feet. Vance, meanwhile, was surrounded by roots rising from the ground like giant earthworms. His blade appeared and reappeared, leaving a trail of blue-tinted faerie blood wherever it struck.

"Hey!" I ran at them, brandishing my sword.

A thick root blocked my path, and a crooning laugh echoed from behind. Anger sparked, and I whipped one of Isabel's explosive spells from my pocket and hurled it at the Lady's face.

A shimmering green barrier appeared, and the spell dissolved before it made contact with the trunk. Her Summer magic might not be at its peak in this realm, but she'd acquired some new tricks since our last fight.

The tree roots continued to circle Vance, slicing and stabbing, but the Mage Lord moved quicker, cutting off any attempts to grab him. As I tried to reach his side, a tugging sensation lurched through my body, pulling me towards the oak tree. I stumbled, no longer in control of my own limbs.

"Shit!" I yelled. "She's using the vow."

"Cease your attack," said the Lady of the Tree, "or I will bind you to me for life."

I had zero doubts that she would. All she had to do was twist the vow slightly and I'd be reduced to nothing but her puppet, doomed to do her bidding for the rest of my mortal existence.

Vance halted, his sword held defensively between himself

and the tree roots. The tugging sensation released me, and my feet stopped moving forward of their own accord.

I glared at the Lady of the Tree. "You'll get what you asked for, but if you hurt either of us, you'll regret it. And if you kill me, I'll make a point of coming back to haunt you personally for the rest of *your* immortal existence."

A deafening shriek rang through the forest as the Lady threw back her head and released a cry of anger. Roots stabbed upward and blue light flared as my own magic reacted to defend me, but before the Lady's attack hit, Vance's hand closed around my arm and the world disappeared in a whirl of motion.

I staggered away from Vance and caught my balance against a fence. We'd landed on a road, not one I recognised at first.

"Damn," I said, shaking bits of soil off my clothes. "That was a close call. Where are we?"

I scanned the detached houses lining the street. Judging by the neat lawns and the fancy cars parked in front, we'd ended up somewhere on mage territory. Vance's mouth was a tight line, and black scales covered his wrists and hands.

"Vance?"

He shook his head. Gradually, the claws replacing his hands began to recede, until the sharp scales disappeared into skin.

I peered at his unmarked hands. "Does that hurt? The scales?"

"No."

I raised an eyebrow at the slightly dismissive hint to his tone.

"Not anymore," he elaborated. "Shifting is... uncomfortable, at first, though no more so than magic is."

"Magic," I said. "Yeah. Mine pulled me into *Death*, so I get it. Anyway, I don't know how to use it to do what the Lady asked. What does the heart of a tree even look like?"

He shook his head. "I can't say I know, but a source of pure faerie magic in this realm wouldn't go unnoticed for long."

"There is that."

Vance's grey eyes darkened. "Unfortunately, the sort of people who will be inclined to seek out this object are no doubt the ones we least want to get their hands on a store of Faerie's power."

"Tell me about it." My thoughts flickered back to Calder. "Guess we'll have to talk to the Chief again. He might know."

The guy had barely begun to regain control over his territory after Calder's power play had sent him on an unexpected misadventure into Death, but that wasn't my problem.

"That should be our first move, yes," Vance said. "I would hope the last two weeks have opened his eyes to the serious damage that can be inflicted if he neglects his duties."

"Better hope so."

I re-sheathed my blade, then brushed some stray bits of dirt from my new jeans. The whole outfit was new, in fact, down to the leather jacket and boots. Vance had—completely without my permission—replaced all my clothes the other week. I hadn't begun to consider how I'd repay him for it, though I appreciated how he'd respected my taste rather than forcing me to adopt the style of the mages. I'd look ridiculous in a smart suit, though Vance managed to make formal attire work in pretty much any scenario.

"The Chief has been occupied with arresting people involved in the recent incidents," Vance said. "But I'll try to secure us a meeting."

"He's Seelie," I said. "Well, half of one. Maybe he'll be able to sense where this source of Summer power is. I sure as hell can't."

"Perhaps," said Vance. "Regardless, he can no longer bar us from accessing his territory. His refusal to accept my help cost many lives. He has blood on his hands, and he knows it."

"Yeah." What with spending the last week in recovery mode, I hadn't seen the full aftermath of the chaos when a bunch of his people had fallen under a drugged spell. "Doesn't mean he'll be pleased to see us, though. Last I saw of him, we were both dead."

Vance's eyes darkened. "No, you weren't. And I won't let that happen again."

Damn if it didn't warm me all over to hear the protective undercurrent to his voice. "Don't worry. I don't plan on dying anytime soon." I checked that my sword and the daggers on the sheaths inside my sleeves were in place. I generally carried two at a time, secured so they wouldn't get dislodged when, say, a faerie dangled me upside-down.

"Ready?" asked Vance.

"As I'll ever be."

Which is to say, not at all. What an absolute mess. If the Lady of the Tree had gone back to Faerie when the veil cracked open, had others, too? Had someone sneaked into Summer and stolen the tree's heart, or had the thief already been inside Faerie itself? I'd always thought the human and faerie worlds were far enough apart that people in this realm, even faeries and half-bloods, were generally unaware of anything that might be occurring on the other side of the veil.

Except *them.* The outcasts, like Velkas and Avalin. Might other Sidhe have come here, like they had during the invasion? More to the point, why the hell would anyone steal a powerful magical object and bring it into the *mortal* world?

The Sidhe hated our realm, and their power sources were all but useless this side of the veil.

Unless someone *wanted* the Sidhe to lose their power.

Someone like... a lord of the Grey Vale.

2

Even with the dominating presence of the Mage Lord at my side, I remained on guard for hidden traps as we approached half-blood district. High hedges circled the territory, while the gate bristled with sharp thorns. Nobody waited outside, but at a small gesture from Vance, the gate swung open.

"How'd you do that?" I squinted at the thick hedges from which the gate appeared to have sprouted, but I saw no mechanism by which to open it.

"Used my abilities on the lock," Vance said.

"There's a lock?"

"If you look closely."

I grinned. "Didn't know you were into breaking and entering."

He flashed a smile at me in return. "Let's say I had no concept of limits when I was first exploring my powers."

Interesting. I suspected it'd take a while to get used to the idea of being this deep in the Mage Lord's life, and him being so deep in mine. Not just because Vance was head mage, but the idea of someone knowing and understanding the hell the faeries had put me through, and pursuing me anyway, was at total odds with everything I'd experienced over the last ten years since my return from Faerie.

Vance was also my employer, technically, though my contract was with the mages as a collective. I was reasonably sure he wouldn't screw me over, but until recently I'd been at the mercy of Larsen Crawley, owner of the local mercenary guild and the single worst employer on this side of the veil. For the mages, I'd be doing the same job for ten times the pay and the added bonus of insurance should something nasty cause me a life-threatening injury.

Speaking of life-threatening. As we stepped through the gate, a voice shouted, "Mage Lord!"

The words rippled through the territory, and half-faeries stopped to watch us enter. Most were dressed casually in regular human clothes, but several wore the armoured coats of guards. While faeries often didn't bother with clothing at all, the warmth of Summer had given way to the frosty tint of Winter magic, and the chill in the air made me glad for my leather jacket. Despite the weather always being in one Court's favour, Summer and Winter fae intermingled without argument in a way that they never did in their own realm. Seelie fae favoured bright clothing that complemented their vibrant green eyes and hid any less humanoid traits they might have, like hooves or feathers. The Unseelie, by contrast, wore dark colours for the most part, and were more likely to expose their claws or fangs on show for the world to see.

And every single one of them was staring at the pair of us.

I rolled my eyes at Vance. "If you wanted to sneak in without being noticed, you missed your chance."

"That wasn't my intention."

"Sure it wasn't." I returned my attention to our rapidly growing audience, and my heart dipped when I heard someone whisper my name. They knew me, and the odds were high that they also knew I'd fought Calder and stopped him from ripping open the veil. Maybe they even knew I had their magic, if the Chief had told them. Most looked more curious than afraid, with the exception of the guards eying my iron blade with tight-lipped expressions.

Vance strode forward to address a group of armoured warriors. "We're here to speak to the Chief about a confidential matter. Can you take us to him?"

"Chieftain Taive is too busy to speak with mortals," said a silver-haired guard I vaguely recognised as the guy who'd given me my first introduction to half-blood territory.

"That's his name, huh," I said. "Well, the Chief and I have an understanding." Namely, that he knew I had the magic of a Sidhe Lord, and I'd sincerely prefer it if he didn't tell anyone else. Having faerie magic was one thing. Killing a Sidhe Lord, even an exiled one, was the sort of crime that had got Lord Avalin exiled from the Courts in the first place. Some half-faeries would hate me on principle, if they didn't already.

"You're carrying iron," said the guard.

"I have reason to expect to defend myself." I gave a pointed nod to the gathering crowd. Alain wasn't amongst them, and her unpleasant boyfriend was presumably locked up for murder, if not dead. "I've been attacked here before."

Angry whispers passed amongst the half-faeries, but Vance spoke over them. "As leader of the Mage Lords, I request an audience for Ivy and myself with the Chief. I might remind you of who was pivotal in preventing the recent riots from consuming your territory."

The silver-haired guard cast a glare at the visible hilt of my blade but stepped forward. "We will take you to him. If you use iron, we will treat you as we would any other criminal."

"That won't be necessary," said Vance. "Provided we're given no reason to defend ourselves against attack."

A slight breeze accompanied his words that warned he was prepared to unleash his power if necessary. The silver-haired guard beckoned, and a dark-skinned Summer female with armour made out of overlapping bark-coloured plates joined him. Together they led the way through the winding path alongside a river. Summer had long gone, and dead leaves were all that remained of the once abundant flowers blooming at every corner.

Vance didn't speak, and I wasn't in the mood to start a conversation with the faeries, so we walked in silence until tall blocks of flats loomed over us on both sides. It wasn't compulsory for half-faeries to live in this territory—and some of them had human families—but most flocked here to the area that mimicked Faerie itself better than anywhere else in the city.

When I'd returned ten years ago after escaping captivity in Faerie, I'd been horrified to find that Faerie had also infiltrated the human world. Yet now, the thought of the half-bloods' desperate attempts to win their way back home brought a twinge of sympathy I hadn't previously acknowledged. Calder had fooled the half-bloods into thinking he'd take them home, then drugged them into killing one another. He'd never intended to let them share in his glory if his plan had succeeded.

My lingering hatred for Calder dimmed the sympathy rising inside me. I couldn't afford to identify too much with people who, for all the human blood in their veins, belonged to a world that was poisonous to mortals. And given the circumstances of our last encounter, I figured their Chief would be as pleased to see me as I was to see him.

Our path took us out of the warren of flats and into wilder territory. Thick, woodsy smells crowded the air, underlaid by the faint scent of rot. Winged half-faeries flitted behind tree branches, while dryads peered from inside their trunks. I gave the latter a wide berth, reminded too much of the Lady of the Tree. Faerie played havoc on the senses and made it easy to fall into obvious traps, and while no one would be foolish enough to attack the Mage Lord, I kept one hand on my sword's hilt at all times.

The two guards led the way through a thicket of trees to a cottage that looked far smaller than I might have expected of the home of the half-bloods' leader. At first, I puzzled over the size and the apparent lack of defences, until I saw the shimmer of light on the walls indicating a heavy glamour.

Against my will, my own magic shone in response. From the way the two half-faerie guards stiffened, they'd also noticed the blue light rising around my arms. Crap.

I turned back to the cottage. A curtain had been drawn across the window, but it had to be much larger than it appeared on the outside, and the whole house gave me a fairy tale vibe that made my skin prickle even with Vance at my side.

"Chief!" shouted the silver-haired guard, rapping on the door. "Mage Lord's here to see you."

The door opened, revealing a hallway easily four times the size of my flat and an interior more like the mages' head-quarters than the tiny house it appeared to be on the outside. The polished wooden floor reflected a ceiling overhung with vines and other dangling plants laden with thorns that made my hand jump to my blade. Bloody reality-distorting faeries.

"Another visitor?" The voice came not from the Chief, but from a man standing beside a side door into the entrance hall. He had a silvery sheen to his dark-brown skin and the bright-green eyes of a half-Sidhe. "Taive, I think it's the Mage Lord."

You think? Who was this dude? Given that he was in the

Chief's house and had used his actual name, I assumed they were friends or romantic partners, though with the Chief's general temperament, I was surprised he had either.

"Mage Lord." The Chief strode out of another doorway, back at full power compared to the wreck he'd been the last time I'd seen him. Not that that was saying much. He was scarcely taller than me and carried a staff that looked more like a stage prop than the powerful talismans wielded by true Sidhe lords of Faerie, while his gold-trimmed crown might have come from a charity shop. Now that he wasn't covered in dirt or bleeding, his inhuman handsomeness was more evident, but I had zero interest in his too-pretty face or silky dark hair.

"Chief." I raised a hand in greeting. "Nice to see you're back to normal."

The Chief's watery green eyes narrowed when they passed over me, and he didn't acknowledge my presence. "Leave us," he told the guards. "You too, Killian," he added to the other half-Sidhe.

"Do you always let him boss you around?" I asked Killian, who retreated through the side door. "Not cool, Chief."

The Chief spun on me and growled, "You will not talk to him."

Okay, romantic partners, then. That he'd found someone willing to tolerate his unpleasantness was more of a revelation than that he'd let us into his house.

With an imperious gesture, the Chief beckoned Vance and me into an office carpeted in what looked like actual grass and decorated with beds of blooming yellow and purple flowers. I positioned myself in front of an oak desk that was formed from the actual stump of a dead tree. The smell of decay didn't touch this place, and I stood stiffly on the spot, trying not to look at the creeping vines snaking along the ceiling and wishing we'd opted to meet outside instead.

I'd had some level of curiosity about how the half-bloods ran their territory, but I'd recently concluded the answer was 'badly'. The Chief had been fully aware of the Trials despite their illegal nature and had refused to put a stop to them even after Vance's warnings. Avalin's son Calder had turned out to be the one responsible, offering supposed faerie blood as a prize that turned out to be a drug designed to drive half-bloods into a killing frenzy. After several people had died, including another Mage Lord, I'd infiltrated the Trials myself. That had spurred Calder to put his true plan into motion. He'd trapped every half-faerie in the city he could reach under the effects of the drug so that he could channel their power into breaking the veil.

The Chief was supposed to save everyone. Instead, he'd been knocked out cold by a death stealer, and with him incapacitated, I'd been forced to speak the Invocation to seal Calder's magic myself. I'd damn near died in the process, but from his sour expression, the Chief had no intention of thanking me for it.

I regarded him with my best pissed-off mercenary glare. "Have you recovered from your injuries?"

A ripple of anger passed over the Chief's face. "No thanks to you. You left me to die."

"I thought you *were* dead," I cut in before Vance could speak. "We had to stop Calder. It was nearly too late, because you decided not to listen to our warnings."

"Enough," said the Chief. "You people deal in lies—"

"Like you're the paragon of truthfulness," I interjected. "Have you told the others about the Grey Vale yet?"

His silence said it all. I'd figured he wouldn't want to deal with the fallout of telling the other half-bloods that that the miracle Calder had offered wasn't the chance to return to the Courts but to certain death. Most faeries didn't know about the Grey Vale unless they'd been exiled there. I'd barely escaped alive myself, and certainly not unscathed.

"They'll figure it out eventually," I warned. "Or someone'll try to scam them again. Calder wasn't the first. Does the name 'Lord Velkas' mean anything to you?"

"I'll have no more attitude from you, Ivy Lane."

"If you don't already know, Velkas was an exiled Sidhe Lord," I went on. "He decided it'd be fun to open the veil via the human world and invade the Courts. Just in case you wondered where Calder got the idea."

"It hasn't escaped my attention that both times the veil has opened, *you've* been at the centre."

"Because I closed the damn thing." Blue swirls of magic danced off my skin in response to my growing annoyance. "You have some nerve accusing me. Besides, I'm not here to talk about that."

Vance spoke. "We're here because a faerie told us that Summer is losing its magic. She claimed that the heart of a Great Oak had been stolen and brought here to this realm."

The Chief's mouth fell open, his fury giving way to shock. "What?"

"It's true," I said. "I'm bound by oath to find this missing heart. Unfortunately."

"You're what? How can you..." His eyes flared a deeper green. "Humans should not be privy to the deepest secrets of our kind. You are not one of us."

"I don't want to be," I returned. "But I've been strongarmed into securing the Lady's missing property, so you're stuck with me until I do. She'll kill me if I can't fulfil my end of the bargain, so I have incentive enough to tolerate your attitude."

"You're lying." The Chief's Summer-bright eyes narrowed.

"Nobody could possibly have brought the heart of a tree from Faerie here to the mortal realm."

"Whether it's true or not, Ivy is bound by a promise to find and return the heart to the Lady of the Tree," said Vance. "Whether it exists or not, she certainly believes it does."

"The Lady of the Tree left her sanity behind in Faerie." He tapped the edge of his staff against the floor dismissively. "She is not to be trusted."

"Yeah, I figured," I said. "But if I don't obey her, I'll die, so I kinda have to take her word for it that this heart is findable."

"You think I care for the lives of mortals?"

"You *are* one." Annoyance bubbled to the surface. "Pull your head out your arse and accept you aren't in Faerie, however much you'd like to pretend you are."

The Chief slammed the heel of his staff into the ground. "You haven't the right to come in here and talk to me like—"

"She does," said Vance, "because, as Mage Lord, I have appointed her as my chief liaison for dealing with the faeries."

I did my best not to show my surprise. "What he said. Also, I saved all your hides, in case you've forgotten. You owe me."

"Get out," snarled the Chief. "You'll get your information, if and when I have it, but you'll never set foot in here again."

The floor opened underneath our feet. I fell, legs kicking, arms flailing as I tumbled down an earthen tunnel. A second later, my feet hit the path outside the cottage. Bitterly cold wind struck me in the face, and I staggered against Vance.

"Damn," I said. "Why not just show us the door?"

3

Outside the Chief's house stood the two guards from earlier, their swords unsheathed as though to ensure we didn't set foot in there again. From the way the temperature had notably dropped, Vance was pissed off.

"You will come with us," said the silver-haired guard. "Your meeting with the Chief is over."

"We can see ourselves out, thanks," I told him. "Tell your boss that if any of you start losing your magic, it's his fault."

I fell into step with Vance, though he didn't speak on the way out. His grey eyes had turned cold, and the air crackled with suppressed power. I didn't blame him. The half-faerie Chief was an irritating little shit who'd deserve any consequences that came from not helping me find what the Lady of the Tree wanted. But I refused to die for his stubbornness.

I held my tongue until we reached the gate. Once outside the hedge, I let out a stream of expletives that I'd wanted to call the Chief right there in his territory.

"The incompetent fuckwit," I exploded. "He can't come

crying to me if this missing heart turns out to have side effects for the other Summer faeries."

"No," Vance said. "I confess I expected Chieftain Taive to be more accommodating this time."

"I guess nearly getting killed once wasn't incentive enough." I shook my head. "Disregarding the Chief, do you know anyone else who might be able to track down this missing heart? Maybe someone related to a high-born faerie from Summer?"

"The half-faeries don't all know their parentage," said Vance. "Particularly those living with their human families. The Chief might know who does, but he's not required by law to disclose the histories of people living on his territory."

"Dammit. We're at a dead end." I blew out a breath, frustrated. "The Lady of the Tree probably wants me to fail."

"Do you think he's right?" asked Vance. "About the Lady being a liar?"

"She certainly twists words, like she did when she sent us into that train station," I acknowledged, "but I'm magically bound to solve this, and it's pretty unambiguous that I'll suffer some grisly side effects if I don't find this heart. Wherever it is."

"There are a relatively small number of hiding places for magical artefacts that will enable them to stay undetected." His phone appeared in his hand. "The other Mage Lords are requesting a meeting. I have to go, but we'll pick this up later."

"Can't you tell them we have important business?" He'd been with me all morning, admittedly, and Calder's attack on the city had left him a hell of a mess to clean up. "What time is it?"

"One o'clock. As your boss, I'm giving you the rest of the day off."

"Thanks for reminding me."

"You'd rather forget I'm your boss?" His phone vanished from his hand as he leaned in and his lips brushed mine. I let his subtly charged scent wash over me, a combination of clean air and muskiness, tinged with a cool hint of the power he was capable of conjuring with a single hand.

"Pretty sure you aren't supposed to do this to your employee," I mumbled, then kissed him properly. My fingers dug into his shoulders, feeling the corded strength under his thick coat.

The air whipped around us, and the next thing I knew, we stood on my doorstep.

"Unfortunately," he said, breaking off the kiss, "I really do need to be at this meeting. I'll call you in a couple of hours to see if we're still on for tonight."

Oh, I'm there. "I'll see if Isabel has any ideas to help me with the Lady's request."

"Do that. And please try to stay out of trouble."

"Can't make any promises." Grinning, I all but skipped into the house, startling Isabel on her way out the flat door. The large handbag she carried over one arm told me she was on the way to deliver a pile of charms to the coven leader.

"Someone's happy," she remarked. "I assume the faeries didn't ruin your day after all?"

Damn. There went my good mood. "Yes. Actually, they did. In an epic way."

Isabel sighed. "Oh, boy. Luckily, I have a bit of time before I need to drop in at Francine's. Tell me."

We went back into the flat and I ran through what had happened since I'd last seen her that morning. Which was a lot. I'd come out of a weeklong convalescence and confessed to Vance that Calder's ghost had threatened to kill him and scared the shit out of me. Then he'd asked me on a date, only to be interrupted by the Lady's inconveniently timed faerie vow dragging me halfway across the city.

By the time I got to the part about the Chief throwing us out, Isabel was shaking her head. "I should put a confinement spell around the flat for a day or two to keep you out of trouble, shouldn't I?"

"Trouble's found us here before," I reminded her. As if to emphasise my point, a loud thud from upstairs shook the ceiling. The Cavanaughs' young son, George, had probably knocked over another ornament.

"Fair point." Isabel shook her head again. "But really, if you don't help this ancient Faerie find this missing… heart, whatever it is, you'll *die?*"

"Yep." I headed to the kitchen to scrounge for some food and threw a sandwich together. "I don't even know what the heart looks like, but Vance seems pretty confident that a powerful magical artefact won't be hard to find."

Isabel, who was sweeping up bits of discarded spell from the living room floor with a dustpan and brush, flashed me a concerned look. "I know you walked over the veil into Death the other day, but a faerie vow is unbreakable, isn't it?"

"Yeah, enough to outdo pretty much any other kind of magic. Or even the laws of physics." I referred to how I'd challenged Avalin to a duel via the rules of Faerie combat based on a vow that I'd get to escape the faerie realm if I won. When I'd slit his throat with his own sword, the vow had caused his magic to transfer over to me, because the only way home was to use his magic and open a shortcut across the veil into the human world.

"Got it." Isabel tipped the pieces of spell into the bin. "I'll ask the coven if they've seen anything odd."

"Cheers." I tossed the butter knife into the sink. "I figure someone will have. Like Vance said, magical objects tend to attract attention."

"Unless…" Her gaze drifted over to the map peeking out

from underneath a stack of elastic-band-shaped spells on the coffee table. "Unless they hid it on the Ley Line."

Yeah. There is that slight issue. "Might be. I'll work it out. She might even have given me a clue already that I missed. Faeries have a thing for wordplay."

She blinked at me. "What, this missing heart might not be in the city at all? Did she give specifics?"

I thought. "You know, I don't think she did. For all I know, the thief flew to Australia with it."

"I mean, you can always get Vance to take you with him. It'd be a nice holiday."

"Nah." I walked to the sofa with my sandwich. "He can get across the city, I think, but Australia's a bit of a stretch."

The destruction wrought in the invasion two decades ago had kind of put a wrench in the possibility of overseas travel, to say the least. Even if any planes had survived the carnage, the idea of getting into a flying machine was markedly off-putting when a wild burst of faerie magic could send it spinning out of the sky. Even leaving the city was a tall order most of the time. I *hoped* the missing heart was within range. The Lady of the Tree wouldn't have set me an impossible task.

Who am I kidding? She was a faerie who hated my guts and had good incentive to see them strewn all over the forest. I'd been lucky she hadn't twisted the vow to request that I offer her the favour of sticking my head on a chopping block.

I heaved a sigh. "You know, I was supposed to be going on a date with Vance tonight, and it looks like we'll have to spend it talking about the bloody faeries again."

Isabel cleared her throat. "It's the full moon tonight. Did you forget?"

"Oh." That explained the crashes upstairs. While the biggest part of the shifter population lived behind the metal fence surrounding their territory, others chose to live amongst humans and lock themselves away on the week following the full moon. Like our upstairs neighbours. Henry and Disha were peaceable and ordinary individuals three weeks out of every four. Then they chained themselves up in their own flat when they transformed, and Isabel and I usually had babysitting duty. It was an unorthodox relationship, but it worked. Except if we had babysitting duty, that meant no date.

"Sorry," said Isabel. "I have to go to a coven meeting this evening. I'll take over babysitting tomorrow night."

"It's cool." Vance and I would have other date nights. I refused to let the faeries thwart all of them. "I honestly forgot. If this is the first day…"

"Then we have six more days of babysitting," said Isabel. "We can alternate. I have two more coven meetings, but you'll get your date night, don't worry." She winked. "I'm glad you two made it up."

"Yeah. I'd still be with him, but the other mages dragged him into a meeting." If not the faeries, I should have figured the other supernaturals would make a valiant effort to thwart my attempts at a love life.

Isabel picked up her shoulder bag. "I'll see you tonight, okay?"

"Sure." I took a bite of my sandwich. Honestly, it was my fault for not checking the dates. Isabel kept an eye on the moon's phases for coven meetings, but I'd spent the last week hiding in my room in recovery mode. Come to think of it, maybe the full moon accounted for Vance's slightly off behaviour earlier. He was only a quarter shifter, but he did have some of their traits. Like the claws. And the predatory vibe he gave off, which I was all too happy to have on my side rather than against it.

Enough, Ivy. Thinking about him wouldn't help me forget my disappointment.

After I finished my sandwich, I picked up the map Isabel had left out, figuring I might as well search out possible spots in which someone could have hidden a powerful magical object. Vance likely had a more detailed map of his own, but it wouldn't hurt to get an overview. Key points were areas of the Ley Line with particularly strong magical energies, and I'd been to several already, so I marked those first and wondered if it was worth asking the other supernatural leaders if they'd detected anything odd in the last few days.

The necromancers were on my shit list and vice versa, but they'd been forced to engage with the public recently after a surge of undead had followed Calder's antics on the Ley Line. Oh, and Lord Frank Sydney had tried to recruit me as some kind of liaison between the dead and the living. He'd claimed the current leader was too incompetent—which was true—but the necromancers would sooner swap out their dark cloaks for neon capes than form an alliance with the likes of me. My abilities gave me a connection with the veil that overlapped with theirs, to some degree, though I didn't have the spirit sight in the usual sense.

I'd used those skills to recruit an apprentice via the spirit world to find the document containing the cure for the serum that turned half-faeries into bloodthirsty killers. I might have worried the apprentice would tell tales on me, but he wouldn't want Lord Evander to know he'd been rummaging through the necromancers' secure documents. Not that theft was my biggest crime where the necromancers were concerned, but it was another strike against me, another reason they wouldn't shed a tear if the Lady of the Tree skewered me.

I doubt they'll be of any help, I told myself, putting the map aside. *Besides, I'm done cleaning up their problems.*

After an hour of marking out possible hiding places, I needed to blow off steam, so I found a clear floor space and ran through my combat forms. I wasn't welcome at the mercenary guild's gym anymore and Vance was occupied, but I didn't quite dare use magic in the flat. Or weapons. Swinging a sword in a narrow space packed with magical paraphernalia was just asking for trouble, even if I used a fake one, so I pretended to duel an invisible opponent. A faerie warrior, armed with a sword like—

I halted mid-strike. Stepped back. Didn't the Sidhe forge their weapons from the hearts of their trees? Oh, damn. How had it slipped my mind? Avalin's sword had once stored his magic before I'd taken it, and Velkas had been the same. Even Calder had carried a blade forged from an ash tree, and he'd certainly made an agreement with the Lady of the Tree.

In fact, had *she* given him the sword, and the armour, too? He'd never gone into Faerie, never met Velkas in the flesh, but it made an awful kind of sense.

So did her asking me to retrieve the heart, if it was truly a sword, too. Even the Lady of the Tree might struggle to best a Sidhe talisman, but I'd done so, and sending a mortal on an impossible quest to retrieve an enchanted sword was just the kind of story a fae might come up with.

My phone buzzed on the coffee table. I wiped sweat from my forehead with my sleeve and answered. "Hey, Vance. How'd the meeting go?"

"The other mages aren't pleased with the Chief's utter lack of responsibility."

"Can't they tell him that directly rather than complaining to you?"

"No," he replied. "Given the lack of tact some of my fellow Mage Lords are known to display when discussing the half-bloods, I think they would cause irreversible offence if they were to set foot in their territory."

"Right, some of them hate non-humans. Or non-mages." I pulled a face. The younger generation of mages had a more open-minded attitude towards those outside of their ranks—and anyone who didn't match their definition of what the mages should be, come to that—but there were some who held the opinion that half-faeries were too dangerous to be allowed to live in close proximity to humans. The recent incidents had doubtless not helped that impression in the least. "Ah, I just thought of an idea. Did I ever tell you that the Sidhe Lords' blades are usually forged from the hearts of their trees?"

"The missing heart." Understanding filled Vance's voice. "You think it's hidden in a weapon? A talisman?"

"Makes sense," I replied. "It'd explain why the Lady didn't go after it herself and dumped the task on me instead."

"That gives us something to work with, if it's true," Vance said. "Now we need its location."

"I've been working on that, too," I said. "Isabel has a map of the Ley Line and I've been marking possible hiding places. Oh, and we can ask the necromancers if they've sensed anything screwy. I need to speak to them anyway, but... well. You know my track record there isn't exactly stellar."

"I did request an audience with Lord Evander. He claims to be busy restoring the awakened dead to rest."

"Still? He's had a week." Typical. "Well, try to get hold of him, if you can. If he only wants to meet at night, I'll do that, too, but I can't make tonight."

"Our date?"

Ah, shit. "Would you believe I have babysitting duty? The shifters upstairs are going dark until morning."

"Right, I forgot you have shifter neighbours."

"Sorry." I tried and failed to come up with a subtle way to ask my next question. "Are you... er, shifting?"

"No," he said. "I'm quarter-blooded. I don't go through a full transformation."

"Okay. Just checking you aren't going to sprout claws on me this week."

"I could." I heard the laugh in his voice. "But I rather think it'd spoil the atmosphere for our date."

"So we're okay to reschedule? Say, for tomorrow?"

"Of course."

Sorted. I had twenty-four hours to avoid trouble, while babysitting a shifter kid all evening. What could possibly go wrong?

4

"**N**o," I said, for the fifteenth time, leaping from the sofa and dragging George's dirt-stained hands away from Isabel's bookshelf. "I said not to touch those."

He moved instead to the Ley Line map I'd left on the table, grubby fingers scrunching up the edge. I pushed the books back into their proper place and reached to move the map aside, but he'd already grabbed an elastic band I'd left underneath. There was a popping sound, and a torrent of purple glitter exploded all over the floor. *Dammit, Isabel.* I'd been joking when I'd said a fountain of glitter would be a great weapon to deploy on Larsen if he ever showed up at the door again.

"Or those." Our flat was the definition of a danger zone for anyone, let alone an overly inquisitive four-year-old shifter. His parents were currently chained up in their room, and with Isabel at a coven meeting, I'd been left solely responsible for not getting him killed. George was an adorable kid, but I was kind of tempted to set up a caging spell around the safe area of the flat before he triggered one of Isabel's explosives.

So far, he'd thrown Erwin the piskie across the room and nearly started a fire, so babysitting was going about as well as it usually did. I'd thought I'd cleared the floor of anything hazardous, but with this being a witch's flat, even the floor was a hazard in some places. I reached for a cleansing spell and scooted George away from the glitter explosion so I could clean up the mess before everything in the flat ended up covered in purple sparkles.

Erwin flew past, shrieking, and George made a hissing noise that was downright startling coming from a four-year-old. Shifter kids were moody at the full moon even if they couldn't transform yet, but I'd never heard him make a noise like that before.

"Whoa. Stop that." I made to grab the piskie, but he flew out of my reach and smacked into the bookshelf, knocking a stack of papers into the spelled candle on the windowsill. Luckily, the candle wasn't lit, but bright-purple wax stained the corner of what I sincerely hoped wasn't an important document. Erwin, meanwhile, landed feet-first in the candle, kicking bits of wax everywhere.

"Hey!" I lunged to grab him, but I'd made the mistake of taking my eyes off George. He picked up another charm, and before I could snatch it off him, the elastic band snapped.

A sharp clap of thunder whipped through the air. George dropped the startling spell, howling, and crawled under the coffee table.

"Ow." I held my hands to my own ears as George continued to sob loudly. How did you calm a hysterical four-year-old shifter? I couldn't even plonk him in front of the TV as a distraction, because our ancient television had bit the dust ages ago and we hadn't been able to afford a replacement. Usually, my idea of entertainment was helping Isabel create new explosives. "George, it's okay. It's only a spell—"

Another crash sounded as Erwin knocked several spell-books onto the floor.

"Whoa. Don't get wax or glitter on those. She'll murder me."

I fished the textbooks out of range and shooed the piskie off the shelf. He zigzagged past the coffee table, and George stuck his head out, hissing again.

"Go away!" he yelled, throwing a pencil at the piskie.

Except it wasn't a pencil, but a spell. To be more precise, one of Isabel's point-and-shoot explosives. Sparks began to fly from the end.

Panic shot through me. I jumped to my feet, magic arcing from my hand. The bolt of blue energy struck Erwin, and his winged body dropped out of the air as my faerie-quick instincts took over and I seized the explosive device in mid-air. Swooping down, I plunged the pencil into the cup of water I'd left out on the table, and it stopped sparking.

"Shit. Shit." Never mind not swearing in front of a kid. Had I *killed* Erwin? He lay prone on the coffee table, and I let out a sigh of relief when he fluttered his wings.

"Bad faerie," he muttered.

"I'm so sorry." I was, too. Erwin was a pain in the arse, but he'd lived here for years, and I'd developed a weird affection for the hyperactive little menace. "It was an accident."

Behind me, George crawled out from under the coffee table, his eyes as round as saucers. He'd seen... damn. What had he seen? My magic was invisible to anyone without the Sight, but I'd knocked Erwin down without even touching him. Kinda hard to explain away.

"Ivy, you scared me," he whimpered. "You're like the elf lady."

What? "Who?" I asked, my tone unintentionally sharp. "What elf lady?"

He flinched away from me. "I told you about her before. I see her outside sometimes."

A chill raced down my back. "You saw a faerie... outside the house?"

He bobbed his head. "Through the window. I didn't talk to her. Like you told me."

"Good." Whichever faerie he was talking about, I sure as hell hadn't seen them. *Creepy.* The wards kept out anyone who intended harm, but they only extended around the house, not outside. "Never talk to the faeries. They're dangerous, and some of them like to kidnap child—people," I amended, not wanting to freak him out too much. I was doing a shitty job at this, but the idea of someone from Faerie running off with this kid, because of me—no fucking way. I'd kill them first.

"Yeah, but don't worry." I crouched down and offered him a tentative smile. "Your parents'll keep you safe. And when you're here, *I'll* personally make sure no faeries set foot in here."

He eyed Erwin.

"Except him," I added. "He's a piskie. Harmless. You don't normally mind him. What's with the temper?"

George shrugged, his shoulders wiggling. "Dunno. Just got angry."

Shifter thing. "That's fine. I get angry sometimes too. Just... you know. Don't pick up any of those pencils."

I looked for a distraction and picked up my phone, finding that the internet had connected for once. I downloaded a few silly free games for him to play and opened one which involved throwing piskies into a net. When he was suitably occupied, I cleaned up the mess on the floor and deposited Erwin in a corner to sleep off the shock. He had no memory to speak of and would probably forget this by tomorrow, but a nagging sense of unease persisted. Not just because of George's surprising display of temper, but because I'd used magic without conscious thought. Until recently, it had been something I kept a close lid on, but even now, wisps of blue magic lingered around my hands and arms.

Why? I hadn't been over to the Grey Vale during the last conflict, though admittedly I'd tapped into some serious power when I'd spoken the Invocation. This might be an aftereffect. I didn't know. Faerie magic was the least under-stood of any kind of magic, especially by humans, and mine was doubly complicated because I'd stolen it from someone else. Avalin had been a Lord of Winter before he'd been exiled, but my power didn't manifest like the other Winter half-Sidhe. I'd never been able to throw a snowball or conjure a blizzard. Just energy, which gained strength from pain and anger, both mine and others'. Not pleasant by any means, but I wielded the power now, not Avalin. I intended to make it my own.

When I went to the bathroom to wash the glitter from my hands, I couldn't help studying my reflection in the mirror to see if there were any changes. Were my eyes a shade brighter, too, or was my imagination playing tricks on me? Likely the latter. Shaking my head, I left, and a faint, fragrant smell wafted over my shoulder. I turned around, my spine prick-ling. My bedroom door lay slightly open, though I was sure I'd closed it.

"George?" I peered into the living room, where he lay curled up on the sofa, sleeping.

Who'd opened my door, then?

I went to grab Irene before heading into my room. Every-thing was as I'd left it, save for the bouquet lying on the bed. A bouquet of... roses?

The click of a key in the lock sounded—the building's front door opening—and I broke into a run. I slammed out of the flat, blade in hand, and Isabel took a startled step back. "Er… Ivy? It's me."

"Yeah. I think someone else was in the flat, though."

"George?"

"He's asleep." I glanced behind me, my head spinning. "I went in my room, and someone left roses on my bed. I think the faeries are fucking with me again."

"Roses?" Isabel followed me into the flat, walked to my room, and peered over the bed. "Ah."

"See?" I folded my arms, my hands shaking. "I didn't hear anyone come in."

"Probably because he can teleport." Isabel held up a piece of paper, wearing an amused expression. "He also left you a note."

"What?" I stared at the note, my fear melting away to embarrassment. "No—he wouldn't."

Yes, he would. And I was officially the biggest dimwit this side of the faeries' realm. Well, Vance couldn't have known the memories I associated with the smell of roses. How could he? I'd never told him.

I turned away from the roses with a groan. "Why didn't he warn me? He scared me to death."

"He'll be pleased to hear that." Isabel's laughter followed me back into the living room. "What's with the glitter?"

I groaned again. "Don't ask."

We checked George was still asleep and then I told her everything in a whisper, including my general incompetence with small children.

Not that Isabel was much better. "Damn that glitter spell," I muttered, flicking purple sprinkles off my jeans.

"At least we know it works," she said. "So we can defend ourselves against Vance's romantic gifts."

"Ha ha. How was the meeting?"

"We cut it short early. The shifters got rowdy outside. I heard one of them went missing this evening."

My heart sank. "Missing?"

"Yeah… near half-blood territory." Seeing my face, she added, "She probably went to sleep in a hedge or something, but you know what they're like. It's a little scary out there, with them howling and screaming behind the fences."

I shivered. "I can imagine. Just, you know, nothing good ever happens on half-blood territory."

"We'll see what they say in the morning," she said. "I'll sleep on the camp bed out here tonight. I owe you."

"Hey, we're a team." We usually alternated, like with babysitting duty, and someone would need to make sure George didn't wake up in the night and set off another glitter spell. "I don't mind, though."

The smell of roses would linger in my room for a while, and part of me remained paranoid about that 'elf lady' he'd referred to. While not everything meant a faerie conspiracy, I knew I couldn't fool myself into thinking it was no big deal. I gave it twelve hours before my life imploded again.

———

Sure enough, I woke to a rapping on the flat door. My phone buzzed. I got up, dislodging glitter from the bed, figuring the Cavanaughs had come to collect their son.

Then I saw the time. Six a.m. The Cavanaughs wouldn't have transformed back into human form long enough to undo the wards keeping them locked in their flat yet, would they? I didn't feel particularly human myself. Rubbing my eyes, I checked I was vaguely decent before leaving my room.

Another rattle. I yawned and opened the door to the flat. "It's kinda early, isn't it, Henry—"

"Nice," said Vance, eyeing my glitter-specked navy-blue pyjamas. "What's with the glitter?"

"Oh, for fuck's sake."

He arched an eyebrow. "Sorry I woke you. I just met with Lord Evander and I thought you'd like to hear what he had to say."

"Why'd he want to meet at the crack of bloody dawn?" I ran a hand through my hair. I hadn't combed the tangles out of it yet. "Is it about the…" I cut myself off, glancing over my shoulder, but George hadn't woken. I'd also forgotten I'd left the roses in an empty glass jar on the sideboard. "Thanks for scaring the shit out of me yesterday."

He frowned. "What? The roses?"

"I thought the Lady of the Tree came into the flat. Don't do that."

"You thought I was a faerie trying to kill you?" He stared incredulously. "That's a new one. I thought roses were pretty unambiguous."

To most people, yes. "You've never met the Princess of Thorns. Flowers and I… don't get on. Or most plants, really. Except possibly cacti."

"I'll keep that in mind. You don't like music, you don't like flowers… what objection might you have to going to Alfonso's this evening?"

"None, because I've never been there." Probably because the fancy Italian restaurant on mage territory was several miles outside my price range.

"Good. I'll get us a reservation. I take it you're otherwise unoccupied tonight."

"Uh." I licked my lips. Vance's closeness, and scent, weren't doing much to wake up my scrambled brain cells. "Isabel and I are trading shifts, so it's her turn to take over babysitting. What did the necromancer have to tell you?"

"Nothing suitable to say in front of a small child," said Vance, his shoulders stiffening. A cold breeze kicked up, and goose bumps prickled all over my arms at the sound of footsteps.

"Who are you?" Henry Cavanaugh walked downstairs, glaring at Vance. He was in human form in jeans and T-shirt, but judging by the faint claw marks on his face and the dark circles under his eyes, it'd been a rough night.

"Mage Lord Colton," said Vance. "And you are Ivy's neighbour, right?"

"Cavanaugh." He reached the foot of the stairs but kept a steady distance from Vance.

"Colton. I thought I knew the name. Your uncle—"

"—has nothing to do with me." The air turned cold as Vance's eyes darkened to the grey before a storm. I braced my feet, clamping down on the instinct to flee.

Henry's own eyes flashed yellow, and alarm shot through me. "Hey—!"

When I moved towards him, Vance placed himself between me and Henry. "If you have a problem with me, we'll take it outside."

"I have a problem with your family," said Henry. "Briana hasn't come back."

"Who?" Wait. "The missing shifter? Isabel mentioned… but Vance had nothing to do with that."

Henry ignored me. "Your uncle has been stirring up the other shifters. He has some nerve roaming our territory when everyone knows what a liar your grandfather was."

"Quiet," said Vance. "I am not responsible for anything my family might have done, but if you go within a mile of my uncle's house, you'll have to answer to me."

Oh boy. Vance's cousin Anabel lived with her shifter father, with whom I gathered Vance did not get along in the least. Common sense told me to stay out of this one, but I really didn't want to watch Vance fight with my neighbour either.

"Hello?" I said loudly to Henry. "Your son's right behind me, in case you've forgotten."

Henry's gaze drifted past Vance, the yellow tint to his eyes fading slightly. "I will not allow my son to be subjected to your influence."

"I haven't spoken a word to your child," said Vance in the condescending tone I'd once despised. "Nor do I have any control over my uncle's behaviour. As for your missing shifter, perhaps you might apply yourself to the matter rather than expecting the mages to fix your mistakes."

A flush suffused Henry's face. "Get out of my home."

"Hey!" I stepped between them. "You can't give him orders. And Vance, the same applies to—"

He disappeared in a gust of wind that rattled the front door. Henry's wide eyes returned to their usual pale-brown colour. "What... magic was that?"

Him trying to intimidate you. And succeeding. "He's Mage Lord. What was that about?"

"I'm sorry," he said. "He—Colton—isn't a friend to shifters. His family certainly isn't."

Curiosity stirred, but annoyance won out. "We were discussing something important. I know it's the full moon, but you can't chase people out of my flat just because you don't like them."

"Ivy?" George mumbled from behind me. "What's going on? Dad?"

"Here. Come in." I beckoned Henry into the flat. With reluctance, he followed.

"George? What's that glitter for?"

Here we go again.

———

By the time the pair of them had gone, I was thoroughly rattled, not to mention reluctantly wide awake. Once I'd showered, properly dressed and stocked up on coffee and a stack of toast to wake myself up, I assessed my options for the day.

"I have two choices," I said to Isabel. "See Vance and ask him about the necromancer or go back to half-blood territory and poke around further. Preferably without anyone attacking me."

"See Vance first," said Isabel, munching cereal on the sofa. "Knowing you, if you go into half-blood territory alone, you'll get chewed on by a kelpie again."

I gave her a look. "Nice to know you have faith in me."

"I know what you're like. Anyway, I thought you wanted to hear what the creeps in cloaks had to say."

"Not really. They still haven't apologised for taking away my money."

"They haven't? Dicks."

The doorbell rang. Well, that saved me the bother of messaging Vance. I walked out into the corridor, assuming Vance hadn't teleported inside because he thought Henry was still here. Bloody shifters and their mood swings.

I opened the flat door. The postman stepped away from me. "Good. No sword this time."

"What?" I said blankly, before it registered that he'd had placed a considerably large box in front of me. "What is this?"

"Special delivery. Sign here."

I obliged, signing the paper. What had Vance done this time? He'd already bought me half a department store's worth of clothes. And shoes.

The answer… cacti. A dozen of them. I stared into the box, like the prickled plants would reveal the secrets of the universe.

Isabel came up behind me. "What's that?"

"Trouble."

"Of the romantic kind? Or magical?"

"I'd rather deal with magic right now," I said. "I don't even believe this."

"He figured you didn't like the roses, then? This is an alternative?"

"I mentioned cacti in passing." I sighed and picked one of them up. "I didn't say, 'please buy me twelve and park them on the doorstep.' What am I even supposed to do with these?"

"Keep them. They'll add character to our flat."

"You do realise we're supervising a small child for the next week, right?" I gave an eye-roll. "Tell you what, put them on the lawn. Might deter the creepy faerie lady who's watching our house."

"Watching our house?"

I picked up the cacti box and carried it into the hall. "George seems to think there's an 'elf lady' watching him. The way he described her sounded like one of the faeries. When he saw me use magic..." I trailed off, frustrated. "I don't understand how it even happened. It's like my magic has a mind of its own."

The thought sent a fresh wave of worry crashing over me. I'd barely begun to claim the magic as mine, but what if it was too tied to Avalin for me to ever be able to fully control? I was pretty sure I was stuck with the power for life, so ditching it wasn't an option, and it wasn't like there were a dozen older, wiser people to ask advice from. As far as I knew, no human had ever taken magic from a Sidhe Lord before.

"Don't worry," said Isabel. "You've had a rough go of it lately. Bound to be some side effects. At least you aren't turning into a giant wolf every night."

"Fair point."

Once we'd carried the cacti into the flat, I grabbed my phone and messaged Vance. *Hey. Where are you?*

Outside your door.

I shook my head, a smile forming despite myself. I hadn't put him off coming back here, and neither had my neighbours. Not that I had a bloody clue what to do with all those cacti.

"Vance Colton," I said, opening the flat door. "I should have left a dictionary for you in return so you could look up the word 'overcompensating'."

"Someone's prickly today."

I groaned. "Please, for the love of fluffy kittens, tell me you didn't buy a dozen cacti so you could make that pun."

He smirked. "If I said yes, would you admire me for forward thinking?"

"I'd be surprised the Mage Lord didn't have better things to do with his time."

"Few things are as entertaining as winding you up. I remembered you were working on tripwire spells to prevent faeries from attacking you, so I thought I'd contribute."

"I think glitter might be more effective."

"They're a hybrid species. Didn't you read the note?"

"No…"

"Witch-charmed cacti that can destroy any other plant which comes into contact with them. Just in case the Lady of the Tree decides to use more extreme methods to make you fulfil the vow."

"That's…" Good thinking, actually. "I hope Isabel finds the note before she puts them anywhere near her flowerbeds. Are you going to tell me what Lord Evander had to say?"

"Yes, but not here."

He took my hand and transported us into his office. "Unfortunately, you're not going to like it."

Oh, boy. "What?"

"Lord Evander agreed to refund the money he took, but on condition that neither you nor anybody associated with you goes near the guild again."

"Even if we're being chased by zombies?" Dammit. I'd have to find another way to speak to old Frank the ghost again. "I suppose it won't help if I told him Frank wants me to be a liaison between the living and the dead."

Vance's eyes flashed light grey. "I didn't tell him. He might be harmless if incompetent, but it's not information I want to pass into the wrong hands."

"Me neither," I said. "I guess if I pay fewer visits, it'll be easier not to let slip that I sent his apprentice to steal from his office."

"What... oh, the cure for the drug."

"Yep." I'd done so as a ghost, but that made no difference to the necromancers, who pretty much made a hobby of hanging out in Death. "He didn't mention seeing any faerie artefacts lying around? I mean, near the Ley Line?"

"No, but I made note of some possible locations yesterday."

"So did I." We'd probably picked out the same spots. "Listen... what was the deal earlier?"

His eyes darkened, all traces of humour vanishing from his expression. "Your neighbour crossed a line."

"By talking about your family? Your cousin's family, right?" From what he'd said, I'd gathered Vance's uncle was also part shifter, but that he lived over on shifter territory instead of with the mages. "He's not going to go near her, you know that. He's got a kid of his own."

One look at Vance's face told me I wasn't getting answers.

"Okay. You know all *my* secrets, though. It's only fair that you share something with me." I tried for a flirtatious tone, but all my worries had risen to the surface again with the reminder that a shifter had gone missing the previous night, too. "Ah—did you know about this disappearance? Did they report it to the mages?"

"No, they didn't." Vance looked down at his phone, which had jumped into his hand. "The half-faerie Chief has agreed to another meeting."

"Since when?"

"He sent an emissary to the manor," said Vance. "His territory is experiencing a magical drought and he's been inundated with complaints."

"Wait—really?" A drought? Thinking about it, their territory had seemed more and more subdued the last few times I'd been there. I'd assumed that it was mimicking the changing seasons of the outside world. "Huh. You don't think it might be an effect of that missing heart from Summer?"

Most half-bloods might not necessarily be able to tell, if they didn't possess strong magic, but the Chief would be hard-pressed to ignore the issue if it had started to affect his own people.

"It might," Vance agreed. "It's worth looking into."

"All right," I said. "Let's see if the Chief agrees with us."

5

This time, the Chief met us at the gate. One glance confirmed why he'd felt the situation was serious enough to merit a visit to the mages. The colours behind the gate were muted, the leaves from every plant drooping and rotten. More crucially, no vibrant green magic poured off everything like the first time I'd been here, and I didn't see any bright-blue glow to indicate the coming of Winter either. In Faerie, Summer was lush, verdant, bursting with colour, while Winter was the stark opposite, ice-cold and wreathed in power that fed on death. Yet I saw no traces of magic in the air as well, and the dying flowers looked more... well, mortal. Impermanent.

The Chief wore his oil-black hair tied back and his body clothed in armour depicting a leafy pattern that looked painted on. The dark wood staff he carried might have been made of plastic for all I knew, and the same went for his tarnished gold crown. I didn't like the guy, but I liked the idea of the half-faeries running around without leadership even less. Or worse, with someone like Calder in power. I wondered if he feared the others would blame him for their magic fading, and that was why he'd asked for Vance's help.

"Ivy Lane," he said. "The Mage Lord says you know why we are experiencing difficulties with our magic."

"The heart of one of the trees of Summer is missing," I told him. "I told you yesterday."

His pale-green eyes narrowed. "You disrespected me in my own territory."

You did the same to me. At a warning look from Vance, I stifled several less savoury remarks. "The Lady of the Tree coerced me into helping her find the location of this… missing heart. That's how I know. I can only assume it's having some kind of knock-on effect on the magic in this realm, too, but that's guesswork on my part."

"The Lady is a weakened shell of her former self, unable to leave her forest."

"You're dead wrong there," I said. "She bound me by a vow when I went looking for information on missing children a few weeks ago. Her information was useless, but I still owed her a favour, and when she dragged me over to her side, she ordered me to find this missing heart. Trust me, I don't want to be involved in this any more than you do.

"If you make a deal with a faerie, you can expect to deliver on your promise," he said coldly. "Even one as weakened as she."

"She's not weak. She nearly gutted me. Several times."

"If you provoked her, as I'm fairly certain you did, it's your own fault."

"I didn't. Much. That's not the point. If I don't keep up my end of the bargain, I'll die—and believe me, you don't want that. I've saved all your hides twice this month." Not to mention by killing Avalin, I'd probably saved a few hundred more.

The Chief's forehead creased in a frown. "I will not assign the responsibility of my people over to you, but the Mage Lord tells me you've encountered similar… artefacts, to this heart."

I glanced over at Vance, who watched the Chief with a neutral expression, letting me do the talking.

"He told you I think it might be a talisman?" I guessed. "I don't know too much about them, but I heard they're forged from the hearts of your trees, and I figured that's why the Lady picked me for the job."

"Under normal circumstances, only another Sidhe can interact with a talisman without adverse side effects," he said. "Or someone with Sidhe blood."

Or someone who stole their magic. I'd handled a talisman myself, when I'd cut Avalin's throat with his own sword. I'd already claimed his magic at the time, though I hadn't known it yet. His sword had once been the source of the power flowing in my veins, and even now, I detected a pale-blue glow around my skin.

"Who might that have been? Calder didn't have equally evil siblings, did he?" I'd never found out if Avalin had other kids. He might have had a hundred affairs with mortal women. Calder had hidden within this very city for his whole life without me having a clue he existed.

"I've told you before, we don't keep a register of half-Sidhe. People come and go all the time, some decide to embrace their human side, and then there are quarter- or eighth-blooded born without magic…" He shrugged in a decidedly un-Chief-like gesture. "It's not up to me to track everyone in the town who might have faerie ancestry."

"It should be," said Vance. "What about the ones you arrested the other day?"

"In jail, of course," he said. "They've all been questioned

and sentenced, though the majority were under the drug's influence and have few memories of that night."

"And might any of them have Sidhe blood?" I asked.

"Not that I'm aware of. Not all Sidhe tell their children of their parentage when they leave their offspring in this realm."

"You're all absolutely delightful, aren't you?" I said, my temper spiking. "We need to find a missing object and we have no idea what it looks like, nor where it is, or who even stole the damn thing in the first place—"

"If it's truly a talisman, it'll be a staff or another weapon," he said. "All the Great Oaks were used for a similar purpose, to my understanding. The Sidhe cut them down centuries ago."

"She acted as if the tree got cut down last week." She hadn't specified, though, and now I saw how easily I'd let my own presumptions shape the meaning of her words.

"The dryads have long memories," he said. "Undeniably the Sidhe did them wrong, but the faerie realm is a place where the weak die and the strong remain so long as they cling onto their power with everything they have."

"Sounds thrilling. I can see why you guys are all dead set on going back."

"Do *not* mock me," snarled the half-faerie. "You're a human interloper who has no idea what wielding a Sidhe Lord's magic really means. Soon, you'll overstep your boundaries and another faerie will rip it away from you. I confess I'd like to be there when it happens."

The air turned cold. I held still as Vance stepped forward, power crackling from his skin. The Chief took a step back, then two, trying and failing not to let his terror seep into his expression.

"Do not speak to my employee like that," the Mage Lord

said in thunderous tones. "If you do so again, expect no mercy from me."

"Mage Lord." The Chief swallowed, his gaze darting around to avoid looking into Vance's eyes. "I meant no disrespect to you."

"You sure as hell did a good job disrespecting *me*," I said, determined not to let Vance get the last word in. Though damn if I wasn't enjoying the show. "Luckily, the feeling's mutual, and I'll even accept *your* help if it means not being skewered by a living tree."

"The Lady is the most ancient dryad in this realm. She might be weakened and her mind clouded, but her power remains and so does her grudge."

"Grudge?" Against the Sidhe who'd stolen from her? Assuming they'd done so at all. I wished I'd taken note of every word she'd said so I could tease out any hidden meanings. I was in way over my head when it came to parsing the riddles uttered by a fae who'd lived a thousand of my lifetimes. "Tell me what you know about the Sidhe and their talismans. Why did they decide to cut out the trees' hearts in the first place?"

"In Faerie, the most ancient have the strongest magic," he said. "Magic builds over time, gaining strength with each passing century. The trees are even more ancient than the Sidhe, which is why they possess so much power at their cores."

Interesting. "Then the swords were designed to harness that power?"

"Yes, and it's my understanding that most Sidhe choose to store their magic in a talisman to ensure its maximal capacity," said the Chief. "Any who are exiled are stripped of their talismans beforehand. It is the ultimate shame."

Not all of them. Avalin and Velkas had both claimed theirs *after* being exiled, which implied that the Courts weren't exactly keeping a close eye on their valuable magical objects.

"And who takes them?" I queried. "After they're confiscated?"

"I assume whoever is currently in power in that Court. I'm not privy to the details." Bitterness tinged his voice, though I decided against offering comment. I already knew that being out of touch with Summer bothered him a lot.

"Do *they* know the Grey Vale exists?" I asked. "The Courts, I mean?"

"That I cannot say," said the Chief, a nervous expression crossing his face. "When they exile people, they must know they're sending them beyond reach, but the idea of another realm entirely… if they do know, they must assume it's not a threat to them."

"It's a threat to *us*." And Velkas and Calder had both wanted to draw the attention of the Sidhe who'd cast them out. "Back to the sword. How common are talismans? I mean, I assume I'm not likely to find one on the market?"

"No," said the Chief. "They're rare—incredibly so, especially in this realm—and none of the weapons we carry here are directly from Faerie itself."

I'd suspected his own staff was all for show, but I'd encountered no fewer than three true talismans in the comparatively short time I'd been involved with Faerie. What were the odds?

"There are only so many places a magical artefact might be hidden," Vance said, "and I expect you're aware of most. Namely, key points on the Ley Line."

"That is not my area of expertise," he said haughtily. "My people do not live on the Ley Line."

"They're still being affected," I pointed out. "How'd it take you so long to notice your magic was fading?"

"Our territory is sustained by our collective magic." A

flush darkened the Chief's face. "It did occur to me that the balance might have shifted, but I assumed Winter was about to take over."

Not that Summer was losing its power. "Well, other than the Ley Line, I don't know where else to go looking. I can't go into Faerie. I'm not Sidhe."

"No, and the Sidhe would tear the magic from you with your heart still beating," said the Chief, with rather more enjoyment than I liked. "The answers must be in this realm. Very well... I will send out some of my people to investigate the Ley Line."

"Good," Vance said. "Some of my fellow mages are already patrolling the area, but Summer half-faeries will likely pick up on anything amiss relating to the faerie realms."

"I know," the Chief all but snapped. "Don't presume to have won this, Mage Lord. I will do what is necessary to protect my kin. As for *you*, Ivy Lane, I'd strongly advise you to tread carefully. If you find this sword, you will give it to me, and I will return it to Faerie myself."

"Gladly," I shot at him. "After I've made it clear to the Lady of the Tree that I've fulfilled my end of the bargain. Considering she also met with Calder, I think you and she need to have a chat about her motives."

"Absolutely not," he said. "As I've repeatedly told you, I'm not responsible for every faerie outside of this territory."

"Then I'm not responsible if the faerie in question ends up impaled on my sword."

His teeth bared in a snarl. "You try my patience."

"And you're trying mine. Look, I don't want to die, and you don't want to lose your magic. Until we've solved this problem, we'll have to agree to a truce." As little as I cared about him losing his magic, I *did* care if the half-faeries started a war, and unfortunately, hunting down the missing sword meant being stuck with him for the foreseeable future.

"Precisely," Vance said. "Let me know if you find anything out. I'll come back here tomorrow in any case."

The Chief's eyes narrowed. "Send an emissary first. It's difficult to reassure my people that they are under protection when you insist on defying our laws and appearing on my territory without any warning."

I laughed under my breath as Vance and I turned our backs and walked away. "You teleported in here?"

"Chieftain Taive refuses to join the twenty-first century and acquire a mobile phone."

"I don't think *he's* a villain." It was nice to know one person in the supernatural community wasn't plotting to destroy the world as we knew it, though he'd be equally happy to see me dead. *Can't have it all.* "Though he barely has control over his people. They could be hiding the talisman in front of his nose."

"He'd know if they did," said Vance. "The nature of faerie magic… the power of a talisman tends to warp and distort the reality around it. It's not meant to fit into this realm."

"Who told you that?" I was surprised that even the mages had access to that level of knowledge.

"The council did, when they handed me the keys to the depository," he said, referring to the place from which we'd taken the Invocations that I'd used to stop Calder's plan. "There are no talismans in there, but that's one of few places capable of storing one without causing adverse side effects."

"Same with the Invocations." I fought back a shiver at the memory of the way the glyphs had flared to life, had warped my vision so that I could read a language I didn't speak, and had ripped me from my body in the process. Warping reality. I'd seen the worst of that in the Grey Vale, and then some. "Might be why *my* magic is acting up, too."

His grey eyes watched me. "Your magic?"

I nodded, unease skittering down my spine. Even now,

the instinct arose to keep my secrets close to my heart. "It's kind of... erratic lately," I admitted. "Last night, the piskie went berserk and I panicked and shot magic at him without meaning to. I worried I'd hurt him. Kinda scared the kid, too."

At Vance's sympathetic look, I wished I hadn't spoken. I didn't think Vance of all people would judge me, but the past couple of days had made me conscious of just how in the dark I was about my own abilities.

"If the Chief wasn't such a dick, he might have been able to give me pointers," I said. "Sure would help to have a tutor."

"He's from Summer, not Winter," said Vance. "That said, most types of magic have commonalities. If you want to practise, you can come to the manor whenever you like, even when I'm not there. There are usually other mages in the training ground."

I gave him a grateful smile. "All right. What're you doing now?"

"Checking in with the mages who are patrolling outside the necromancers' guild," said Vance. "I sent them to keep an eye out just in case, though without alerting Lord Evander."

"Is this what you used to do?" I asked. "I mean, before all this mayhem started, did you always go around pissing off every head of each supernatural community in the city?"

"Sometimes I pissed off the ones outside the city as well."

I burst out laughing. "Vance, I think I'm a bad influence on you."

"You may be right." He smiled. "And the mayhem isn't a recent development. You've just never been at the centre of it before."

"I want a holiday."

He chuckled. "I wish we could move our date earlier, but I need to make sure Drake hasn't set anyone on fire."

"Is that likely?"

"With necromancers? Yes, unfortunately."

I had to admit he was probably right. "Okay. You go and check on your mages. I'll go and make sure the Cavanaughs have calmed down from earlier. Isabel's in charge of babysitting tonight."

"Good." He swept me in for another bone-shaking kiss.

"Tease," I mumbled against his lips.

"See you later."

And in a rush, we were on the doorstep of my flat. A brush of his lips against mine, and he was gone. Heart considerably lighter than before, I skipped into the hallway and nearly collided with Henry. "Ah—sorry."

"You were with the Mage Lord?" His nostrils flared. "He's been outside, too."

"Of course he has. We're dating." Might as well get it over with.

Henry's eyes went wide. "You're human."

"So's he." Mostly. "What does it matter?"

"It matters because shifters and humans aren't the same," said Henry. "As the Coltons should know already."

"Look, I've no idea what you're talking about." And to be honest, I was sick of his attitude. "Vance is a quarter-blooded shifter. His uncle lives on shifter territory, right?"

"Unfortunately."

Okay... "What's your issue with him?"

"It's not him," said Henry. "Most of the shifters bear a grudge against the mages, and with good reason. Thanks to the rules the Mage Lords put into place, my people were decimated during the invasion."

"So were his." I knew that much. "His parents were killed fighting the Sidhe. They didn't do anything to your people."

He shook his head. "It's an old grudge, one that goes beyond the invasion, but it's not my place to reveal other people's secrets."

"I'll ask Vance himself, then. On our date." I'd never had a particular argument with Henry—unlike most other neighbours I'd had—but his tone grated on me and so did his apparent desire to blame Vance for his family's actions, including ones who were long dead.

"Don't go near shifter territory," he said. "Briana still hasn't been found."

"She's dead." Henry's wife, Disha, descended the stairs, her face easily as haggard as her husband's. Brown-skinned and burly, she towered over me, her denim jacket hugging her wide shoulders. Hints of the tiger she shifted into were visible in the lighter streaks in her black hair that might have seemed orange in the right lighting, and the reddish tint to her pupils. "They found her body."

Oh, shit. "What—who killed her?" I shrank back when Disha's catlike eyes pierced me, with a similar effect to being stared out by a hellhound.

"Faeries," she snarled. "Traces of their magic were found at the scene. They tore her to pieces."

I swallowed, fighting the instinct to cower away. "I'm sorry."

"You were with the half-faeries today, weren't you?"

"Vance and I met with the Chief, yes." Why would a faerie kill a shifter? Might have been a random murder—both groups were volatile as hell, after all—but shifters didn't leave their territory at the full moon. They knew the consequences if they did. And even if the shifter had been completely out of control, a half-faerie wouldn't want to risk the consequences of violating the shaky peace between their groups and committing murder. No, it was more likely to be a rogue fae that had done this, but that she'd gone missing near their territory was a shitstorm waiting to be unleashed.

"Someone will pay for this." Henry's nostrils flared again. "Briana was a good person. I have to go—"

"—check on George," said Disha. "He's sleeping. I'm going to see what happened to Briana. She was found on the boundary with half-blood territory. There will be blood for this."

"No—"

She cut off my words with another blazing stare. "This might mean war, Ivy. I'd stay out of it."

She swept out of the house. Her heels snapped on the pavement as my eyes followed her down the garden path. Following her would be downright risky, but how else was I supposed to figure out what had really happened to Briana? Why would a shifter have been near half-blood territory to begin with?

I turned to Henry instead. "Why'd one of your people leave shifter territory last night?"

"You aren't to get involved, either," Henry growled, his eyes lighting with the merest flash of yellow. He was a wolf in shifted form, though not as scary as his wife. God only knew what kind of creature George would end up turning into when he reached puberty. A tiger-wolf hybrid?

"All right." I spoke carefully. "Just, you know, it's technically my job to help solve supernatural cases involving the faeries."

"You're working for the Mage Lord." Henry sighed. "I don't want to argue with you, Ivy, but trust me when I say the man's untrustworthy and his family is worse. As for this death… your involvement with the faeries puts you at risk of being accused yourself if you try to interfere."

That figures. "I can't stop the Mage Lords getting involved, though."

"Then they'll have to take responsibility for any consequences that might rebound upon them." Henry moved closer to the stairs. "I'm going back upstairs to check on George. Don't go to shifter territory."

"Gotcha."

I'd never been good at obeying orders. Sure, going to shifter territory directly would be a bad move, but the last time a half-faerie had lost it and murdered someone, they'd been acting under the influence of Calder's drug. I couldn't overlook this.

Besides... I did have a way to do some investigating without the shifters being aware of my presence. If I was careful.

6

I slipped out of the flat, concealed beneath a shadow spell. The sky wouldn't darken for a few hours yet, but the overcast day made it easier to stay out of sight. Fallen leaves skittered through the street, some pursued by piskies. I never did catch all the ones that escaped the other week, but luckily, none of the others had decided to stay at our flat. Erwin was quite enough to handle on his own.

The wind whistled into my coat and bit at my arms as though to warn me off, but I had time to kill, and a shifter death near half-blood territory was nothing if not suspicious. My shadow spell ensured I wouldn't be seen by anyone, human or otherwise, but I walked the long way to half-blood territory to avoid venturing near the shifters' homes. I sincerely hoped no half-faeries were out roaming the streets. Not only would an encounter with the shifters end in exactly the bloodbath I was hoping to avoid, but my shadowy illusion wouldn't mask my magic if it decided to make an appearance, given its recent volatility.

The shifters, as I'd suspected, were already at the scene. When I neared the hedges circling half-blood territory, I heard the distinct sound of a half-dozen or so voices from a nearby alleyway. I veered that way, half-wishing I'd waited a couple of hours until the sky was darker and the shadows more pronounced. I slowed my pace, one hand on the hilt of my sword, when I saw a group of shifters standing in the alley's entryway. Scarlet dots scattered on the pavement, darkening to thick smudges.

My heart sank in my chest. *Oh, no.* Was this where they'd found Briana's body? The half-bloods' gate was scarcely ten metres away. No wonder they'd been suspicious.

I edged closer, even as a primal instinct urged me to flee, both from the beasts in human form standing in the alley, and from the killer whose presence lingered in the form of the carnage they'd left behind. Blood spattered the alley floor and walls where the dead shifter lay sprawled on the ground, her body ripped open from stomach to throat. I choked back vomit and then stifled a gasp. Fanning out from the dead shifter's open chest, threads of green light spilled onto the ground. *Faerie magic.* She hadn't been torn open. Someone had hit her with magic hard enough to blast her body apart. Skin hung in bloody fragments from her exposed organs. I swallowed bile, willing myself not to throw up and alert the others to my presence.

I tuned in to their conversation instead. The rumble of voices became more distinct. A deep male voice was saying, "...declaration of war."

"Don't jump to conclusions," said a female voice. "The half-faeries don't want another war any more than we do. Some of them were under the influence of a drug last week. The Mage Lords said—"

"The Mage Lords are liars who want to save their own skin," interrupted another, louder male voice. "They all but abandoned us after the invasion, even knowing what we lost.

They don't want another war, because it might jeopardise the positions of power they wrongfully took."

I held still, keeping my eyes on the pavement rather than on the shifter's broken body. I'd known not everyone liked the mages—hell, *I* hadn't until recently—but I'd had no idea the shifters held that much of a grudge. Henry had been telling the truth, and while his hatred of Vance made a little more sense now, I wanted to know more.

"I don't disagree, but we don't know exactly how she died," said another. "It might not have been one of the fae."

"They're sadistic animals," said a female voice that I recognised as Disha's. "Of course they did it."

Oh boy. None of them would be able to see the light, so to their eyes, their friend had been ripped apart by an unseen force. My Sight made it impossible to miss the glow of magic igniting the whole alleyway. Green meant Summer. A Summer faerie had committed the murder.

But there's hardly any magic in half-faerie territory.

A chill raced through my blood. How could anyone commit murder using magic during a magical drought that had affected even the Chief? The only person I thought capable of this level of sadism had been Calder, but he was dead, and he used Winter magic besides.

I was missing a clue, but if I stuck around for much longer, I'd risk exposing myself. Or the half-faeries would come out to see why a bunch of shifters were outside their territory and all hell would break loose.

All right. Time for a diversion.

I slipped a hand into my pocket and pulled out one of Isabel's explosives. Aiming carefully, I threw it at a nearby dustbin.

The resulting explosion went off like a thunderclap, startling all the shifters. And me, too, admittedly. I shielded my arms, retreating from the shower of refuse. The shifters peeled away from the alleyway to look for the source of the noise. The smell of burned rubbish ought to mask my scent, but two shifters lingered near the alleyway, and I hoped their sharp senses didn't pick up on me creeping past them.

I moved fast, whipping a spare glass container from my pocket to take a blood sample from amid the mess splattered on the alley wall. Job done, I darted back around the corner, narrowly avoiding a collision with another shifter returning from investigating the remnants of the bin's contents that now littered the pavement. He paused, sniffing the air, but the stench was strong enough that he didn't look in my direction.

Once I'd put enough distance between myself and the shifters to relax my guard, I found another deserted alleyway and took out one of Isabel's tracking spells. After setting down the spell, I tipped the container of blood into the middle of the circle. My hands met the light flaring up at the circle's edge, and I prepared to relive the shifter woman's unpleasant death.

Green light trailed up my arms. My vision clouded over, darkening rapidly. Shadows stretched along the road as the light of the full moon hit the buildings alongside the pavement. I watched through the eyes of someone who was much shorter than me—in fact, when I looked down, I saw clawed feet on the pavement. *Briana.* She'd been in shifted form when she left her territory… but why come here to begin with?

A dazzling glow caught my gaze. Though tracking spells showed no colour, there was no mistaking the vibrancy of faerie magic. I held my breath, watching as a figure appeared within the glow. From my position on the ground, the figure appeared tall enough to blot out the light of the moon. I couldn't make out their features—couldn't see anything but a slim figure whose curves suggested femininity—but their hand held a long, sharp object, which they pointed towards me.

The light became a torrent and rushed towards me like a bullet, and everything went black.

I blinked back into my own body, tasting Briana's panic on my tongue. *Damn.* I hadn't got a close look at the killer, but I'd confirmed that they'd used Summer magic. And…

My mind replayed the images. The killer had held a weapon, though they'd committed the murder with magic. I hadn't seen closely enough to be certain if it was a sword, but a sudden suspicion seized me. Magic might be draining from half-blood territory, but someone had recently stolen a powerful magical object from the Summer Court itself.

And they'd brought it here.

Did they use the talisman to kill a shifter?

Even if they had, I couldn't possibly tell the shifters that. No way.

Shit. I had to tell Vance, at least. First, I cleaned up the spell circle's remains, leaving no traces of either the spell or the blood I'd used. As I was leaving the alley, my phone buzzed in my pocket. I'd misjudged the time. My date with Vance was in less than two hours.

His deep voice sounded in my ear as I walked. "What've you done now?"

"Nothing," I said with a touch of guilt. "I heard from Disha—Henry's wife—that they found the shifter who went missing. She was killed by… by faerie magic. Right by half-blood territory."

Guilt choked me, urged me to explain what I'd found. But if he came over here, the shifters would turn on both of us and the half-faeries would likely be drawn into the melee as well. They'd never listen to reason while Briana's body was still fresh.

"I'll send a team," he said. "Don't go there alone."

I chewed on my lip. I'd sworn to stop lying to him, if just because it wasn't a healthy way to start our relationship. "Already went there. I'm on the way home. Nobody saw me."

"Ivy." His tone somehow conveyed both concern and exasperation at the same time.

"I'm not the one who's lying dead in an alley, Vance. I'm fine." I hoped the shifters' acute hearing didn't pick up on my voice from several streets away. "I'll tell you everything when I'm home."

"I want you to be safe. That's all."

My annoyance melted a little. "Yeah, I got it. Just you know. Independent by necessity here. I pay my bills by poking around."

"You don't need to do that anymore."

"Maybe I do," I muttered. "This is... it's bad. The death took place on the half-bloods' doorstep and the shifters have already decided it was one of them. It wasn't. I used a tracking spell."

He sucked in a breath. "Come to the manor."

"I will..." I pulled the phone away from my ear, seeing someone else heading right for me. Disha. "Call you back," I whispered quickly, and ducked out of sight.

Disha passed by my hiding spot and paused for an instant, head raised as though she'd picked up on a trace of my scent. A second later, she resumed walking again. I breathed out, waited thirty seconds, then returned to the street, relieved that she was at least leaving the scene of Briana's death. If the others had done the same, there wouldn't be a standoff tonight. I'd need to take off my disguise first, but maybe when I got back to the flat, I could try to reason with her and Henry.

I followed her path, putting enough space between us so she wouldn't smell me. In a few short hours, she'd be chained upstairs in beast form, and Isabel would watch over George. As for me…

A shadow fell over me from behind. My feet left the ground as someone far stronger than I was lifted me into the air. Struggling, I twisted to face my attacker—a hulking man I didn't recognise, though from his size and his long, matted hair, he must be a shifter. His beard was equally thick, and his eyes flared yellow. "I knew I smelled a rat."

"What gives?" I squirmed, fighting against his iron grip. Shifters at the full moon were far stronger than regular humans, even during the day, and he held me off the ground one-handed while his other hand searched my pockets, pulling out two daggers and the witch spells I'd been carrying.

"Let me go." I reached for the magic waiting below the surface, and blue light burst from my arms. He released me with a snarl of surprise and I launched into a run, using my faerie-enhanced speed to propel myself over the road.

I ran smack into another hulking figure. Wait, the same one. How the hell had he moved so fast?

Damn shifters.

"Who even are you?" I swore and struggled when he reached out and lifted me one-handed into the air again. I wriggled, kicking at his kneecaps, but he held me at arm's length. "I said let me *go.*"

"You're meddling in something that doesn't concern you, Ivy Lane. I think you deserve to be taught a lesson."

"Here's a better idea. You let me go, and I'll help you solve this murder."

A thump. Stars winked before my eyes, and the world dissolved into blackness.

"Ivy." A hand waved in front of my face. A transparent hand.

"Oh, for god's sake," I said. "Don't tell me the fuckwit killed me."

"He tried," said Frank the necromancer. "Very luckily, your healing spell worked. You'll wake up in a minute."

"Healing spell? I didn't use a healing spell." What the hell was going on? Like my other disembodied experiences, the surroundings were little more than hazy greyness from which Frank's indistinct face peered at me. How could my head hurt so much if I was a ghost?

"People don't realise that hitting someone over the head with a hard object is more likely to kill them than knock them unconscious."

"I'll tell them that, when I'm *alive*," I said pointedly. "Wait. Is there a shifter here?"

"Right here? No. There's an angry one beside your battered body in the waking world."

"Were you always this annoying?" I rubbed the back of my head. My hand passed right through it. Ack. "I was investigating a dead shifter. Didn't intend to come here. Didn't know I could, in fact, with the veil back to normal."

"Well, now you do," he said dryly. "A dead shifter, you say?"

"Yes… is she here?" An obvious possibility hit me. "Can you find her? Reach through the veil and grab her ghost?"

"No," said Frank, helpfully. "Is that blue light your magic?"

I looked down, seeing that my body was there, albeit transparent, and undeniably shrouded in blue light. "I guess it is. Why can you see it? I thought you needed the Sight."

"I imagine the same rule doesn't apply to the dead. Every time I've seen you in Death, Ivy, you've been surrounded by the same blue glow."

"My magic lets me pass through Death." That was how I'd crossed to the Grey Vale, after all. "But why's it happening now? The veil's not acting up. Right?"

"The veil is fine," said Frank. "No more disturbed than usual. I think your magic binds you to the veil, if you can pass through Death. That would also make you a valuable asset to the necromancers."

"They've refused to have anything more to do with me." Of all the times to get myself excluded by the necromancer guild. Even if they'd refused to help me find the missing talisman, they might at least have been able to call up the shifter's ghost to ask her who the killer was. I couldn't set up a summoning circle myself without the proper equipment. "Can you talk to them?"

"I have tried, many times. Lord Evander is incorrigible."

"That's one way of putting it." I scowled. "It's bad enough that I'm supposed to handle the half-faeries, too. They're going to be accused of this murder if I don't find out who really did it. Trust me, you don't want a war between the shifters and the faeries any more than I do."

"This is all out of my area." Frank's forehead creased.

"However, I *can* give you instruction on how to cross the veil voluntarily. If you accept the risks. With apprentice necromancers, even under controlled conditions, there's always the chance that they might never return to their bodies."

My heart sank, fear flooding me. Weird how I got the physical symptoms of having a body when mine wasn't present. "To be honest, I'm *not* okay with that, but tell me anyway."

"Normally, necromancers use a summoning circle to tether them to the real world while they step out of their bodies," said Frank. "With magic like yours, though, I'd wager you don't need one, given enough practise."

"Seriously?" My brows shot up. "I thought I came here because the veil was breaking open. Not..."

"Your magic brought you here."

"Whoa." Not only was the magic a pain in my arse in the waking world, it followed me into Death, too? Undoubtedly, Frank's ability to teach me was limited by the fact that he didn't have any faerie magic to speak of, just plain old necromancy. "I didn't do it consciously, though. How does that work?"

"It's hard to demonstrate when you're already in Death, but I can show it to you in reverse."

"All right. Hit me."

Frank leaned forward, grabbed my shoulders and shoved me. I yelped, falling back, clouds of blue magic rising around my transparent form. The grey faded and all my senses returned in a dizzying rush as my eyes flew open. "Jesus, Frank, I didn't mean literally hit me."

"What?" snapped a voice. Definitely not Frank. The big, bearded dude from earlier loomed over me, and he'd brought an equally big and bearded buddy. Great.

"Thanks for nearly killing me, dickhead." I tried to rise

but fell to my knees; tight ropes bound my wrists and ankles behind my back.

"Ivy Lane," growled my kidnapper, baring his teeth in a wolf-like gesture. "You'll pay for what happened to Briana."

"What?" My head felt like it had been stuffed with cotton wool, and my physical body reminded me of its presence with a hundred aches and pains. Evidently, they'd beaten me while I'd been unconscious, and new pain stabbed me in the ribs. From what I could see, they'd brought me into a room, or a cell, with earthen walls covered with wood in some places. The ceiling was maybe seven feet above, also covered in wooden slats. "I didn't even know Briana, I swear."

"She was killed by one of the faeries, and it's all thanks to you."

"What?" I shook my head, baffled. "I don't own the faeries. Pretty sure they want me dead, actually."

The second giant shifter stepped forward. Like the first guy, he was heavyset with shaggy black hair, and he held a sword in both hands. A familiar-looking sword.

"Give that back, dickhead. Irene is mine."

"You named your sword?" The two men exchanged blank looks.

I sighed. "Just tell me what I'm supposed to have done, so you can untie me and we can put this mess behind us. What do you say?"

"I don't think so," said the first shifter.

Typical. My first date in months and I was stuck in a hole instead. I fought against the bonds, but all I managed to do was rub a layer of skin off both my wrists.

"Seriously, I had nothing to do with Briana's death," I said. "And neither did the half-faeries."

"You're working with them," said the first shifter. "I saw you on their territory."

"I got kicked *off* their territory. I work for the mages, and most of my cases involve dealing with murderous faeries. In fact, I'd be happy to help solve Briana's murder if you untie me and give me my weapon back."

"We don't need your help," said the first shifter. "If you and the faeries are planning another invasion, you'll have to go through us."

"Why the hell would anyone want another invasion?"

"You tell me."

He pressed his foot to my ribs. I yelped. Definitely bruised or broken. A snarl issued from his mouth, and the second shifter had backed away, dropping my sword.

"Don't mishandle Irene." I squirmed away, my back fetching up against a cold earthen wall. "Isn't it nearly sundown?"

A growling noise issued from the second shifter, whose head bowed. *Yes. Yes, it is.*

"For god's sake." I tried to stand, but the first shifter pushed me downward. "Get me out of here. And you should probably run, too."

Shifters didn't distinguish between prey and their fellow shifters while in a frenzy, but the growl in his throat told me he was succumbing to the shift, too. His lips peeled back from his teeth, which were rapidly elongating, fur sprouting from his forehead. *Oh, fuck me sideways.*

Fur sprouted from his body, too. His clothes didn't tear but disappeared outright, a detail I might have found interesting if I wasn't trapped in an unknown enclosed space with two transforming shifters. There was no way to reason with a shifter when they were in beast form.

Come on, magic. I need you.

Blue light erupted and my hands burst free of the ropes in the same instant that the two huge wolves leaped at me.

I ducked and one wolf soared over my head, colliding

with the other. One thing I knew about shifters was that they'd once lived in packs, but ultimately found their beast instincts won out and they ended up killing one another. Given that these two had been foolish enough to end up in a confined space together at the full moon, I didn't mind if the pair of them tore each other's faces off, but I'd prefer not to be in the pit myself when they did so.

Blue threads wrapped around my hands. I directed a burst of magic at my ankle bonds, freeing my legs, and lunged for my sword.

A clawed foot stomped down inches from me. One shifter had overpowered the other. Drool dripped from his curved teeth, and the manic glow in his yellow eyes told me he'd left reason far behind. I ducked and rolled, but my sword had clattered into the far corner, and my ribs screamed with each movement.

The two shifters clashed with a force that shook the earthen walls. Jaws snapped, claws swiped, and the clamour of their fight reverberated around the enclosed space. Packed earth walls meant we must be underground. There was no door, but narrow handholds marked the walls, small enough for a human to grab but not a shifter's clumsy paw. A smart move, though I doubted either of these two goons had been responsible for building this place. It must be some kind of underground bunker designed for a shifter to wait out the night while in beast form. Through a gap in the roof, the full moon alighted on the wolves' jet-black fur. I rolled to the side again to avoid being trampled, another stab of pain hitting my ribs. Dammit, I couldn't leave my sword behind.

One of the shifters rose upright, blood and drool dripping down his face. I rolled, dodging his paw, and his teeth snapped close to the back of my neck. I rose upward and punched him in the jaw, but the wrenching pain in my hand suggested I'd hurt myself more than the wolf. Hitting a shifter was like punching solid rock, but it had distracted him long enough for me to get a second punch in, this time with magic to back it up. Blue light blasted him backwards into the wall and I dove for my sword again, my hand closing around the hilt.

Blue ignited the air, showing me handholds on the roughly dug-out walls leading up to a gap in the roof. I climbed upright and reached for the nearest with my free hand, but the second shifter's paw struck me in the back and sent me staggering. He was bleeding from multiple wounds but was still conscious, and his next swipe gouged at my legs. I didn't dodge in time, slowed by my injured ribs, and pain flared up both legs from deep gashes. *Ouch.*

Cursing, I lifted my blade and drove the point into the shifter's shoulder. He sank, howling, one leg useless, while his companion gained on me from the side. I lifted my palm and sent a blast of magic at him. He flew back in a burst of blue light and hit the wall.

"Stay here and think about what you've done," I muttered, sheathing Irene at my waist before reaching for the handholds again. The movement burned my injured thighs as I clambered up, cursing through my teeth. My vision wavered. *Hang on, body. Pass out later.*

Snarls arose from below and I hung on grimly as the wall trembled with an earth-shaking thud. The shifters couldn't follow me, but if they shook me loose, I was dead. I dug my hands in and drew on my magic, pushing myself higher, until my hands hit wood and not earth. Grasping the edge of the roof, I pulled myself upward.

The bunker trembled beneath me, but I rolled off the flat roof and onto soft grass. The world spun and danced around but I stayed conscious, the shifters' roars rising from below. Assuming they survived the night, they'd both have a hell of a headache when they woke up in the morning, but that wasn't my problem.

"Shouldn't have fucking kidnapped me," I said, but all that came out was an incoherent croak. With a groan, I shifted onto my back. The sky seemed unnaturally bright, the moon a giant staring eye looming over me. A cough rattled my body that further jarred my broken rib. Or ribs. Ow. My hand reached into my inner pocket, fumbling for the healing spell I kept tucked inside my coat. I tugged my phone out, too. I couldn't see to hit the call button, but the healing spell activated in a flare of blue, adding to the magic already cloaking my skin.

For a brief moment, the vision of the faerie with Summer magic played behind my eyes again, a female figure haloed in green light.

The world danced around some more, and the next thing I knew, Frank hovered at my side.

I jumped upright. "Please say I didn't die."

"No. You crossed over again. You should probably stop doing that."

"I didn't do it on purpose!" I glared down at the bunker, visible through the haze next to my inert body. That was creepy. Like looking at my own corpse. "Why'd they get themselves locked in a confined space together before they transformed?"

"They didn't seem like the brightest bulbs," said Frank.

"No shit." I heaved a sigh, glad that my ribs no longer hurt. "Great. I missed my date and got the crap kicked out of me instead. Can you send me back again? Or did you change your mind about speaking to that shifter? I know she's here. We aren't near the Ley Line. It's safe."

"Meddling with death is never safe, Ivy Lane."

"Yeah, all right. Safe by comparison, then. There's a nasty killer out there and I want to know who it is."

"Ivy Lane." A hint of disapproval entered his voice. "Do you have any idea how many people die every day?"

"No, and I probably don't want to. But this place is localised, isn't it? People who die in this city come to you. There are other necromancers in different parts of the world—even in this country—aren't there?"

Frank paused for a moment. "Yes, but Death itself has many layers and few linger on this side."

"She recently died, so she must be around here," I pressed. "*Please.* This is important. Not just to stop a war between half-faeries and shifters—though that is pretty fucking urgent, if you ask me. No, I'm pretty sure she was killed by a powerful faerie talisman, and you know what happened the last time I encountered one of those."

Frank gave a sigh. "I'll see what I can do, but I'm not the only necromancer here, you know. The others might not like it if I single out a lone spirit who should have moved on."

"Tough shit." I frowned when a sudden lurching sensation tugged at my feet. "Wait a minute. I think I'm—"

I fell back into my own body. The brightness of the moon silhouetted the very tall person towering over me, and I scrambled away, hands brushing against dusty spell fragments. I blinked, my vision clearing.

Vance bent over me, concern on his face. "Ivy?"

"Why... what are you doing here?" I sat up properly, brushing bits of discarded spell and dirt off my legs. "How'd you find me?"

"Used a tracking spell after you called me and made incoherent noises into the phone." He sounded more worried than amused, though. "I didn't expect to find you so far from the city. What happened?"

"Got myself kidnapped by two dickheads who accused me of working with the faeries. Don't worry, I took care of them." I pushed to my feet. The shifters had brought me further from home than I'd realised, and we stood in a field divided by low stone walls. Beyond, the shapes of houses rose and fell, silhouetted against the indigo sky. I spied the underground bunker nearby and stepped in front in case Vance got any ideas. "They're alive but in beast form and probably beyond reason. Don't go in there."

"They should be reported," said Vance, the hint of a growl in his own voice.

"You can't arrest them while they're in shifter form," I said, rubbing the back of my neck. My hand came away covered in dirt. So much for our date. "Next time I'll be the one to rescue you, I swear. I'll even carry you out."

His mouth quirked a little. "I'll keep that in mind. You need to get home. It's not safe here."

"Yeah. Good advice. Where even are we?"

"On the boundary of shifter territory. How badly did they hurt you?"

Vance's concern stabbed me in the chest. I hated lying to him. All I'd wanted was a stress-free date, but I couldn't keep this a secret, and he'd been fine with my last earth-shattering revelation.

He wrapped his hands around mine, then we stood on my road, outside my flat. I drew in a breath, and explained everything, ending with my impromptu trip into Death.

Vance's eyes darkened with every word. The air grew colder, biting at my arms. My heart sank.

"Uh, anyway," I finished. "I want to see if I can talk to necromancer dude again—"

"Don't." The word whipped out, and I stepped back, startled. I'd hardly seen him this angry, at least not with me. I opened my mouth, but no sound came out.

"You passed over the veil," said Vance, in a flat, cold voice. "Into *Death*. There's a reason that necromancers receive extensive training before attempting to do so."

"Relax, Vance. The necromancer dude—"

"Is already dead," said Vance. "And a bloody fool, whoever he is. He should know better than to bring someone who isn't even an apprentice over into Death."

"I did it myself," I told him. "Accidentally. And he offered to train me. He can help. Listen—I asked if he can call the shifter's spirit, but we could ask the necromancers, if you'd rather. It's the easiest way to find out who the killer was."

"The shifters will never allow it."

"You know this is about more than a single death." I'd told him all my suspicions, but he'd fixated on my trip over the veil and not on the possibility of the killer wielding the very talisman the Lady of the Tree wanted me to find. "If we find the killer, we might find who stole the talisman. Then I can give it back to the Lady of the Tree and wash my hands of any promises I made her."

"If your vision was any indication, the shifter couldn't see her attacker." The air grew heavy and thick with tension. "Necromancer apprentices have a one in twenty chance of never waking up from their first attempt to cross the veil, and that's with the proper precautions in place." He spoke with all the emotion of someone reading from a textbook, but fury simmered in his eyes.

"Vance, I—"

He turned away, and I caught a glimpse of scales creeping up his arm. "I have to report this to the council. Please stay out of trouble for one night."

And he disappeared.

I swore at the cacti Isabel had brought out onto the lawn earlier, kicking the gate open. Whether Vance approved or not, I needed to know who the killer was. And if crossing the veil would get me answers, I'd do it again. Sure, the rational side of me knew it was risky as hell, accidental or not, but the faeries had killed someone. The shifters had blamed me for the murder and wrecked my date. On top of that, I still hadn't escaped the Lady of the Tree's bloody vow.

A howling sounded from the flat's top floor. Okay, maybe someone was having a worse night than I was. Aside from those two shifters I'd left in the bunker, of course.

The thought was no consolation whatsoever.

8

"Yes, I know it was a bad idea," I said wearily to Isabel. I hadn't been able to give her a proper explanation until George had gone back upstairs with his parents that morning, and despite sleeping in my own bed, it'd been a restless night of tossing and turning. "I told Vance repeatedly that I didn't do it on purpose, but I might as well have tried to share your cookies with those two shifters."

The cookies were the one bright spot in this shitshow of a week. Isabel had taken one look at my face when I'd come in last night and declared an evening baking session, to George's absolute delight. Now the inside of the flat was covered in flour as well as glitter.

Isabel looked at me from the armchair where she sat, one of her witch textbooks open on her lap. "I can't find anything in here on people accidentally skipping across the veil using faerie magic as a rope. Congratulations, Ivy. You've invented a whole new brand of necromancy."

"Whoop-de-fucking-do," I muttered. "I get that it's

dangerous, but the living necromancers won't help, and if I can find out who killed that shifter…"

"That Frank guy offered to help, right?"

"He also offered to teach me, but Vance acted like I'd taken up an apprenticeship with Satan." I bit into another cookie. "Who else is going to explain, though, really?"

"It'd be useful if there was someone alive who could teach you."

"No shit." I chewed, savouring the cinnamon-flavoured goodness. "You know what the half-faeries think of me, and besides, my power came from the Grey Vale. Not Summer or Winter."

"You can't be *that* special."

"I'd know if there were ten of me running around." I shoved the last piece of cookie in my mouth. "Never mind my magic. I want to find this killer, but Vance said he'd ask the necromancers, and I'd rather not talk to him until he's calmed down."

I rubbed my sleepless eyes and tried to think. Doubtless I'd have to see the necromancers if I wanted any answers at all, but I was pretty certain skipping over the veil without their permission violated their code in a dozen ways, and I'd never be able to explain how I knew Frank without admitting how we'd met.

"Maybe I should sneak into Necromancer HQ and steal their books," I said. "They must have a 'Crossing into Death for Dummies' somewhere in there."

Isabel put her book down. "Ivy, I know you did it by accident, but please don't make a habit of crossing over. If that necromancer hadn't been there, you might have been stuck."

"I know." I also knew there was someone potentially lurking over in Death who I did *not* want to meet again, in the flesh or otherwise. Someone who'd sworn revenge on me… and on Vance.

Wait a minute. If I could cross into the veil at any time, did that mean I could go into Faerie, too? Without the veil in turmoil? Sure, I didn't *want* to take a voluntary trip into the Grey Vale, but it struck me as the sort of thing I ought to figure out before my enemies did it for me. *I really need a tutor.*

A rapping on the door. *Vance?* I should have called him, but my blasted pride had got in the way after he'd taken off on me the previous night.

Steeling myself, I opened the door. Henry Cavanaugh looked even more rough than he had during our last encounter, shadows darkening his eyes and clumps of hair missing as if he'd pulled them out with his own claws.

"Oh, it's you." I didn't even try to disguise the contempt in my voice. "Thought you already took George home."

"Ivy… I wanted to apologise for how I spoke to you yesterday."

"Get in line," I said, before I could stop myself. "Two of your people kidnapped me and tried to beat me to death last night."

"I know," he said. "The Mage Lord brought them in."

"Wait… what?" He had?

"He subdued them while they were in shifter form, the foolish human. They're in jail, but the other shifters are restless. There was another death yesterday. We need your help." He paused for an instant, but not long enough for me to absorb the impact of his words. "I want to hire you."

I stared at him, hardly able to believe what I was hearing. "Someone else died?"

"Who?" Isabel watched us enter the flat, her eyes widening. "What happened?"

"A shifter named Perry. He disappeared just before curfew and was found a few hours after dawn."

"And—how did he die?" I knew how. While I'd been here

feeling sorry for myself, the killer had struck again. Damn it all.

"Magic," he said. "Faerie magic. Their scent was found near the body. And… and it wasn't near half-blood territory this time."

"Shit." I clenched my fists. "I could have stopped this, you know."

Henry avoided my gaze. "If you can stop whichever monstrosity is killing my kin… I can't promise the others will be agreeable, but I'd like you to help. I'll pay, of course."

My mouth parted. This would be strictly freelance, because he was hiring *me*, not the Mage Lord. I hadn't yet figured out how I'd split my time between taking on jobs for the mages and freelance cases, but this overlapped enough with what Vance and I were doing that I'd have suggested visiting the manor if not for Henry's irrational grudge.

"All right." A rustle of paper told me Isabel was retrieving one of our contracts. "You're probably familiar with how I handle cases. Just sign that."

Isabel passed him the contract and a pen. "You'll be needing one of my tracking spells, I expect."

Henry nodded, relief flashing across his face. "Yes. Thank you. I'd be grateful for your help."

"Pity someone had to die for it."

Isabel gave me a look. Oops. My filter went walkabout on a regular basis at the best of times, but I'd crossed the line from mildly pissed off to hopping mad some time ago. Henry bent over the desk to sign the contract and handed it back to me, his expression not exactly wary, but with the hint of a predator sensing potential danger. Good.

"I'll need to use a tracking spell at the murder site," I told him. "To get the most accurate results. Also, if it's really the faeries who did this, I'll have to look around in person, too. I can see through glamour. I'd prefer for the other shifters not to know that, though."

If I was going to use my abilities to investigate, it would be easier if he knew, though I didn't like the notion of the shifters suspecting I had any ties to the faeries. Aside from the ones they were already aware of.

"You can?" Now he looked wary, his nostrils flaring, his eyes gaining a yellow tint. I'd thought the beast was caged during the day, but maybe not.

"Yes." No point in beating around the bush. "I don't know what I'll find at the murder scene, but we're looking at an uncommonly powerful fae. One that can overcome a shifter in beast form. The culprit isn't on half-blood territory."

"Not everyone would agree with that assessment."

"I can trust that they won't confront me?" I pressed. "If I'm going to help, I want a guarantee that I won't encounter resistance."

"I can't offer that."

Figures. "Let's go, then. Isabel, are you coming?"

"Sure." From her worried frown, she had reservations, but we were partners, and Henry was marginally less likely to fly off the handle at her than at me.

When dealing with shifters, keeping my own emotions in check was the best move, but the recent kidnapping coupled with Vance's apparent attempt to take matters into his own hands had thrown me off completely. He must have teleported straight back over there after he'd left me last night. Hadn't he cared if they took him to pieces? More to the point, the killer had been right by shifter territory last night, and if Vance had walked into them…

I cut off that thought and focused on the more immediate issue of a trip into shifter territory at their crankiest time of the month. Isabel and I followed Henry past high fences reinforced to keep the shifters from breaking out and terrorising everyone, and he led the way to a padlocked door near which a crowd had gathered. My stomach lurched when I saw the blood.

"The murder was committed right outside the victim's home," said Henry. "I believe Perry was trying to get back into his house when he died."

Damn. Someone had killed a shifter right outside their own door this time? That was tantamount to a declaration of war.

Heads turned at our approach. I let Henry take the lead so that if anyone tried to start a fight, he'd be first in line.

"What're they doing here?" demanded one of the shifters.

"Helping us to find Perry's murderer," said Henry. "Ivy and Isabel are freelance investigators and witches with expertise in this area."

"Well… we haven't investigated a *lot* of murders." Isabel took a wary step back as a heavily muscled shifter peeled away from the group and advanced on us.

A tattoo ran down one side of the man's shaved head, a pattern of symbols etched in black ink, but his beard was thick enough to make up for the lack of hair on his scalp. "Well, what're you here for, then?"

"To use a tracking spell." Isabel's voice trembled a little. I planted myself at her side and directed a challenging stare back at the hostile faces watching us.

"Why?" growled the shifter.

"Tracking spells can show the immediate past," Isabel said. "It'll show the last person who came here, but… well, you guys have walked all over the crime scene."

Six pairs of eyes flashed. *Yikes.*

"It's true," I added. "We do spells, not miracles."

"And just what are *you* doing here? You're the Mage Lord's new lapdog, right?" asked the tattooed man.

"I'm a freelance investigator," I said. "I specialise in

beating the shit out of sick fucks like the killer." I rested my hand on the hilt of my sword, looking the shifter in the eyes rather than at the crime scene behind him. I could already tell it was messy. Blood covered the entire area outside the gates, and everything was wreathed in green light.

"You aren't to come near him," said the shifter, seeing my gaze shift to the blood despite myself.

"I need access to the scene to effectively use a tracking spell," said Isabel. She was handling this much better than I'd expected. Shifters terrified anyone who, unlike me, had a healthy sense of when to run for the hills. "If the killer left traces at the scene, the spell might pick up on them."

The leading shifter's nostrils flared. "Fine, but you aren't to touch him."

Isabel and I exchanged glances that said, *Who the hell would want to touch a dead body?*

"I'll do it," I offered. "The spell will work the same for both of us." And I'd already seen the killer in action before. Not that I had any intention of admitting so in front of six furious shifters.

Isabel passed me the tracking spell with a grateful nod. "I'll wait here."

"Good call." I waited while Henry stared out the tattooed shifter at the front until he moved aside and let me past.

Unlike the first victim, Perry's body wasn't intact. Blood spread in a gory halo around what I could only describe as *fragments.* The man's arms and legs lay a foot away from his torso, and his neck had been half-severed. His chest, ripped open with enough impact to tear off his limbs. I stared numbly for a few seconds, too shocked even to feel nauseated.

"Well?" growled the shifter. "Get on with it and then get out."

I shuffled forward. Green light wreathed the alley, more

obvious when I stood in its midst. I dropped to my knees, the spell shaking in my hands. My skin felt cold and clammy, and I closed my eyes for a moment to clear my head.

The spell activated at my touch, and light spread from the circle to my arms. Behind my eyes, I saw the same street that I knelt on in the waking world. Darkness filled the spaces between moonbeams that illuminated someone sprinting down the street on four paws. A more human-sized figure pursued the beast, as indistinct as the last time. Too far to make out their features, but the gleam of a sword in their hand was as stark as the green light that flared out—

I let go of the spell before I saw the shifter's gruesome end. Swallowed bile. *Damn. I have to tell them.*

"I can't be sure," I said slowly, "but I think the killer used… Summer magic."

"Half-bloods," spat the tattooed shifter. "Murdering scum."

"It's not them." I rose upright and brushed spell dust from my knees with shaking hands. "That faerie was way too powerful to be half-blood. More powerful than I've ever seen in this realm."

"In this realm?" echoed the shifter. "You've been *there?*"

"Not voluntarily." *And this conversation is over.* "Listen, I know what I saw. I can talk to the half-faeries' leader. I guarantee he'll want to find the killer as much as you do."

"Wrong." His voice was a guttural growl. "The fae care nothing for anyone other than their own."

They aren't the only ones. "This faerie is a potential danger to everyone, not just you. I… I imagine your people were targeted because they're the only ones out at night this week."

Guesswork—and they normally *wouldn't* be out at night—but I could see no other connection between the two deaths.

"How do you know that?" Henry asked.

"I've met the Chief of the half-faeries. He barely had more magic than a troll, and he's the strongest they have." Not strictly true, if the way he'd kicked Vance and me out of his house proved anything, but hey, they didn't need to know. "Trust me. It's not them. Though… have any of you spoken to a necromancer?"

A ripple of anger spread through the group of shifters. A female shifter with biceps thicker than my thighs said, "No. They're all lying scumbags."

"That, I can agree on," I said, "but if we contact Perry's spirit, he might be able to tell us anything else he saw before he died. The tracking spell didn't reveal enough for me to know what the killer looked like."

"Absolutely not," growled the tattooed man, and the others echoed his words. If they'd been in shifted form, their fur would have been bristling.

"We don't allow our people to be violated in such a manner," said the female shifter. "Not at all. No exceptions."

I raised my hands. "Okay. We'll have to rely on guesswork, then."

Or rather, I'd have to go behind their backs again. Assuming Vance was amenable to the idea. I did need to talk to him again, not least to confront him over his clash with those two shifters the previous night. I walked past the shifters, whose eyes followed me, and saw Isabel vomiting into a bin on the other side of the road. I averted my eyes, fighting nausea myself, and turned to Henry instead. "It really would be easier if I could speak to the necromancers."

"No," he said, "and don't tell the Mage Lord either."

I raised an eyebrow at him. "It's his job to keep an eye on any incidents in the supernatural community that threaten the peace, remember? Pretty sure murder qualifies as such."

"Then tell him to stay out of this," said Henry.

"Don't tell *me* what to do," I retaliated. "Whatever your

personal problem with him is, the mages' goal is to maintain order. They wouldn't beat me up and dump me in a hole in the ground and then shift into werewolves, either."

Henry's face flushed. "They shouldn't have done that. The pair of them have already been apprehended. The Mage Lord saw to it they won't be walking again anytime soon."

"Good," I snapped, wishing I'd been the one to break their kneecaps. "I'll help you with this case, but you'll have to accept I'll use all my resources if necessary, including the mages and the half-bloods."

"I would rather you didn't speak to the Chief either, and many would agree."

"You must know you're being ridiculous." I sighed. "I highly doubt the Chief wants a killer loose in the city any more than I do. He's not prejudiced against shifters." No more than he was against humans in general, anyway.

I understood Henry's reservations. The faeries were a menace, but the half-bloods… I didn't quite know how to feel about them. Despite our shared mistrust, the incident with the drug showed they were as prone to being manipulated at the hands of the Sidhe as the rest of us. Most were simply trying to survive, and for many, losing their magic meant losing their lives.

"You don't understand," he said. "When the faeries came, the disruption on the Ley Line forced all shifters into their animal forms. Everyone transformed, losing their humanity and reason in the process, with tragic results. It's not something my people will forgive."

"I'm sorry for that, but the Sidhe killed millions of other humans, remember? None of us were untouched by this. Including the half-bloods."

Henry uttered a faint growl. "Fine. Speak to whoever you like, but half-faeries and mages won't be welcome in our territory. Nor necromancers, either."

"Right." I didn't need to bring the necromancers to shifter territory to call back the victims' ghosts, assuming I could wrangle an agreement from their leader. "I'll see what I can do."

I went in search of Isabel, who'd finished being sick and was wiping her mouth on a tissue. "That—how could anyone—?"

"Faeries," I said. "They don't have morals. Humans are like toys to them."

Isabel gave a shudder. "What now? Going to see your boss?"

"I should probably call him first."

"Do that. Last night was weird. I don't think he's mad at you. He's worried about you. There's a difference."

"I wanted a date, not a dead body." I pulled out my phone and hit Vance's number.

"Vance," I said. "I've been—" The sound of a dial tone interrupted me. "What the hell?"

"He's not there?"

"Nope." I hung up, fury beginning to simmer. "Fine. I'll go it alone."

I walked, Isabel hurrying to keep pace with me while the high fences of shifter territory gave way to houses and gardens. "Er... where exactly are you going?"

"To see the necromancers. If I'm going to be sensible and not hop over the veil, I'll have to do it the legal way. Otherwise known as the bloody impossible way, because Lord Evander hates me."

Isabel chewed her lip. "Not alone. Let me come with you."

"To the necromancers?" I hesitated. "I suppose they're less dangerous than the half-bloods or shifters. But bring salt. Lots of it. They've had trouble controlling their undead lately."

"Yippee," said Isabel, in such an accurate impression of me that I laughed.

I tried to call Vance twice on the way home, but my calls went straight to voicemail. Giving up for the time being, I left a message telling him to call me back as soon as he had a free moment.

When we reached the flat, Isabel ducked inside and returned carrying several saltshakers.

"Good call." I took one from her and stashed it in my pocket. "Last time I visited the necromancers, a half-faerie ghost showed up as well as the undead."

"I didn't know you could see ghosts."

"Only when the veil's thinner than usual." I secured a second saltshaker in my inside pocket, too. "Should be normal now, but you never know."

"Good," said Isabel. "I'm glad you aren't turning into a full-fledged necromancer. No offence, but they're creepy as hell."

"Gotta agree with you there." I zipped up my coat. "If we're lucky, Lord Evander won't have figured out I stole the recipe for the drug's cure from his office."

"Wait, *that's* where the coven got it?" Isabel, who was in the process of locking the door, dropped the key on the floor. "You never mentioned that."

"I didn't technically steal it myself... it's complicated." I retrieved the key and handed it back to her. "It's the least of the reasons he has to be pissed off at me, really."

"Ivy." She shook her head at me. "I'm starting to think Vance has good reason to want to keep a close eye on you."

"As if that'll stop me." I flashed her a grin. "Shall we hear what Lord Dickhead has to say for himself?"

9

The first thing I did when we reached the necromancers' headquarters was check on the locked gate to the cemetery next door in case there were any half-faerie ghosts lurking around. Nothing appeared to be amiss, but the squat, jet-black building seemed to push the sun's rays as far away as possible, and the black-curtained windows made it impossible to tell what might be happening inside.

"Do they sleep during the day?" Isabel whispered. "Like vampires?"

"Good question." Vampires weren't a thing as far as I knew—not the blood-drinking variety, anyway—though there were plenty of fae who fit that description. "Nah, I think they're just allergic to light and happiness."

The door opened. My heart sank. I'd hoped the leader of the necromancers wouldn't answer the door in person, but no such luck. Lord Evander—short and slight, dressed in a smart suit that made him look more like a politician than someone who raised the dead on a regular basis—glared at me. "Ivy Lane. I thought I informed your boss that you aren't welcome here."

I let my dignity slide away. "I wish to hire a necromancer. I'm investigating a murder and require your services."

"Absolutely not," said Lord Evander. "The last time you were near a summoning circle, people died. Specifically, you *killed* one of my apprentices."

I swallowed. "He was possessed. I acted in self-defence. I didn't mean to kill him."

"I don't think you do anything by accident, Ivy Lane."

I kept my expression neutral, with difficulty. He was asking for a punch to the throat. "Whatever you think of me is irrelevant. I'm asking you in a professional capacity."

"Then let *me* hire you," said Isabel, stepping forward. "I'm investigating this murder case, too. I'm happy to pay your rates, whatever they are."

Lord Evander scowled at her. "Witch, are you?"

"The Laurel Coven's Second," said Isabel. "I can call my leader to make the request directly, if need be."

"That won't be necessary."

I gaped at little. Isabel of all people didn't threaten anyone. I was the sharp-tongued one, usually, but her words had the desired effect.

Lord Evander's expression flattened. "Fine. I'll ask one of my apprentices to assist you. Ivy Lane, you aren't to go within a metre of them."

"I need to speak to the ghost in person." I didn't, but I wouldn't let Isabel go in there alone. "I swear I won't touch anything."

"Fine."

He swept into the building. The gloomy hallway led into an equally gloomy room, wide and high-ceilinged. The outline of a big circle had been chalked onto the shiny metal floor with unlit candles placed at intervals around the edges. More candles burned in tall carved sconces on the walls, casting long shadows upon the summoning circle.

"Why's the room made of metal?" I asked.

"Iron," said Lord Evander. "It was once believed that iron repelled spirits in the same way that it does faeries."

Interesting. I hadn't heard that one before, but it'd at least be a handy way to keep half-faerie ghosts out. Lord Evander halted before the circle and two other cloaked figures I hadn't seen before stepped out of a corner. Evidently, 'lurking creepily in corners' was part of necromancer training.

"Colby," said Lord Evander, gesturing towards a scrawny young man. "Your assistance is required."

The man—boy, really—was barely out of his teens, and his wary gaze rested on the sword at my waist. *Wait a moment. Is that...?*

Yes, it was the same apprentice I'd met in the spirit world and asked to steal the recipe for the drug's cure from his boss's office. I sincerely hoped he didn't recognise me in the waking world.

"We need you to contact a spirit," said Isabel. "A man named—" She looked at me.

"Perry," I said, crossing my fingers behind my back that the apprentice didn't give the game away. "A shifter. He was murdered last night. We wish to question his spirit."

The apprentice swallowed, throat bobbing nervously. "Okay. If he was killed violently, though, his spirit might try to attack us. He might not know he's dead."

"It'll be fine," said Lord Evander, in a surprisingly reassuring tone. "The spirit will remain caged within the circle. He won't be able to get out."

The apprentice shuffled forwards. "Okay. You two... stay away from the circle while I'm doing the ritual." He mumbled the words, like he wasn't used to giving orders.

Still showing no signs of having recognised me, he crouched and fiddled with one of the candles at the circle's edge. A whitish light flared up. He then moved around the circle and did the same to the other candles. I'd figured they weren't regular candles, but they appeared to activate with some kind of switch on the side. When all twelve flared up, the apprentice began to chant in a language that sounded vaguely like Latin. The candles burned brighter, their flames more white than yellow. The lights blurred around the circle's perimeter, enclosing a rapidly growing patch of grey smoke.

The veil.

Shivers ran down my spine. The room was already like a refrigerator, but the icy wind billowing out from the circle almost made it feel like the candles exuded coldness, not warmth. Isabel's teeth chattered next to me, while I spied a few more necromancers who'd entered through open doors off the room. They'd obviously come to watch the show.

The apprentice necromancer, Colby, walked up to the circle. Even from a safe distance, I could tell his knees were trembling. He spoke again in that strange language, and then said the name *Perry*. He must be calling the shifter's spirit.

The grey smoke began to swirl, picking up speed like a miniature tornado contained within the magical boundaries of the summoning circle. Dizziness swept through me, but I couldn't look away. The smoke thinned out, turning into fine mist. The outline of a man appeared, indistinct and blurred, but recognisably human, though his corpse had been in such a state that I couldn't have said for sure it was the same guy.

I closed my eyes against a wave of nausea, and when I opened them again, he'd moved to the circle's edge, placing his hands outward as though a glass door sat between him and the way out of the circle. "What—what is this?"

"It worked!" said the apprentice, sounding startled. When

Lord Evander cleared his throat, he gave his boss a guilty look and turned back to the ghost. "Ah… there's someone who wants to talk to you."

I stepped forward. "Hey. I'm Ivy. I wanted to ask you some questions about last night."

"Last night?" His forehead scrunched up. "What happened last night?"

"You tell me. Do you remember what you did yesterday evening?"

"I was… I went for a walk."

"Before shifting?"

"I didn't—" He broke off, looking vaguely puzzled. "I don't remember going for a walk. What time is it now?"

Crap. He didn't know he was dead. Well, this would be fun.

"Tell me everything you remember about last night," I said. "Remember any faeries?"

"Faeries?" He stared at me in puzzlement. "Why is everything grey?"

"Because… we're underground." Great job there, Ivy. Well, it was the necromancers' job to break the bad news to the newly dead. Not mine.

"Why? How did I get here?"

I shot a desperate look at the apprentice, but he gaped at the circle as though he couldn't believe he'd managed to conjure up a real spirit. *Great.*

"Answer our questions and I'll tell you." If he refused, the necromancers could deal with the fallout. It wasn't my problem.

"Who *are* you?" His eyes rounded. "There's blue light all around you."

My heart plunged. Could the dead see faerie magic? Or just mine, because it was tied to Death itself?

"Never mind," I said, wishing the necromancers didn't

have to hear all this. "Someone was murdered yesterday. I have reason to think you might have seen the killer. Did you see any faeries last night?"

"Aside from you?"

My heart performed a sickening dive. "What?"

"You're glowing like one of them." He stared into the distance. "I remember… but how can that be possible? What *happened* to me?"

"You remember something?"

"A… a woman." His brow scrunched up. "A beautiful woman."

A sudden suspicion seized me. I thought back to what I'd seen of the killer through the blurred vision of the tracking spell. The figure I'd seen had been female. She'd carried the talisman. And…

Wait, Ivy. I needed to check with Vance before I did anything rash. Because I knew one female faerie who'd recently visited Faerie and had recently regained her youth and power.

"Did you see what her face looked like?" Isabel spoke in hesitant tones. "The woman."

"Beautiful." He seemed to fold in on himself, his form becoming even more indistinct. "Where am I?"

"We don't have long." I pressed on. "Do you remember if this woman was carrying… a weapon? A sword, maybe?"

"I don't know." He faded even more. "Please. Why won't you tell me where I am? I don't remember how I got here."

"Be glad you don't," I said quietly, thinking of his dismembered body. "Guys, help me out here," I called to the necromancers. "At least tell him the truth."

The apprentice seemed to have frozen into a statue. Lord Evander, typically, was nowhere to be seen.

Fine. "You're dead. Sorry. You were murdered last night."

The shifter stared at me a moment. The smoky miasma

surrounding him spilled outward, beating against the circle's boundary. "I'm *not*."

"Enough," Lord Evander said loudly from behind the circle. "Colby, banish him."

The apprentice snapped back to life. "Yes, sir. I—what are the words again?"

Lord Evander made an impatient noise. "You practised every day for the last three years. Say the words."

Colby tripped over the strange language, and the smoke began to churn within the circle. The ghost vanished like a light snuffed out beneath the thickening smoke, which once again coalesced into a vortex of grey. My vision doubled, and within the grey, a shining silvery light caught my eye and I glimpsed a narrow passage. No, not a tunnel, but a path leading between tall trees clad in silver.

Holy shit.

I could see the Grey Vale.

I looked at the other necromancers, but none had reacted. They didn't see what I did, surely, but a familiar chill bit into my bones. We weren't on the Ley Line. I shouldn't be able to see this.

Lord Evander bellowed something in possibly-Latin, and the smoke dissipated like he'd scared it away. My legs unlocked, having frozen to the spot, while my hands and feet had gone numb. I moved from one foot to the other to get some sensation back into them as the necromancer leader marched over to me.

"Ivy Lane," snarled Lord Evander. "I did not give you permission to cause the spirit unnecessary distress."

"He was already distressed," I pointed out. "You clearly weren't gonna tell the guy the truth. Someone had to."

"It's not for you to decide," said the necromancer. "And what exactly were you asking him? A faerie murderer, is there?"

"It's a confidential matter between myself and my client," I said smoothly. I'd used the same line to get out of questionable situations a dozen times, but Lord Evander was less easily dissuaded.

"I don't believe a word you say," he said. "Ivy Lane, I'm holding you in custody here until you tell me exactly what you're planning."

"What?" What had he decided I was doing? "I'm solving a murder that I'm positive was committed by a faerie, if you must know."

I was also pretty sure I knew who the killer was, though her motives were a total mystery.

"I won't have any more of this," he snapped. "The veil has been in a dire state since you started poking into matters that don't concern you, Ivy Lane."

"You aren't the centre of the universe," I informed him. "Two shifters were brutally murdered. Forgive me if I don't think coddling your insecurities is more important than people's lives."

"Don't talk to me like that. You aren't the Mage Lord, and you're speaking above your station." He moved closer, and a chill lifted the hair from my scalp. Not the sort of cold breeze that Vance's power conjured, but more of an icy, soul-sucking coldness that sucked at my bones and leached every last vestige of warmth from my body. His eyes were cold and dark as the grave.

"I'll call the Mage Lord," I said, falling back on the one surefire way to make him back down. "He's a busy man, but I'm sure he'll make time to explain to you that these murders have the potential to affect the entire city. Including you and your people, Lord Evander."

I didn't like the idea of Vance bailing us out either, but it wasn't fair to get Isabel trapped in custody alongside me.

Lord Evander hissed out a breath. "The man is a fool to ally with the faeries."

"Nobody's allied with the faeries," I said. "In case you didn't hear me the first time, they killed someone. Blasted them to pieces. You might be next."

"Don't you dare threaten me—"

"I'm giving you a warning, you absolute fuckwit," I exploded. "Not a threat. There's a difference. Besides, you're the one who threatened me first."

Lord Evander's face darkened to purple. "You—how dare you speak to me like that." The words tripped over each other on the way out of his mouth, and I took advantage of his shock to slide my phone from my pocket. I'd had two missed calls from Vance already. About bloody time he got in touch.

I skimmed my finger over the call button. "I did warn you."

"Ivy Lane—"

Too late. "Hey, Vance," I said brightly. "I'm at the necromancers' headquarters and Lord Evander is insisting on keeping me in custody on false allegations. I'm sure you'd be happy to come and explain to him that I'm here investigating a murder."

My heart thudded in the silence following my words. Five seconds passed. Ten. Maybe I'd finally tipped him over the edge.

Twenty seconds. "I'll be there."

The phone clicked off. Lord Evander stared at me, his eyes bulging from their sockets. "The impertinence," he hissed. "Ivy Lane, if I ever see you near this place again—"

"You'll use my intestines to hang laundry on. I get it."

"Get *out*."

"Are you sure you don't want to speak to the Mage Lord?"

"Out. Both of you."

Isabel shot him a guilty look as we both hurried to the door, while I spared a glance for the apprentice who'd summoned the spirit. *Still doesn't recognise me, does he?* You'd think he'd have caught on at some point. Maybe I just really didn't look like the same person when I was yanked out of my body.

Once the door closed—or rather, slammed—I turned to see Vance walking up to the entrance. Here we go.

"What did you do this time?" he asked.

No apologies for last night, then. Maybe he thought the necromancers were listening in, or else a bunch of ghosts were lurking behind the cemetery gates. To be fair, that was a distinct possibility.

"I called him a fuckwit after he accused me of working with the faeries. He was going to call you anyway, so…"

Isabel kept her distance, wisely, as Vance and I fell into step with one another. "You really couldn't hold your tongue?" His eyes were underscored with dark shadows like he hadn't slept, and stubble shadowed his jawline.

"He's a dick."

Vance grunted. "Why did you even come here?" He glared at the gates to the cemetery like they'd mortally offended him. "I didn't think any of your clients worked with the necromancers."

"Didn't you get my voicemail message? Someone else died on shifter territory. Killed by the same person as the last one."

He stopped walking. "Another death?"

"Yes, and Henry wanted to hire me independently," I added, before he got on my case about getting involved. "He wants to keep the Mage Lords out of it. The other shifters are furious."

"That doesn't surprise me in the slightest," Vance said. "I

take it you came here to question the shifter's ghost. Did you learn anything?"

He was taking this better than I'd expected. "Not enough, but he got blasted to pieces with Summer magic. It's… it's got to be the person carrying the sword. The talisman."

Vance's eyes flashed light grey, like the sky before a thunderstorm. "They must have struck after curfew. I did have people watching out on shifter territory, but we couldn't cover every inch."

"Speaking of, why the hell didn't you tell me you went after those twats who kidnapped me?"

"Because you took enough risks yesterday."

"There's a murderer on the loose blasting people into bloody pieces." I choked on the words. While I'd had no intention of those shifters getting off easily, Vance had some nerve lecturing *me* about taking risks. "At least tell me before you decide to fight my battles for me next time. How do you think I'd have felt if I'd woken up to news of *your* murder this morning?"

Vance continued to walk, his tone calm. "I didn't know about the second death, but you're right. I didn't think before I left you last night."

"That's better." Where the hell was the guy who'd delivered a dozen cacti to my doorstep? "Because as gratifying as it is to think of you kicking the shit out of those dudes, I'd rather you'd have spent the evening with me instead."

"I apologise for that," he said, not looking at me. "To be honest… I think the energy surge from the recent events at the Ley Line is still affecting everyone with shifter blood in the area. Shifters are prone to emotional outbursts, but the two who attacked you yesterday were entirely irrational even in human form. Your neighbour, too."

Wait. "Is that why everyone's blowing up at one another so easily?"

"Perhaps," he said. "I initially went to check on those shifters to see if they'd taken any drugs similar to those that affected the half-faeries. They hadn't, but when I tried to ask more questions of the other shifters, they refused to speak to me."

"They wouldn't speak to you?" That figured. "I guess arresting and beating two of them up doesn't give the best of impressions."

"They deserved worse," said Vance. "That aside, didn't you see your neighbour's eyes change when we spoke? That's not supposed to happen when shifters are in human form, even on nights of the shift."

"It isn't?" The image of a dozen flashing eyes replayed in my head. "Crap. The same happened with all the shifters who'd gone to check out their dead buddy. I mean, they had a good reason to be pissed off anyway, so I didn't think anything of it."

"Shifters generally need to exert an effort to remain in control of their emotions," he said. "That they aren't—even given the circumstances—suggests the energy levels on the Ley Line aren't back to normal."

"The necromancers said they were." I hoped he'd think I meant Lord Evander, not the dead guy.

"Shifters are particularly sensitive to the Ley Line at the full moon," he said. "Other supernaturals, not so much, so they're less likely to pick up on any anomalies."

"That includes mages?"

"Exactly," Vance said. "I've managed the change for twenty years and usually I barely notice the difference in shift season. This month, it's different, but whether it's due to the recent events the veil or has another cause, I can't say."

"Nor me. Does that mean you'll try to keep a lid on your temper?"

"Yes, if you stop to think before you act."

"I'll take it into consideration the next time I get kidnapped." Before he could object, I added, "As for you, if I so much as hear a rumour you're wandering around shifter territory without telling me first, I'll hit you with one of Isabel's glitter spells. Try being subtle then."

His eyes widened a little in disbelief, then he smirked. "Is that how it is?"

"I keep my word. What now?" I asked. "I didn't interrupt anything important, did I?"

"No. I left Wanda in charge. I've also ordered Chieftain Taive to conduct an investigation into Calder's possible allies in case one of them is involved in this."

"That's possible, but… well, the killer used Summer magic. Not Winter." Unease trickled down my back, and I became abruptly conscious of how close we were to the gated fields that housed the dead. "I'll drop by the manor later, if you aren't busy."

The question, *what about our date?* hovered on the tip of my tongue.

"Come in an hour," said Vance. "I have some things I need to take care of first."

Before I could respond, he'd gone. Like smoke on the wind.

10

I caught up to Isabel outside the flat, thoroughly pissed off at the universe in general. "Right," I said. "I'm heading off again."

"Where?"

"To see the bloody Lady of the bloody Tree."

"Didn't she try to kill you last time?" Isabel swivelled to me. "You can't go there alone."

"She needs my help." She also might be the murderer we were looking for. It'd be just like a word-twisting faerie to hire me to find a missing object she'd stolen herself and used to commit murder with, and I didn't want Isabel within a mile of her regardless.

Yet again, I wished I'd taken careful notes of our last encounter so I could pick apart every word later. She'd cleverly avoided using any references to a specific time, as far as I remembered, and she also hadn't said she'd never handled the stolen object herself.

Then again, maybe I was letting my grudge against the Lady of the Tree cloud my judgement. She hated humans, yes, but so did every faerie this side of the veil. If she'd murdered the shifters, drawing my attention right before-hand by invoking the vow wasn't a wise move. Why risk me finding out the truth, especially if she already had the talisman and didn't need me to help retrieve it?

She left her sanity behind in Faerie, the Chief had said, but she'd struck me as someone who had at least some sense of self-preservation, considering she'd survived in the mortal world for twenty years. She wouldn't throw her own safety away over a talisman that was allegedly too strong for a non-Sidhe to handle. Right?

Checking I had all my protective spells and weapons in place, I said goodbye to Isabel. "I'll call you in an hour. If not, tell Vance. You have his number, right?"

"Yeah. Be careful, Ivy." Her tone suggested she knew I'd do the exact opposite, but there was no help for it. I didn't like to imagine what the Lady of the Tree would do if I failed to fulfil my end of the bargain. I'd heard stories of people being literally ripped to pieces for breaking a promise to a faerie, and without the faerie in question so much as lifting a finger. Not that I expected the Lady of the Tree to use a hands-off approach.

Walking to the Botanical Gardens cleared my head some-what, but my apprehension returned when I reached the forest. As soon as I entered, sprawling trees extended in every direction, and every noise seemed twenty times as ominous without Vance at my side. I gritted my teeth and marched forward, Irene in my hands, reminding myself that forest wasn't Faerie, however much it liked to pretend so. That much was obvious from the fallen leaves carpeting the ground and the weak sunlight painting shadows on the path.

Far sooner than I expected, I reached the clearing with the giant oak tree resting in the centre. Vance and I had walked for at least fifteen minutes the first time we'd come here. Not five. Had the forest shrunk, or was this some faerie trickery? I'd bet my sword on the latter.

The Lady of the Tree's newly youthful face appeared within the tree and gave me a broad smile. "What do you have to say, Ivy Lane?"

I kept one hand on my blade, keeping well away from the roots criss-crossing the clearing. "Did you kill a shifter?"

"Why would I harm a mortal?"

"You didn't answer the question."

Her smile turned into a dark scowl that marred her perfect features. "I should remind you, mortal, you are bound to me, not the other way around."

"Have you been murdering shifters?" *Are you also the Elf Lady George saw?* Because if she hurt that kid, I'd rip her roots out. "Two shifters have died. Both saw their attacker was a female faerie who used Summer magic. On your own account, Summer magic is dying. To use that amount of power—"

"—means tapping into the talisman," she said, a melancholy expression crossing her face. "Someone is using magic that belongs to Faerie alone."

It isn't you? The last time I'd seen her put on the *I'm so sad* act, she'd followed up by trying to bury me alive. I didn't trust her an inch, but outright accusations would get me nowhere, and if I pushed too far, she might twist the vow to some grisly purpose. She'd never said she needed me in one piece to fulfil my end of the bargain.

"Chieftain Taive tells me the talisman is likely to be in the shape of a sword," I said. "I'm having difficulty believing someone could just stride out of Faerie carrying a weapon of that power under normal circumstances without being detected. Much less wander around the city with it."

"No." She spoke in a whisper, her mouth forming a grin.

"No, but you must have noticed its effect upon half-blood territory. Their magic is fading."

"I thought that was why."

She sounded positively delighted at the prospect. Creepy old hag.

"Then who carries it?"

"Only the very best can handle a talisman."

"A Sidhe." I gave her a pointed stare. "You knew who stole it from the outset, didn't you?"

"One could easily guess, Ivy Lane. Nobody but a Sidhe Lord would have the audacity to steal what isn't theirs. Nobody until you, that is."

She knows I stole... wait. Which exile from Summer had I recently encountered who'd fought with a powerful blade? A blade I'd left behind after his death, abandoning both in the Grey Vale?

Ah, fuck.

The Lady looked at me expectantly with those too-bright green eyes.

I scrambled for a reply. "Me? I wouldn't wander off with a Sidhe's sword. I'd get mugged as soon as I took it on the bus."

No... I'd left the sword exactly where it had fallen, beside Velkas's dead body. *Anyone might have picked it up afterwards.*

"But you did steal Lord Avalin's magic." Her eyes were shrewd, calculating.

"By accident." Or necessity. My fingers itched to grab my blade. "I doubt anyone has missed him. How long has the talisman been gone from Faerie, exactly? You never specified how recently it was taken."

Her lips curved into a smile, but she didn't answer.

"Yes, I know you've been fucking with me," I said. "Did *you* steal the talisman?"

"No."

"Did you ask someone to steal it for you?"

"Such accusations, Ivy Lane. No, I did not."

Damn. She couldn't lie. So much for that theory.

"Then you want to help Faerie out of the goodness of your heart?" I narrowed my eyes at her. "Or do you want the talisman for yourself? Is that what this is about?"

She'd told me to bring her the heart. She hadn't said she intended to return it to its owner, and with the faeries' vows, every word mattered.

"That's enough questions from you." Her creepy smile turned positively feral. "If you have no new information for me on the whereabouts of what I asked you to find, I'd advise you to leave."

She's not innocent. Killer or not, I doubted she wanted to return the talisman to Summer at all. It was obvious she wanted it for herself, and failing to retrieve it for her meant my own death.

A root crept underneath my feet. Magic rose to my hands, its blue light reflected in her green eyes.

"That magic of yours won't save you, Ivy Lane."

"Sure about that?" My heart thumped, a warning that challenging her was a bad move, and an ominously hungry expression stirred in her eyes.

"You cannot access its full potential," she told me. "Not here."

No. But I can in Faerie. In the Grey Vale. "Does the same apply to the talisman?"

If so, and it could cause *that* much damage while suppressed, I didn't want to see what it was capable of in Faerie. Didn't want it in her hands either.

The roots continued to move around my feet, causing the ground to shift sideways. I grabbed my sword, intending to strike first, and a waterfall of earth rose before my eyes. I turned tail and ran, not at all keen on the idea of drowning in soil. Earthy fragments pelted me in the back, and the wave crashed over my head.

As it turned out, getting hit in the back with a wall of earth hurt like a bitch. I fell forward, scraping my knees on tree roots, and crawled a metre forward before the second wave hit me. Spitting out soil, I squeezed my eyes shut and splayed my hands. Blue light ignited, burning the backs of my eyelids. A cracking sound shot through the air, followed by a scream.

I turned to find the giant tree had split down the middle as though struck by lightning. Maggots crawled out of the rotting trunk, and decaying magic hung in the air like miasma. The stench was overwhelming, yet no traces of the Lady remained.

Was she *dead?* Surely not. I hadn't hit her that hard, and if the vow bound us, I ought to have felt something when she died.

A sudden burst of high, horrible laughter echoed through the clearing. *No, she's not dead.*

"Really creepy." I raised my sword, half-expecting her to burst out of the nearest tree like the creature in that *Alien* movie. I didn't know what game she was playing now, but she needed my help. Why she'd let me destroy her tree was a mystery, but given the maggoty state of it, it'd been dying on the inside all along.

"When I come for you next, Ivy Lane, you won't be able to resist my call," said the Lady's voice. "Be warned."

I backed away, my sword useless against the shifting soil, but no more earthly tidal waves hit me on the way out of the clearing. Cursing under my breath, I kicked clumps of earth off my boots and stomped along the forest path.

If I'd been in trouble before, I was in the deep end now. Giving up was out of the question. Finding the talisman, potentially fatal. Handing the talisman over to Faerie before the Lady got hold of it, without breaking the vow in the process? All in all, the odds of me dying before Vance and I actually got a proper date were depressingly high.

When I finally reached the forest's edge, my phone rang in my pocket. A quick scan confirmed Vance had been trying to reach me for a while, but some effect of the Lady's forest had killed my signal.

"Hi, Vance." I decided against adding, *Can I come over and have sex with you before someone kills one or both of us?* Because he'd think I'd gone as barking mad as the Lady of the Tree. Pun intended. "Sorry. Signal got cut off, I think."

"What happened this time?" asked Vance.

"How'd you guess?"

"I'm psychic," he said dryly. "It's you, Ivy. I leave you alone for ten minutes and you've made a hundred new enemies."

"That's an exaggeration," I informed him. "I didn't make any *new* enemies, anyway. The Lady of the Tree buried me in soil."

"Of course she did," he said. "Come here. I want to keep an eye on you."

Funny how he could make even *that* sound seductive. The Mage Lord was back, apparently.

"I'm covered in mud. It's not a pretty picture."

"You've been covered in mud or blood most of the time I've known you."

Touché. "Give me a chance to shower and I'll be there."

11

Forty minutes and a quick shower later, I left the flat. I locked the door, turned around, and walked smack into Vance.

"Jesus!"

"Not quite."

I hit him in the arm. "Please tell me you weren't standing out there for the last half-hour."

"Five minutes. I did send you a message."

I made to pull my phone out and check, but he transported both of us into the conservatory of the manor before my fingers reached my pocket.

"Let me see the last two clients out and I'll join you in a minute." He strode off while I smoothed down my hair and looked around to see if anyone had witnessed our sudden arrival. The answer was no, apparently.

As before, the main feature of the conservatory was the grand piano in the corner, while potted plants had been artfully placed around its edges. Glass windows overlooked the immaculate gardens, which contained rows of aesthetically arranged flowerbeds on one side and fields designated for practising magical duels on the other.

"Ivy?" Wanda walked into the conservatory through the open door. "Didn't know you were coming."

"I didn't get much warning." I shook my head after the Mage Lord. "Nice to see you anyway. Are things busy around here?"

"No more so than usual," said Wanda. "What did you do to Vance? He's acting downright surly."

Great. I didn't want the whole world knowing our drama. "Nothing. He decided to beat up some shifters who kidnapped me last night."

Her eyes widened. "You were kidnapped?"

On second thought, maybe I'd rather talk about our argument instead. "I stabbed them and escaped, but Vance flipped a lid and went after them without consulting me first."

"That… doesn't surprise me in the slightest," said Wanda. "If someone he cares about gets hurt, the entire mage council could stand in his way and he'd run them down."

"I thought we'd established I can fight my own battles. Besides, running after shifters at the full moon isn't something a rational person would do." I stopped before I said his anger issues were probably a shifter thing, remembering she might not know. Or maybe she did. Anyone who'd seen Vance fight would surely have seen his claws.

"Neither is making a bargain with a faerie," Wanda said. "Which you did, according to him."

Oops.

"The Lady of the Tree. I owed her a favour, and it got… complicated." I didn't know if Vance had told her the details about the talisman and its possible links to the killer, but I'd err on the side of caution. "There's no breaking a promise to a faerie. Trying to go against it would literally kill me."

Which made it all the worse if the Lady did turn out to be

behind the shifter murders. Maybe she really had been lying all along, but how, and to what extent? And why use the vow to rope me into helping her anyway?

Wanda's eyes grew wide. "A promise can kill you?"

"Yeah, that's the faeries for you. Anyway. Enough about my impending doom." I cracked a smile. "How're the clients?"

"Terrible, as usual," she said. "We've had endless complaints about the noise the shifters are making at night, a dozen shifters who've come in here to tell us to arrest the half-faeries, a botched spell that turned someone into a piglet…"

"Never a dull day," I said. "How'd you end up working for Vance, anyway?" I'd never asked before, but I'd wondered a few times how she'd snagged the spot as his assistant, which had to be highly coveted.

"My parents died in the invasion," she said. "I'm half-mage, half-witch, and I didn't develop my abilities until quite late on. The mages took me in anyway, so they're like family. My grandmother survived, but she retired from the council a while ago."

"Ah."

I hadn't known. In my limited interactions with the mages, I'd found out most of them had an unhappy history around the invasion. Wanda was younger than me, around twenty-two, so she'd have been a toddler when the Sidhe came. Not old enough to really remember it.

"As for the assistant job," said Wanda, "Vance gave it to me when I proved I was the only person in the manor who can find things when he displaces them. It drives the rest of the council out of their minds. Of course *he* knows where they are, but the number of times important papers have gone missing…"

Vance re-entered the room, preventing me from hearing the rest. Shame, but now I had some ammunition to tease him about, and it was amusing to imagine those stuffy old council members tearing their hair out because Vance had moved things around.

"Wanda, you can leave," he said. "Tell Quentin to clean the ectoplasm off the walls."

Wanda didn't bat an eyelid. "I will."

"Ectoplasm?" I asked.

"Someone decided to sell a ghost eradicator like the ones the necromancers use on dangerous spirits," said Vance. "They sold it to someone who assumed he was buying a music box and got a nasty surprise when he opened it."

"Someone exploded slime all over your office?" The mental image was too funny. I snorted.

"Didn't you have glitter everywhere in your flat the other day?"

"All right, it's not a contest." I rolled my eyes. "What did you want to talk about?"

"The case," said Vance. "I hazarded a guess you came up with a theory."

"The Lady of the Tree confirmed the killer's using the talisman. Which means if we find it, we'll also solve the murders." Though I somehow doubted she'd told me to find the talisman for the good of humanity. "I think *she* wants the sword for her own use, but I don't know why she wants me to do her dirty work for her."

"I thought only a Sidhe could handle a talisman."

"So did I, but she's definitely not being straight with me." I didn't believe her act for a second, but as far as I knew, faeries like her were incapable of telling untruths. "I honestly have no idea what her game is."

"There must be a way to pry the truth from her. She's playing with your life."

Didn't I know it. "I might know the talisman was used to commit the murders, but I don't get how they picked their targets, and why. Two people murdered by magic most half-faeries can't use seems calculated to get attention, and I thought they picked shifters because they're more likely to be roaming outside at night. But... I don't know."

"I agree," said Vance. "I don't mind if you keep investigating, but if you decide to cross the veil again, I meant what I said."

"Which part?"

He released a breath that sounded like a sigh. "One day I might be too late to save someone. I won't let it be you."

My heart twisted. *Oh, Vance.* "I'm not helpless."

"You can't fight *death*, Ivy," said Vance.

"I'm not fighting it. I'm just experimenting a little... that's a joke," I added quickly, as his eyes flashed warningly. "Like I said, it was an accident that I ended up there at all. I didn't say a word to the necromancers, but they've pretty much barred me from their headquarters, so any chance of instruction from them is off the cards."

"It's not the necromancers you need help from," he said. "I doubt they've dealt with your variety of magic. They've been around for centuries if not longer, while the first time anyone heard of the Grey Vale was..."

"When the faeries invaded," I finished. "Yeah, I figured. I want this investigation done, too, but the Lady of the Tree flat-out refused to admit to anything."

He gave me a sharp look. "You thought she was the killer?"

"She fits the description. A beautiful Summer faerie with powerful magic. But I don't know why she'd want me to steal something that's already in her possession."

"Yes, but her story doesn't add up." His forehead creased. "If she found out the talisman was missing when she was in Faerie, that implies she spoke to the Sidhe, but they wouldn't entrust the task of retrieving it to a non-Sidhe, from what I understand of them."

"I don't think she spoke to the Sidhe." I thought back to our interactions. "She's acting in her own self-interest, even if she isn't the killer."

"And she didn't specify which part of Faerie she went to."

No. She hadn't. "She said she got her immortality back when she went into Faerie," I said slowly. "She might've meant the Vale instead, but… well, the Vale isn't exactly friendly to Summer faeries like her. If she'd gone there when she was half-dead, she'd have been eaten alive."

"Unless she found a talisman."

My mouth parted in surprise. "You're thinking the same as me?" If she'd gone to the Grey Vale and found Velkas's blade… but again, if that was the case, why would she have come back here? Or had someone stolen the talisman from her and forced her to enlist me to retrieve it?

"I don't know. You tell me." He gave me an assessing look, as though wondering what was going through my head.

"Only if you tell *me* one of your secrets."

Vance frowned at me. "This isn't a game."

"I'm dead serious, Vance," I said. "Shifters are being killed by this talisman, and I can't for the life of me figure out the link, but there has to be one."

"I agree," he said, to my surprise. "What do you want to know?"

"How your family's linked to the shifters. Why they hate you so much, enough that they refuse to let the mages help them find someone who's killing their own."

Vance's mouth thinned. I swallowed my pride and prepared to back down.

"Fine," he said tonelessly. "The shifters and the mages had as little to do with one another as possible before the invasion. My grandfather knew that, but he attempted to adapt and live with them when he married my grandmother. After my grandfather died, his two surviving children—my father and his brother—were quickly inducted into the mages when they came into their powers."

I stared a little. "Two… surviving children?"

His gaze turned downward. "I did say shifter and mage abilities are a lethal combination, especially without the proper training. There was an incident one full moon when a family argument got out of hand that killed everyone except my father and his youngest brother, including my grandmother. Afterwards, the other shifters shunned the Colton family and called them bringers of bad luck. Considering the invasion happened right on their territory, they might have been right."

Already, I regretted asking. I hadn't known I'd drag up such a deluge of bad memories, even if they weren't Vance's own.

"My father's younger brother didn't last long with the mages, but when he returned to the shifters, their grudge remained intact," Vance continued in the same flat tones, his gaze distant. "That was still the case when the invasion forced every supernatural out into the open. Like the other shifters, my uncle escaped the devastation by going into hiding, but beforehand, he and my father had a bitter argument. I never found out the details, but both of them partially shifted as a result of the surge on the Ley Line. Since he wasn't a full shifter, my uncle survived the invasion and he witnessed the devastation that hit the other shifters firsthand. As for my father, he joined the mages in confronting the Sidhe. Every single one of them died."

My insides pitched downward. "And… you?"

"I was ten, younger than most mages are when they come into their powers, but I'd already started to show signs of my ability. I was in a hideout along with the mages who couldn't fight. The Sidhe blasted the wards down and killed everyone inside."

"How did you survive?" My voice was hardly a whisper. This was far worse than I'd imagined, and damn, did I regret letting my curiosity get the better of me.

"My powers reacted in self-defence, destroying most of the house and reducing it to rubble. The Sidhe thought they'd killed me."

"You were buried alive?" Holy hell. I'd never figured he'd got *that* close to the Sidhe.

"The one surviving Mage Lord ordered a sweep of the city for survivors. I was lucky they found me."

"No shit." My legs felt weak. I didn't have a clue what to say. I wanted to give him a hug, and simultaneously beat the shit out of every faerie who came within a mile of me.

"I saw the veil," said Vance quietly. "I saw them take her."

"Your sister?"

"The veil was visible to everyone," he clarified. "The Ley Line went haywire due to the collision of realms. Ghosts roamed the streets, attacking the living. The dead rose as soon as they perished. The aftermath took almost as many lives as the actual invasion did, even as the surviving mages tried to fix the damage."

"Jesus." I'd experienced all of fifteen minutes of the invasion. The real event had lasted a day and a half, a short time for the faeries to overturn a significant part of the civilised world, but it'd slipped my mind that the aftermath would have hit the mages as hard as the actual invasion. "You said one Mage Lord survived?"

"Yes." He indicated a portrait of a grey-bearded man among the row that lined the wall behind the piano. "Lord Rickard. He was already retired at the time, so he opted to protect as many people as he could rather than going into battle. His actions saved many lives, and he rebuilt the city with the help of the new council. But the shifters still harboured a grudge, even though the mages couldn't stop the side effects of the invasion any more than they could prevent their own kind from dying."

"And your family in particular took the heat because the shifters needed someone to blame?"

"Essentially. They were the sole link between the shifters and the mages and my grandfather's reputation lingered long after he left their territory."

"Didn't know Henry was that much of a dick."

Vance's mouth pulled. "The Mage Lords haven't necessarily been kind to shifters in the past. We make the laws, and shifters posed more of a risk to the public than any other group due to their volatility at the full moon. There were many times we had to step in and prevent them from exposing other supernaturals."

"Still, you'd think they'd know that working together is more useful for survival in the long run. Even *I* know that." I edged closer to him. "I'm sorry. I really didn't mean to cross the veil. Or go behind your back. I thought I could solve this. Without *you* getting hurt or killed."

When I'd nearly died after saying the Invocation, he'd seen me as a ghost, and it must have reminded him of his sister's death. And to add insult to injury, I'd crossed the veil twice since, and had talked about doing it again. *Okay. I get it.*

"I know you did," he said quietly. "I'm sorry I left you last night. I couldn't stop thinking about how those shifters hurt you badly enough to push you into Death. I refused to let them get away without punishment."

"I already beat them up." I tried to lighten the tone. "If you keep showing me up like that, the faeries won't be scared of me anymore."

"Destroying your fearsome reputation was the last thing on my mind." The flicker of a smile touched his mouth, though tinged with a hint of something else. Regret, maybe, or sadness. "I apologise for standing you up. Odds are, I *would* have shifted during our date, and I doubt you'd have found my claws appealing."

"Hmm." I impulsively took his hands and flipped them over. He let me, tilting his head questioningly. "Depends if you planned to use your hands for anything important."

The glint in his eyes turned wicked. "You know... we don't need to leave the manor to have all the benefits of a date."

Whoever moved first, I didn't know. Seconds later, his lips were on mine and my hands around the back of his head, messing up his hair. The taste and smell of him flooded me, sent heat running straight to my core. The tension between our bodies bent and snapped like a magnetic pull. My teeth grazed his lower lip, and he made a growling noise deep in his throat.

"Does this mean you still want me?"

"You need to ask? Good god, woman," he said under his breath. "You'll be the death of me."

His hands moved to my waist, leaving a trail of heat through the thin fabric of my shirt. I shuddered at the sensation, not prepared for the shock of electricity through my nerves when his fingers touched my bare skin. Two could play at that game. I slid my hands up his waist, seeking the taut skin under his now considerably rumpled shirt. My jacket disappeared in a rush of air. He'd removed it without even touching me.

"Show-off."

He smiled against my lips. Dear lord. If he removed all my clothes in the same way, I was gone. He'd be the end of me without any bloody faerie vow.

Two seconds later, his hands were underneath my T-shirt and I'd forgotten all about the faeries and pretty much everything else, too. I didn't even mind him touching my scars, because it hit me that he wasn't about to stop. His hands grazed my nipples and slid underneath my bra, and I gasped aloud.

"Vance. For god's sake, move us somewhere more private—"

The door crashed open. Vance's hands dropped quickly, as did mine. Over his shoulder, I saw Wanda back out into the hallway. "Another client. I'll tell him to come back later."

I straightened upright, trying to act dignified and not at all like I had the Mage Lord's erection pressing against my thigh.

Vance pulled away from me with more composure than I'd have expected. "Wanda. I'll be there in a minute."

To Wanda's credit, she barely blinked. "You know there's a glass door over there, don't you?"

She left. I turned to Vance. "Tell me nobody saw us."

"I can't do that. I was… preoccupied."

No kidding. His shirt was untucked, his hair dishevelled, and he'd never looked sexier. Not fair, universe.

"Go find Wanda," I said. "Does she normally find you making out with employees?"

"No, that's usually Drake. And it's more likely to be clients than employees."

"Really?"

"You haven't spent a lot of time here, have you?"

"Not yet."

He grinned, a spark igniting in his eyes again. He kissed me lightly on the lips, then left the conservatory, fixing his clothes as he did so.

Dammit. Foiled again. I glanced around and found my jacket on the piano stool. The smooth bastard. Oh god. I put my head in my hands and sank onto the stool. He was more impulsive than usual thanks to the shift. I had no excuses, except possibly built-up sexual frustration. It'd been a long time since I'd got past the first-date stage of a relationship.

The grand piano wore a fine coating of dust, like no one had touched it in a while. Above, stern-faced portraits looked down at me, and I moved closer to examine the names. All were called Lord something-or-other. Two had the name 'Lord Colton', and both were dated some seventy years prior. Must be his grandparents.

No pictures of his parents, though. Or his sister. That I understood. If any photos of my own family had survived the invasion, I wouldn't have had them on display.

To take my mind off my own bad memories, I explored the rest of the conservatory. Next to the piano was a set of dusty shelves containing books, chiefly volumes of the mages' history. Curious, I flipped one open. Did any mention the invasion, or was it too recent?

A rush of air behind me. "That's not one of my more interesting history books." Vance rested a hand on my shoulder. "Before we got distracted, were you going to tell me anything else?"

"Oh, *shit*. Yeah. I know what the missing talisman is. At least, I think I do." I put the book down and turned to face him. "I think it's Velkas's blade."

12

Vance's whole body stilled. "What?"

"Velkas," I repeated. "Remember when we were trying to find those missing kids and people kept talking about a half-faerie with an ash blade and silver hair? When I duelled Velkas, I assumed he'd been shapeshifting, but it turned out they were talking about Calder all along. Velkas used Summer magic, not Winter. And he definitely had a talisman. That sword of his was no common weapon."

"True," said Vance. "It sounded like Velkas had been living in the Grey Vale for a while, though. Surely Summer would have noticed their missing talisman before then, if he stole it before he left."

"Maybe. Time passes weirdly in Faerie." I shook my head. "The Lady never specified *when* it was stolen from Summer, or even that Summer was involved at all. She just said someone stole it from Faerie and brought it here, if I'm remembering right."

"You are," Vance said, "which leaves no doubt that she left out more information."

"If she *is* the killer, if she took it from Velkas's dead body… but no, she said directly that she didn't steal it." I rubbed my forehead. "I guess maybe it doesn't count as stealing in her book if the person she took it from is dead, but I'm the one who left the talisman lying around in the Grey Vale after I killed him."

"You couldn't have known," said Vance.

I rubbed my forehead. "Whether she's the one who has the talisman or not, I've no idea where she's gone. Her tree kind of rotted to pieces from the inside after I… exploded it."

"Of course you did," Vance said. "Regardless, didn't she say that her magic was less effective here than in her own realm?"

"Talismans seem to be the exception." Though I hadn't faced Calder in Faerie itself, nor had Velkas ever set foot here. Our duel had been in the Vale. "I'm not sure. She certainly got a boost from somewhere."

"Wherever she went, I doubt it'll work out in your favour if you go looking for her again," Vance said tightly. "I do, however, have an alternative idea. We could speak to my uncle about the shifter murders."

"Your uncle?" I'd thought they weren't on speaking terms.

"Yes, though I'd rather avoid involving Anabel in this if I can help it."

Oh. His younger cousin—and, I assumed, the youngest in the Colton family—had been dragged into the faeries' schemes once already. "They still live near shifter territory?"

"On the outskirts. We won't be trespassing if we pay them a visit."

We. I'd get to properly meet his family? "Do you think they might know more about what's going on?"

"Maybe," he said. "They're not full-blooded shifters. My uncle goes through a partial transformation, but he might have been more alert than the others the past two nights, and his wife isn't a shifter at all. We'll go there now, since we have a time limit on when it's safe to venture near the shifters' homes."

"Are you going to warn him we're coming?"

"No. Chances are, he'll close the door in my face anyway. He blames me for what happened to Anabel the other week."

"Harsh. You're the one who brought her back." And I was more to blame than Vance, given that she'd been taken as bait to draw both of us into Velkas's trap.

"My uncle has never forgotten the last argument he had with my father before he died," he explained. "He never did tell me the details, but he also strongly believes the mages shouldn't have taken power after the invasion, and I'm an eternal reminder of that. Luckily, Anabel's mother is more reasonable. She's human, though she has shifter family members."

"So… your cousin is half human?"

"Anabel? Yes, and she's a quarter mage. Given my family history, she's likely to develop some level of magical talent when she's older. She's only nine."

From his tone, I gathered he wanted to train her as a mage. That wouldn't go down well with his uncle, I imagined.

"Is her mum likely to help? Not sure I want to piss anyone else off today if I can avoid it."

"Yes, but I rather hope my uncle isn't around," said Vance. "Ready?"

Not really. I'd had a day of it already, but the sooner we got this done, the less likely we were to end up outside right before the night shift. Pun intended.

Vance transported us both to a country road bordered by green fields where a dilapidated farmhouse nested between low stone walls. The fields were more weeds than grass, overgrown and unkempt, and while I could see the outskirts of the city some distance away, it couldn't be more obvious that whoever had bought this place had done so to avoid having to interact with other humans. The fences alone proved that. Layers of wards had been painstakingly etched over their wooden slats, similar to the glyphs shimmering on the manor's walls, though the effect wasn't quite the same when paired with a lopsided farmhouse encased in white plaster with roof tiles missing and a general air of neglect.

"This is the place?" I asked.

Vance inclined his head and strode to the farmhouse. My skin tingled when the wards pressed against me as I followed him through the front gate, but they must have decided I wasn't a threat because the pressure vanished seconds later.

Vance and I walked up to the red-painted front door, and he knocked.

A pale redheaded woman answered. "Oh—Mage Lord." She glanced over her shoulder. "I shouldn't let you in. Wyatt isn't here…"

"Good," said Vance. "It's you I wanted to talk to. This is Ivy."

Her gaze flickered over me. "I really shouldn't."

"Have you heard about the recent shifter deaths?" asked Vance.

She hesitated for a moment and then nodded. "I haven't seen anything. Not here. I thought you'd come asking. None of the other shifters will talk, will they?"

"I have reason to suspect these murders are connected to a larger disruption affecting the shifters as a whole," said Vance. "Has Anabel been acting oddly? And Wyatt? More aggressive than usual?"

"I… yes." She glanced at me again, as though puzzling me out.

"Can I see her?" asked Vance. "Please."

I hid my surprise. Vance had toned down the scary mage act so thoroughly, he might have been an ordinary guy visiting family. If not for the coat, of course.

"All right. But you can't stay long. If Wyatt gets back…"

"I'll be fine." Vance flashed a smile at the small figure who'd appeared in the hallway, a girl with long dark hair and big staring eyes.

"Vance? I didn't know you were coming." Anabel ran past her mother and hugged him.

"Anabel. This is a surprise visit, okay? Don't tell your dad."

Okay. This is the weirdest day ever.

The house was as plain on the inside as the outside, the living room containing blocky furniture surrounding a fireplace that looked as though it'd never been used. I took a seat on the sofa, while Vance sat on my other side with Anabel clinging to his legs. Anabel's mother, meanwhile, stood by the window, her hands clasped in a nervous gesture.

"I'm Rita, by the way," she said to me. "You're… not a mage. Right?"

"I'm a witch," I said, falling back on my usual story. "I work for the mages, helping investigate cases like these."

"Shifters?"

"Faeries." No point in beating around the bush. "That's what I wanted to ask. The two murders were perpetrated by a faerie or half-faerie with powerful magic. It's possible the culprit is hiding near the Ley Line. Have you seen anything?"

I'd been somewhat thrown when we'd landed so far outside of the city, but I was fairly certain that the Ley Line cut through the fields somewhere out here, and that it would be considerably easier to spot a Sidhe wandering around with a talisman out in the middle of nowhere than in an inhabited area.

"Faerie?" repeated Rita, a puzzled frown on her face. "Not out here."

"She uses Summer magic." I scrambled for other possible clues that someone without the Sight would have been able to see. "Has there been any unusually pleasant weather, or flowers growing out of season? Anything weird like that?"

"Now that you mention it…" She glanced over her shoulder, at the window. "Other farmers have reported finding thorny bushes growing around here. Not usual for this time of year, and nobody can identify what they are. I assumed it was some magical aftereffect of the recent disruption." She shot a worried look at Anabel.

A pang of sympathy struck me. She had no magic, no way of defending herself when magical disasters struck. *Thorns,* however… my mind nudged me with images of tendrils rising from a pit to pull me into their midst. I folded my arms, feeling goose bumps spring up on my skin.

"Might be an aftereffect, sure," I acknowledged. "The Ley Line has an influence on almost all supernaturals."

The thorns might be coincidental, like the summer it had rained frogs and alligators after a couple of half-faeries had started a blistering argument in the middle of a field. But my instincts told me otherwise.

"Where did you see these thorns?" asked Vance.

"Just… around," Rita said. "Not near the house."

"Faeries can't come near our house," Anabel piped up. "Our wards keep them out."

"Good," I muttered.

Vance's cousin frowned at me. "Why? They're not all bad, are they? The one who took me was, but the others aren't, right?"

Oh boy. "Some are. Most are dangerous. Ah… you haven't seen a pretty faerie lady wandering around, have you?"

It was a reach, but her eyes rounded at once. "How did you know?"

My throat went dry. "Stay away from her. The prettier they are, the more dangerous they are."

Vance folded his arms around his niece as she climbed into his lap, fear flitting across her face. "Listen to Ivy. In fact, I'd advise you not to leave the house alone until we've solved this case."

"Again?" An undercurrent of anger entered Rita's voice. "You're putting my family in danger *again?*"

"Not if I can help it." Vance's tone was even, his arms wrapped protectively around Anabel. "But shifters are being targeted by a dangerous killer, and I can't always be here. I'll send some mages to watch your property and alert me if there's anything that I should know."

"You think my husband will allow that?" Rita laughed hollowly. "Haven't you brought enough trouble upon our family already?"

"Vance *is* our family," piped up Anabel. "It's not his fault they took me. Besides, my dad's the one poking around that old grave."

I turned to face her. "Grave?"

Anabel shrank back into Vance's arms. "There's this old tomb they uncovered on the edge of shifter territory. Dad thinks it might be linked to the life-drinker legend."

"The... what?" I asked.

"Life-drinker," said Rita. "The real name's in a language I can't pronounce, but Wyatt can. It's a shifter legend."

"He's digging in an old tomb?" I looked at Vance, trying to convey *we need to put a stop to that* without using words. We'd had enough close calls with death already. "What is this... this life-drinker?"

"Who, not what," said Anabel. "He's the god who created the first shifter."

What? "A god? Like… actual superhuman god?" I looked at Vance, whose expression remained inscrutable.

"So the legends say," said Rita. "Some stories claim the first shifters were descended from this deity. Another version of the story says the man wasn't a god, but a supremely powerful shifter who once lived here, hundreds of years ago. This isn't the first time his tomb's been 'discovered'."

"And why's he called the life-drinker?"

"Because he took life from others into himself to gain power."

My mouth parted. "A shifter did that?"

"He was more than a shifter. Some legends say he carried a weapon, an object that mages would call a talisman, to gain power that no other shifter could access."

Talisman. No way could she mean *that* kind of talisman. The faeries and shifters had nothing to do with one another. Right?

Vance's jaw tightened, but all he said was "I'd tell Wyatt to stay away from that tomb."

"I can't." She wrung her hands. "You know what he's like in shifting season. Best to let him take out his frustration on something else. He's been digging it up for days."

"You do realise undead swarmed the city last week, don't you?" I said, unable to help myself. Even if I discounted the missing faerie talisman, digging up an old grave was a sure-fire way for him to end up joining the dead himself.

"I really can't stop him," said Rita. "Not if he's put his mind to it."

"I'll—" Anabel started.

"No," Vance interrupted. "I'll speak to him myself."

He rose upright, gently dislodging Anabel from his arms.

She hurried over to her mother, giving me another

nervous look. "Daddy said he didn't want to talk to anyone," she said to Vance.

"Don't worry about me," he said, in an unexpectedly soothing tone I'd never heard him use before. "We'll be fine."

"Okay." Anabel gave me a wary look, which threw me a bit. I didn't blame her for being scared—most sensible people would give a wide berth to someone who carried as many weapons as I did—but usually Vance was the one who freaked everyone out more than me.

"Be careful." Rita walked with us to the door, biting her lower lip. Was she scared of her husband? I might be reading too much into the situation, but from what I'd heard from Vance already, I'd have to restrain myself from introducing Vance's uncle to Irene.

Vance let Anabel hug him goodbye, one-handedly ruffling her hair.

She pulled a face. "I'm not that little anymore."

"No, you aren't." A worried note sounded in his voice. Was he thinking about how she'd be close to shifting age soon? "I'll see you soon."

Rita closed the door. Vance watched the house for a moment then turned away. "It's no surprise that Wyatt would insist on making my life difficult. Digging up a tomb... no wonder the other shifters are displeased with him lately."

"I'm more concerned about this faerie lady wandering around." Unease stirred in my gut. "I don't know why I asked, but George said the same. You don't think...?"

"This whole place is warded in iron." He took off at a fast stride, while I hastened to keep pace with him. "Rita knows what to watch out for, but what worries me is that someone might be trying to lure shifters out of their territory. The first murder didn't take place there at all, and the second wasn't at home when the killer began chasing him."

"I guess you're right." This place was in the middle of

nowhere, though. "You think the killer is luring the victims outside using magical means?"

"It would explain why they abandoned their usual caution at the full moon." Vance peered at the glyphs on the fence. "I think I should add a soundproofing spell. That way, if anyone tries to talk to them from the outside, they won't hear."

"Like a siren singing to lure men to their deaths?" I didn't think the Lady of the Tree or any of her ilk had the capacity to charm a person into jumping off a roof by singing at them like some faeries did, but you could never be too careful. "Would Wyatt need persuading, though, if he's digging up a grave on a whim?"

His eyes flashed to a darker grey. "I told you hellhounds' fear magic doesn't affect shifters. Neither do similar magics that affect the mind and confuse the senses. The person doing this is using another method."

"Speaking of which." I watched him conjure a pen-like object into his hand that I recognised as the glyph marker he'd once used to put a mark on me so that I could call him to my side at a moment's notice. "The tomb. This legend... did you know about it?"

"I heard the stories." Vance crouched to draw fresh marks on the fence. "Secondhand, mind, but some shifters are insistent that Eraenar was a real person and that he's still sleeping somewhere underground."

"Era what?" I tried to wrap my tongue around the name.

"Eraenar," he repeated. "'The life-drinker' is a literal translation of his name, but nobody knows which language it originally came from."

"The Sidhe?" Surely not. I didn't even know where to begin with that one, so I changed the subject. "What's the deal with Uncle Colton, then? He's not... he doesn't hurt his wife, does he?"

"Heavens, no," said Vance. "He's an obstinate fool, but I'd skewer him if he raised a hand against Anabel or her mother. He just hates everyone else."

"Including the other shifters," I said. "I gather they aren't fond of him digging up the tomb? I find it hard to believe it's coincidental that it showed up at the same time as someone is murdering shifters."

"Perhaps." Vance paced along the front wall, his mouth pressing into a thin line. "The first thing I ever learned about shifters is that transforming requires a tremendous surge of energy. Each shifter is effectively a lightning rod, drawing on that energy from the Ley Line."

I blinked, not sure what he was getting at. "So… what? The closer to the Ley Line we are, the stronger the shift?"

"Yes, and as with most other magic that's used on the Ley Line, it's possible to harness that energy and channel it elsewhere."

"Harness that energy?" Did he mean like Calder had done with the half-faeries' magic, feeding it into the spell with which he intended to break the veil?

"They say the life-drinker was able to do so on a large scale," he said. "That he was able to draw on the power of other shifters, not just their life force, but the power of the shift itself."

"I don't…" A horrifying possibility hit me. "What, you don't think the talisman is drawing power from the shifters? Their deaths are… somehow fuelling it?"

An image filled my mind of Velkas's sneering face leaning over me as his talisman drained my life force. He'd sucked the life out of me, used it to power his magic, and I'd barely survived the encounter. If his talisman was *here...*

My heart took up residence somewhere beneath the soil. Was the person with the talisman recharging its power using shifters as sacrifices? And was this life-drinker legend tied in somehow?

"That's my suspicion," Vance said. "I had some idea, but when you mentioned that the talisman you encountered in the Vale might be the murder weapon, the pieces started to slide together."

"I bet." Shivers danced down my arms. "Do you think your uncle might be a target?"

"Perhaps, but I'm more concerned for Anabel," he said. "She's young enough not to have shifted yet, but the first transformation is always the most volatile."

"And requires more energy?" *Oh boy.*

"Exactly."

We walked onward, my mind roiling like a tempest. Whoever the killer was, they hadn't shown half of what they could do yet, if Vance was right and they needed to charge up the talisman like a magical battery. And just where did the newly resurfaced tomb fit in? What about those thorns? Vance looked lost in thought, too, his polished shoes treading through the rain-damp grass without picking up so much as a single clump of mud.

"There's got to be an endgame here," I murmured. "If you're right, and the faerie wielding the talisman is targeting the shifters specifically, is this tomb supposed to be a diversion? Or is this life-drinker … I mean, Rita mentioned a weapon. A talisman. And the description sounded the same as the one we're hunting for."

Which made zero sense. The shifters and the faeries were poles apart. Right?

"A distraction, no doubt," Vance said. "A means of luring the shifters outside of their homes."

"I'm not so sure," I said. "How do you know the shifters haven't had any contact with Faerie in the past? This life-drinker's power sounds like the reverse of Summer's magic. The branch that gets you exiled."

To the Grey Vale. Velkas has stolen that magic in the first place, and if his sword really *was* the talisman, who had claimed it after his death, if not the Lady of the Tree?

I tugged at my hair. This made no sense. Assuming the life-drinker legend referred to the same talisman, it couldn't possibly be inside the tomb. Not if someone was using it to commit murders.

What, then, was Wyatt Colton trying to dig up?

13

Vance gave no response to my suggestion that the shifters and the faeries had a history, but he picked up the pace.

My feet skidded in the mud as I hurried after him. "Wait. Where are you going?"

"To find my bloody fool of an uncle. If he's been tricked into doing something that'll put my family in danger, I'll bury him in the same grave he's digging up."

"And you know where it is?"

"No, but I can hazard a guess." He glanced over his shoulder at me. "I studied maps of the Ley Line extensively when I was trying to work out potential hiding places for the missing talisman. The legends say that the tomb is somewhere on the Ley Line, too, which cuts right through this area."

"It's an ideal hiding place for volatile magical objects." Which meant there was a fair chance we'd find both. Maybe I should have asked him to bring backup, but Vance seemed to think he could handle his uncle alone. "Wyatt, though… what's with his grudge against you? I mean, you'd think the invasion would have made you closer, not the opposite. Aren't you his only surviving family?"

"It's complicated." His expression darkened. "My grandfather tried to shield his children from the backlash that came from marrying a shifter, but the other Mage Lords were scandalised, especially his own parents, because he came from a centuries-old magical bloodline. My father ultimately decided to join the mages himself, and my uncle has always resented my father for that choice. When I followed in my parents' footsteps, it was inevitable that he'd see that as a betrayal, too."

"Can't your uncle use magic, being half-mage?"

"He prefers not to use it," said Vance. "My grandfather tried to teach them both, but he backed out of training early despite having the raw talent. He's a weather mage, and I believe the only use he makes of his power is when he unleashes the occasional thunderstorm against an intruder. My family has a propensity for the dramatic."

"I know. I've met you."

I expected a smile, but I didn't get one. He continued to walk, his mouth a thin, angry line. Anger at his uncle or at the faeries, I didn't know.

Vance stopped where the field ended in a wall cutting it off from its neighbour. The wall sat in a slight dip, and further north of us, the dip had turned into more of a hole, a wide one covering a large area. "This is the place. I thought so."

A man crouched beside the hole. When he spied our approach, he rose to his feet. The guy was around fifty or so, his shoulder-length dark hair matted and streaked with grey. He was at least fifteen years older than his wife and had the kind of muscled build of someone who worked outside a lot. With his plain, dirty clothes and slouching stance, there wasn't the slightest resemblance between him and his nephew until I saw his grey eyes. White flashed through his irises at the sight of Vance.

"You," he said. "I thought I told you to stay away from my family."

"Anabel is my family, too," Vance said. "I came to check on her safety and found out you're embarking on this foolish endeavour."

"What I do in my own home is none of your business."

"You're technically outside your home right now, and you're digging up a creepy old grave right after a bunch of undead got loose in the city," I pointed out. "I'd say that's everyone's business."

Vance shot me a warning look and then turned back to his uncle. "Did someone tell you to do this?"

"It's nothing to you if they did." A fresh blaze of white ignited in Wyatt's eyes. "Leave."

"We have reason to believe you were tricked into digging up that grave by someone who wants to hurt your family."

"*You're* the danger to our family." Wyatt lifted his head, claws sprouting from his hands. Scales folded up his arms, black as pitch, and his eyes flashed as a rumble of thunder crackled in the air.

Vance stepped in front of me. I yelled a warning that went unheard as Wyatt lunged at him, and I drew my sword, hitting Wyatt in the head with the hilt. I tried to avoid dealing any serious injuries, but Vance appeared to have no such inhibitions. Scales coated his hands, too, and his first swipe at his uncle spattered the ground with blood.

Horror shot through my core as the two clashed in a flurry of claws. If I didn't intervene, one would rip the other's throat out. Neither was using magic either. While it might not be Wyatt's weapon of choice, was Vance holding back, or had his shifter instincts overwhelmed him?

"Vance!" I yelled.

He didn't seem to hear me. The two grappled with one another, dealing blows that would have knocked a regular person out cold. My heart dropped when Wyatt managed to push Vance down, but Vance swiftly tipped the bigger man onto the ground and reversed their positions. His own claws came down. Blood spurted.

Was he actually going to kill his uncle?

I threw myself at Vance from behind without stopping to think, tackling him around the waist. The momentum sent me crashing down on top of him, and I threw all my weight onto his back, sword and all, as I pointed the tip of my blade at the back of his neck.

Vance might be stronger than me, but he wasn't a fool even in shifter form. He tilted his head, eyes narrowed at me.

"This isn't your fight," he growled.

"No," said his uncle. "Do you take orders from hedge witches now?"

My fists bunched in the back of Vance's coat as I fought to keep him from throwing himself at Wyatt. Hell, *I* wouldn't mind throwing myself at him, but that wouldn't get us answers.

"Will you both calm *down?*"

Vance snarled. "Let go of me."

White flashed through Wyatt's eyes, sharp as lightning, and he and Vance tried to lunge at each other at the same time. I pressed myself against Vance's back and hung on for dear life, forced to relax my grip on Irene or risk stabbing him for real. As he began to rise upward, I thwacked him on the back of the head with the hilt. Not too hard, but enough to make him stop moving.

"You're the bloody Mage Lord!" I yelled in his ear. "Let this dickhead throw a tantrum all by himself."

The dickhead in question roared, his impossibly bright eyes now fixated on me instead of on Vance.

"That's right, I'm insulting you," I shot at him. "Get mad at me if you like. Hell, you, too, Vance, but remember you came to stop your uncle from making a fatal mistake, not kill him yourself."

Wyatt leapt. I fell sideways off Vance, raising my blade. I didn't want to kill Vance's uncle, but the list of non-lethal tactics in my repertoire was lacking on a good day. Back on my feet, I slashed in a figure-eight motion to keep his eyes on my sword and not on Vance. Out of the corner of my eye, I glimpsed the hole he'd been digging. We were only metres from the pit, and while I couldn't tell how deep it was, I was all out of any better ideas. I continued to walk backwards, luring Wyatt closer to the hole in the ground with every step.

"You're not that bright, aren't you?" I goaded him. "I'll bet your daughter's ashamed of you."

The beast roared and leaped, and I threw myself flat. He scrambled for a grip as he fell into the open hole, claws swiping at the earth, but all he succeeded in doing was bringing a shower of soil down on his own head as he tumbled in.

"Good thinking." Vance approached, blood streaming from several cuts on his face.

My heart gave an odd thump. I'd seen him get hit before, but it was rare that I saw the Mage Lord bleeding, and the sight sent a wave of anger through my body. "Are you *sure* he's not drugged?"

"We can find out. Luckily, I didn't completely lose my senses." He pulled a container out of thin air.

"You had time to take a blood sample?"

"He bled all over my coat."

"Thought you had a dirt-proof spell on."

"I do," said Vance. "It wears off over time."

True. Now that I looked more closely, I saw his sleeves were torn and bloody. "You do think he's drugged?"

"I don't know, but we can't interrogate him in this state," he said. "We need to subdue him."

"Tie him up," I suggested. "Or knock him out."

"Does Isabel have anything that can knock someone out cold?"

"I think she has a sleeping potion somewhere." They didn't work on faeries, but a half-shifter would be affected in the same way as a regular human, I assumed. "By the time I get home and come back, he'll have climbed out, though."

"Tell me where it is. I've been in your flat, so I should be able to move it here."

"You can be that specific?" I thought. "Left kitchen cupboard, highest shelf. Small blue bottle. We had to hide them from George."

"Good enough." A small green bottle appeared in his hands, then vanished, to be replaced with a red one. The third time, the correct blue bottle appeared. "Easy."

"That's it?" I blinked. "If Isabel was in the flat, you probably scared her to death."

"At least I didn't leave roses."

I gave him a reluctant smile. His hand and face were bleeding freely, and for all I knew, he might have got cut up underneath his thick coat, too. Those claws were nasty.

"What are you doing?" Wyatt demanded from inside the pit. His face was mostly human, but black scales encased his arms as his clawed hands reached upward, trying to get a hold onto the side of the packed earth.

In answer, Vance disappeared, and there was a thud and a gasp and the sound of a potion splashing. An instant later, Vance reappeared again with his uncle's unconscious form slumped in his arms. The Mage Lord staggered a little and Wyatt fell forward onto the grass.

Vance crouched beside his uncle. He looked a little paler than usual, the cuts on his face bleeding worse than ever.

"You should get a healing spell." I peered down at Wyatt, whose face was splattered with the remnants of the sleeping potion.

"Probably," he muttered, flipping his uncle's body over. "I'm not supposed to use my ability on this level right after shifting."

"On this level…"

"Transporting people," he clarified. "It uses more power than moving objects."

"You do it all the time," I pointed out, watching him lift his uncle's chin and examine his closed eyes. "What're you looking for?"

"I've never been good at restraint." He propped Wyatt up on the grass and peered behind his head, and his eyes widened. "I knew it."

"Knew what?"

Vance pushed Wyatt's head forward and indicated a bloodied spike protruding from the back of his neck. As he reached for it, a thorn came loose in his hands. "This is…"

"Faerie magic." A chill rushed up my back. "No way."

Thorns, everywhere, digging into my skin.

"Scream, Ivy Lane," a voice whispered. "Nobody will ever hear you."

"Ivy?"

I shook my head. "Not a fan of thorns. Sorry. I'll take it to Isabel. She might be able to figure out where it came from, but I don't want it in the flat."

"We can take it to one of my fields," Vance offered. "Faerie magic? Are you sure?"

"I can't think of any witch charm that involves thorns," I said. "Summer magic, though… I once heard of someone who used them as a method of control."

I fell deeper into the pit, thorns biting into my hips and shoul-

ders, and felt my will to resist slide away even as the pain built higher.

I shook the image away. Vance gave me a curious look. "A controlling spell... you mean, influencing emotions or impulses?"

"You could say that." A familiar panic crept up my throat. "It's not as sophisticated as a vow, but I knew a faerie who manipulated humans by using thorns. One scratch and they'd wander straight into her trap and be unable to get out."

"This faerie," said Vance. "Might it be the same one?"

No. Not her. Please, please not her. I'd rather fight the Lady of the Tree without a weapon than go up against the Thorn Princess again.

My nails dug into my palms. Rational thoughts warred against the instinct to grab the thorn from Vance's hand and grind it into dust.

"Let go of it," I croaked. "Please. Before it gets to you, too."

"I'll be careful." He held the thorn between two fingers. "How did the magic work, exactly?"

"A... a blood binding." I blinked hard, trying to knock the images away. "Each thorn was smeared with a drop of her blood and a drop of the person's she wanted to control."

"Then washing off the blood ought to break the spell." He turned the thorn over in his hand. "Once we've used a tracking spell. Right now, it's our only possible link to the person behind this."

I swallowed against my dry throat. "Yeah. I know."

I also knew that it didn't solely affect shifters. Any human could be manipulated in the same manner.

"Wait." I thought back. "Didn't Rita say thorns were appearing everywhere? He must have tried to remove them, and..."

"Got caught in the spell," said Vance. "This tomb, though…"

"Oh, right." In the tumult of the thorn's appearance, I'd almost forgotten the massive hole in the ground. When I moved behind him to peer in, I saw nothing but upturned earth. "Doesn't look like he got very far."

"I'd try to find out, but I've overstretched my abilities already," Vance said. "I'll take you home. If you want to use a tracking spell on these thorns today, we'll do that next."

I nodded. "Are you going to leave him here, or…?"

"I'll drop him outside the farmhouse." He scowled down at his uncle. "It's more than he deserves, but I don't want him getting caught in another spell after I went to the trouble of freeing him from this one."

He heaved Wyatt over his shoulder and carried him through the field. I might have objected, but it was marginally better than him using his ability again. As we walked, I tried to ignore Wyatt's unconscious face dangling over Vance's shoulder.

"There's one thing I don't get," I said. "One more thing, I mean. If the farmhouse is so heavily warded, how'd the faeries get past?"

"When they took Anabel?" A frown pulled at his mouth. "That's a good question. I'd say it's more likely that they got her while she was outside. I wasn't closely watching at the time. I never asked."

"And now?" Unease brewed inside me. "Your uncle's been walking in and out of there the whole time he's been controlled by that thorn, hasn't he? Can their magic circumvent iron wards?"

Vance's jaw tensed. "We need to find out where they came from as quickly as possible."

"Yeah." I stared down at Irene, re-sheathed at my waist.

The one advantage I'd always had over faeries was their weakness to iron. I'd counted on it, even more than my faerie magic. If the thorns could get around that… every human in the city was potentially in danger.

Neither of us spoke until we reached the farmhouse, at which point he deposited Wyatt in the garden. Rita came running out, hands clapped to her mouth.

"He's fine, just unconscious," Vance called to her. "We had to employ a sleeping potion. I believe I removed the spell that had him in a trance, but if you see any more thorns around, don't touch them. Tell Anabel the same."

I watched him speak to her, a sense of unreality washing over me. *She can't be here. She's not supposed to be here.*

I startled when Vance's bloodied hand rested on my arm. "We'll solve this, and make the killer pay for what they've done."

I swallowed and nodded. "Yeah. I'd say I wish I knew what we were up against, but…"

"You're capable of bringing down a Sidhe. You've proved that already."

Yeah. I'd done it twice. Except both times, the circumstances had been the same. "Only in the Grey Vale. My magic is stronger there."

Vance's grip on my arm tightened. "It's a death trap."

"I know, but my power is bound to that place." I met his gaze, willing him to understand. "Even if I didn't keep getting ensnared in faerie bargains, my magic came from the other side. Maybe it's acting up because it *wants* to go back."

"No," said Vance. "It wants an anchor. Didn't the Chief say most Sidhe Lords' magic is contained within an object?"

"A talisman?" I looked down at Irene. "My sword's made of iron. Wouldn't work."

Maybe that was part of the issue, and that if I *did* have a talisman, I'd be more than a match for the person behind this. Unfortunately, the other person in this realm who had any knowledge of talismans was the Chief, who hated my guts, and would hate the idea of me wielding a weapon made solely for the Sidhe even more. *Typical.*

Vance gave the farmhouse one last glance, his expression unreadable. "We should leave. Ready?"

"Sure. Are you—?" I didn't quite get to ask *are* you *ready* before we landed on the road outside my house.

Thorns blocked our path. A thick, dense mat of spines extended across the road. Vance looked from the thorn in his hand to the hedge and back again, while I remained locked to the spot, my mouth gaping open. "Shit."

"Your house is warded," Vance said. "They're not inside."

"No." I unfroze. "No, but someone left them outside to prove a point."

Someone who knew where we'd been. Blistering anger seared my palms and blue energy arced through the air, scissoring into the thorny hedge. It split clean in two, fragments of thorns scattering all over the road.

"Fucking. Faeries." I stormed over to the nearest thicket, raised my hands, and brought magic crashing down like a hammer.

Vance came in behind me. "They need to be destroyed, not displaced. I'll get a cleansing spell."

A spell appeared in Vance's hand, activating with a snap, but the thorns barely receded.

"I thought you said you'd overtaxed your ability," I muttered to him. "Quit that."

"No, I just need to be careful when transporting people." He did look tired, though, and there were lines underneath his eyes that hadn't been there before. "Where's Isabel?"

"Watching George, probably." Oh hell. I glanced over at

the house and saw her staring out the window. When we locked eyes, she ducked out of sight and came running out the front door a minute later.

"Do you have any spells that can help take care of that?" Vance gestured to the thorny bushes.

"Speaking of spells, get a healing spell." I pointed at his bloodied hands and face. "Honestly. You nag *me* about running off and getting into trouble."

"Do I even want to know?" Isabel looked between us and the giant thorny bush in the road, a furrow in her brow. "Who threw thorns at you?"

"Three guesses who." I saw George watching from the window, too, and my heart sank. I'd put a target on our entire flat by meddling. "They moved fast this time. Can we borrow some explosives? Oh, and don't touch any of those thorns. Definitely don't bleed on them. I'm pretty sure they're laced with blood-control magic."

"Noted." Isabel backed towards the house again. "I'll get the explosives."

"Maybe leave out the glitter." Despite my flippant tone, my heart began racing again. *How* had the faeries got here so fast? Vance and I had pulled the thorn out of Wyatt half an hour ago at most.

I returned to the hedge, my heart thumping. Why thorns? Maybe someone had overheard me talking about how much I hated them… or maybe another faerie had slipped out of the Grey Vale alongside the Lady of the Tree.

Images flashed before my eyes. *Thorns thick and dripping with blood. I couldn't move. The thorns pinned me into place, biting into my skin. A tendril wrapped around my right shoulder and squeezed. I screamed, hoarse and loud, but nobody heard me.*

Isabel waved a hand in front of my face. I hadn't even noticed she'd come up beside me. "Ivy? You're zoning out."

"Yeah. I hate thorns." I shuddered. "Is that a healing spell?"

"Yes, I got one for both of you."

"Cheers." I turned on the blue band-shaped spell with a snap, and some of my aches and pains vanished. Another flash told me Vance had activated his. The way his hand automatically jumped to his left arm suggested he'd been bitten or scratched more than once. By his own uncle. We had to stop whoever was targeting the shifters, but if similar thorns had been materialising all over their part of town, how could anyone avoid walking into them?

Unfortunately, the thorns proved resilient even in the face of Isabel's explosives, and we ended up having to sweep the remnants into bin bags. By the time we'd finished, the sun had disappeared in a golden haze behind the rooftops, and we'd had to turn away no fewer than fifteen cars who'd turned into the road to find the way blocked by the thorny bush. The house sat near a cul-de-sac so we didn't get too much traffic, but the mages would have to deal with a line of complainers demanding to know why magical thorns had been blocking the road.

"I bet the rest of the mage council will be pissed off at me." I knelt to clean up the last of the discarded spells.

"I'll take care of it." Vance stood still, his eyes closed. "That's the last of them?"

"Yeah. You okay?"

"I'll be fine tomorrow. You should go home."

"Before another thorn monster materialises in the road." I joked to ease the tightening in my chest. This didn't seem like the Lady of the Tree's work, but I'd got through another day without getting any closer to finding the missing talisman. Instead, this situation kept getting more tangled. More, well, thorny. Ha.

"I'm sending patrols to shifter territory tonight," Vance said. "I've made it clear to my mages not to touch any thorns they might come across, but obviously, they can't stop the shifters from leaving their homes altogether."

Yeah. That's what I'm scared of. We needed answers, but the sun would go down in a couple of hours and we already had a target on our back. Through the window, I glimpsed Isabel, who'd gone back into the flat to check on George. I doubted Henry and Disha would ever trust us with babysitting again after this week.

"I don't get it," I said softly. "Thorns. They're not from the Lady of the Tree *or* Velkas's talisman. I didn't see any thorns when Velkas used his blade to... to suck the life out of me."

"The life-drinker," said Vance.

"Exactly." The coincidence was still too much, but where in hell did the thorns fit into this? "Looks like we have *two* enemies. Both of whom came from the Vale."

Life-drinker. Seelie exiles rarely lasted long in the Grey Vale. Velkas had managed it, which suggested his talisman had no uncommon level of power. The Thorn Princess, too. It made a twisted kind of sense that they'd made an agreement, one that may have passed on to the talisman's new wielder, but I'd really hoped I'd seen the back of both of them.

Vance lifted his gaze to the darkening sky. "It's late. I don't like leaving you alone."

"The house is warded," I reminded him. "I'm not alone, either. There are two cranky shifters chained up in the upstairs flat."

"Strangely, that's not reassuring." He scowled at the road where the thorns had been. "And someone's trying to threaten you."

"Wouldn't be the first time." I leaned closer to him. "You. Get some rest. Stop trying to solve everyone's problems at once. You aren't superhuman."

He looked down at his hands like he expected to see claws in place of fingers. "I'm not entirely human, Ivy."

"That makes two of us. Call me, okay?"

My hands dug into the front of his coat as I kissed him, as though if I held on tight enough, I could anchor him right here with me. He vanished, and I knew, beyond all shadow of a doubt, that I'd walk back into Faerie for him again in a heartbeat.

"Earth to Ivy?" Isabel waved from the front garden. "I thought he was going to take you with him."

"I wish." I walked over to join her. "I'm gonna try a tracking spell out here to see if I can get a clue about whoever dumped these thorns in front of the house. It's not ideal, but some shithead's got their eyes on the flat anyway. I'd rather check while I can."

She nodded. "All right. Then I expect you to come and tell me what you were up to all afternoon."

"I will do." I reached into my pocket and fished out a tracking spell. "I'm still not sure what's going on, though. The thorns are… a new development."

Or an old one. The Vale's worst horrors were infiltrating my life, like an undead that refused to rest in its grave.

"I'll double-check the wards." She began pacing the garden, while I crouched in the road and set up the tracking spell.

Green light swept up my arms, and images rushed through my head, following a familiar trail of streets. I didn't see the person whose eyes I watched through, but I knew enough to recognise where they headed.

Half-blood territory.

I let the spell collapse and swore softly. We'd need to go back there first thing tomorrow, but I wouldn't let Vance know until the morning. He needed a break, even more than I did.

I joined Isabel in checking the wards, while George watched from the window. The poor kid. How many years did he have left until he shifted for the first time? More than Anabel, but not enough. So many lives depended on the killer being caught. Never mind my vow to the Lady of the Tree. I'd make the same decision whether I was bound by oath or not.

14

Screaming woke me.

I jolted upright, disorientated, before my panic response kicked in. The faeries had found a way into the flat. They'd taken George. And Isabel—no, she was the one screaming. I lurched out of bed, snatching up Irene, and ran into the living room.

"Bad faerie!" Erwin the piskie screeched, hanging upside-down from the ceiling light.

Isabel stood by the window, her palms pressed to the glass. Behind her, George sobbed quietly, curled on the sofa. They hadn't taken him. I lowered the blade.

"Ivy," croaked Isabel. "L-look outside."

Heart drumming against my ribcage, I hurried over to her. Then stood, transfixed with horror.

A dead body lay outside the flat.

Well. Parts of a dead body. Two arms were speared on the cacti by the fence. The head sat atop the post at the side of our gate. The rest of the guy lay across the flowerbeds, entrails spilling out in bloody ropes.

I gagged, falling back onto the sofa. "What in the actual living hell?"

"Bad faerie!" screamed Erwin again.

A rattling crash shook the house. The sound of footsteps thundering downstairs, then the front door opening. Henry crossed the lawn, staring in horror at the corpse of yet another dead shifter.

This is bad. Someone had killed the guy, then thrown him *over* our wards. Knowing, I assumed, that a lifeless dead body that wasn't undead wouldn't trigger our security.

"Oh, god," said Isabel, hands over her mouth. "He's going to kill someone."

"Not if I can help it." I ran to my room and grabbed my phone, firing a quick message to Vance. Then I pulled my clothes on and grabbed two daggers in addition to my sword.

In the living room, Erwin continued to fly around, screaming, "Bad faerie! Bad faerie!"

By the time I joined Isabel in the hall, no fewer than twelve people had gathered on the lawn, rallying around Henry. His furious stillness made me wary to get near him, and I kept my hand on Irene as I approached. "Don't do anything rash."

Henry ignored me. "This is undoubtedly a faerie's work. We need to confront them on their own turf."

"Murdering scum," snarled a blond female shifter. From the bloody marks on her face, I could tell she'd had a rough shift. "We'll kill them."

Crap. Things were unravelling fast, and I was barely awake. I grabbed my phone again, but even the Mage Lord might not be able to stop a dozen shifters from breaking down the doors to half-blood territory.

Henry opened the gate and the other shifters followed him out of the garden, while I one-handedly typed another message to Vance on my phone, mouthing to Isabel, *Stay there with George.* Tugging my jacket into place, I ran after them.

"Hang on a moment," I called. "What do you think confronting the half-faeries will achieve? None of them did this."

"You'd say that," said the tattooed shifter dude who'd confronted me over the other dead body yesterday. "Would you say the same if it was one of *your* friends torn up back there?" Yellow flared through his eyes, and two more shifters stepped up on either side of him.

I pulled out my sword, but I didn't dare use it. Even if could have taken out twelve enraged shifters who'd barely turned back into human form post-shift, I didn't want to do any of them permanent damage.

"Henry!" I shouted to him. "Your son's back there. Just think for a moment."

"Disha can take care of him," he growled. "This has gone on long enough."

I kept up a desperate stream of discouragement all the way down the road, but nobody listened to a word. Panic had begun to overtake the sluggishness in my head by the time we reached half-blood territory.

A line of cloaked figures barred the way to the gate. Vance must have got my message after all. The Mage Lord himself stood cloaked and fearsome in front of his fellow mages, who'd assembled in a line in front of the hedge.

"Stop," Vance called to the shifters. "Nobody on this territory committed the murder."

"There are no murderers on my territory." The Chief's voice drifted over the hedge. From this angle, I could see him standing behind the gate with a pair of armed guards on either side.

"You're lying," said the tattooed shifter. "People are dying because of your people."

"Murder is illegal," Vance interjected. "No matter who committed the crime. If this is a rogue faerie, the Chief has agreed to put all his resources towards finding them and bringing them to justice."

From their muttering, it was clear none of the shifters believed him, but even they didn't dare contradict the Mage Lord. Not with at least twenty mages accompanying him, and armoured half-faerie knights behind the gates with an array of half-trolls, ogres and other beasts I'd never thought I'd be glad to have on my side.

"Furthermore," said Vance, "it seems foolish to start a war when one of your own lies dead and unburied."

An angry rumble went through the shifters.

"Don't tell us what to do," said the tattooed guy. "If someone killed one of your fellow mages, you would immediately pursue the killer. Don't deny it."

"Nobody knows who the killer is, including the half-faeries." I wouldn't tell *them* my suspicions. The murderer had blasted three of them to pieces already, and even a fully transformed shifter stood no chance against a talisman. "Starting a war won't bring your friends back *or* find the killer. Henry, you have a kid to consider, too."

Anger flashed through his eyes. "Ivy, this is none of your business."

"But it's *my* business if you planned to start a war here in my city," said Vance. "Whatever your motives, our aim is to avoid a repeat of the tragedies incurred during the invasion. Need I remind you of the losses suffered across the supernatural world at large?"

The underlying threat, accompanied by a crackle of thunder, elicited no response from the shifters. Everyone knew they'd come off worse from the war. More shifters had died than anyone else, and as Vance had recently made clear, a fair few had been killed by their fellow shifters rather than by the invaders.

"This isn't over yet, half-bloods," hissed the tattooed shifter. "If another one of ours dies, we'll take one of yours."

The sharp noises of weapons being drawn came from half-blood territory, swiftly drowned out by a crack like a thunderclap. Everyone braced themselves as the air shook with a gust of wind that ripped leaves off the hedges and sent the retreating shifters staggering.

"Enough," said Vance. "Return home and take care of your dead. You may search for the killer on your own territory, if you so desire, but you will not find anything here."

How do you know? Had he and the Chief had another discussion that I hadn't been privy to? One that confirmed the thorns hadn't come from here, despite what the tracking spell had shown me?

Henry was the last shifter to leave. He shot me a reproachful look, enough to reassure me I'd be getting an earful later. Once he'd cleaned the corpse off our lawn. I hoped Isabel wouldn't get dragged into helping him, or else he might find himself on the receiving end of a glitter spell.

For now, the crisis was averted. The mages looked considerably relieved not to have had to fight a dozen angry shifters, but I knew we'd only forestalled the problem. If the killer struck again, we'd be back to square one. Whatever the murderer's ultimate endgame might be, the shifters' deaths were undeniably a precursor to something worse. And if the veil opened the way it had done in the faerie invasion, every one of the shifters would succumb to the beast inside.

Vance beckoned. I stepped to his side, and the gate to half-blood territory swung open. The Chief was still behind the entrance, flanked by two ogres. Seven feet tall and covered in mottled green skin, they waved huge clubs threateningly at me and Vance when we entered. Either they didn't recognise the Mage Lord or were too thick-skulled to realise who they were threatening.

"Chieftain Taive," said Vance, ignoring the ogres. "We wish to speak to you in confidence."

"What is it?" asked the Chief. "Haven't you done enough here? If you're expecting me to thank you for diverting the shifters you drew to my doorstep with your own actions, you're mistaken."

"In confidence," said Vance, in his most dangerous voice. "I told you that Ivy and I had new information connecting this murderer to the person responsible for afflicting this drought on your territory."

And the thorns. Don't forget about those.

The Chief's mouth thinned. "Fine."

The lawns were packed out with half-bloods, some in armour, some not, and with an equal mix of Seelie and Unseelie. Winter knights with ice-coloured hair and Summer faeries with coats of thorns and eerily beautiful faces watched us pass, and a current of unease travelled through me every time I saw one of the latter. Some of these faeries easily fit the description of the killer, and while I didn't believe for a minute that any were responsible, I could understand why the shifters were less convinced.

I'd never expected to end up defending the offspring of the faeries. What was the world coming to?

The Chief led us down a path to an empty clearing I recognised as the place where Vance and I had once sneaked off with blood from a couple of dead bodies. He then dismissed his guards and ordered them to stand watch. His two ogres sloped off, glowering at us.

The Chief planted his staff on the ground in front of him. "This had better be worth my time."

"I think I know who the killer is," I began.

The Chief's mouth fell open. "You what?"

"Answer a question first," I said. "How effective would a powerful talisman be here on Earth? As opposed to in Faerie?"

His eyes narrowed in response to the order, but he said grudgingly, "That depends on the strength of the talisman. Its owner's strength would also play a part, but there are other aspects to consider. Like the location."

"It'd be stronger near the Ley Line," I confirmed. "And… how would one go about creating a talisman?"

"You're human. You don't need to know."

"Yeah, I do. I think that's what the killer is using on those shifters, and it's also having a knock-on effect here on your territory, too."

"No." He shook his head violently. "That's impossible."

"Coming from someone whose house is twenty times larger on the inside than it is on the outside." I gave an eye-roll. "It won't do any harm if you tell me how a talisman is created. It's hardly something I can try at home."

Pity, because gaining control over my unwieldy magic would be a damn sight easier if it was contained within an object rather than shooting out of my hands when I didn't want it to. As a bonus, with a talisman of my own, I might have a fighting chance against the killer.

"Creating a talisman involves taking a source already infused with considerable power and adding one's own magic to bind it to oneself," said the Chief. "The ancient trees of Faerie are already vessels for magic, so it's natural for them to be used as the base."

"And your staff…?"

A flush lit his cheeks. "My staff has all the power I need."

Translation: his staff was worth fuck all. Which I'd already known.

"I'm positive that someone is using a talisman to kill shifters," I went on. "The damage inflicted on the bodies is way beyond anything I've seen in this realm. Furthermore, I *saw* the killer, through a tracking spell. She was fae."

"She," he repeated, his face paling. "You must be mistaken."

"Oh, I'm very much not," I said. "And unlike the shifters, I'm not accusing you or anyone on this territory of being responsible. But if you want to avoid taking the blame, I'd be a little more open-minded about what might be possible in this realm. There are talismans that are fuelled by the life force of others... right?"

"Life force?" he repeated, his face now positively ashen.

"Yes, you know, like magic used by a Summer outcast. I met one," I added. "His talisman could drain the life out of others. Not something I'll forget in a hurry."

The Chief shook his head. *"Taking* a life is against the rules of the Seelie and Unseelie courts."

"Taking a faerie life," I corrected. "That's what you mean, right? Not humans."

"Does it matter?"

"Actually, yes." I scowled at him. "Legalities aside, I'm pretty sure our killer's taking shifter lives to add fuel to the talisman. Shifters on the verge of a change go through a transformation that generates a great deal of energy. One that might, say, create another energy surge and tear open the veil." Of course, killing humans didn't contradict the laws of the Seelie *or* Unseelie courts, but the killer sure as hell didn't care about Faerie's laws either.

"No," he croaked. "Nobody would dare. The risks..."

"We're talking about a murderer willing to go to any lengths to achieve her goals," I said. "Someone like... oh, the Lady of the Tree."

The Chief's washed-out green eyes sharpened. "No."

"Look at the facts," I pressed on. "She hates humans. She even went as far as to hand innocent children over to Velkas because he promised her immortality. If anyone's capable of brutalising shifters to boost her own power, it's her."

"You—you're being absurd," the Chief spluttered, a scarlet tinge creeping up his neck. "The Lady might be powerful, but she's no Sidhe."

"But she's ancient," I said. "She's also recently regained her youth and her magic. The killer I saw—and that the murder victims saw, too—is a beautiful female Summer faerie who carried what looked awfully like a talisman. Coincidence?"

"The Lady may be ancient, but she's far from the only pure faerie in this realm," said the Chief tremulously. "She'd kill you for accusing her."

"She's likely to kill me anyway," I said. "She's already bound me with a vow to find this missing talisman, which I can only assume is the one being used to commit the murders. No idea why she wants me to find something she already has, but it's that or a faerie who looks just like her is using the talisman to frame her." *And the thorns?* a voice whispered in the back of my mind. *What other monstrosities came into this realm when the veil opened?*

"True fae cannot lie," the Chief said.

"They can mislead," said Vance. "As she's already proven, several times."

"Exactly." I looked around the clearing, at the leafless trees and grey-brown undergrowth. "This place is dying, isn't it? So's your whole territory. The Lady of the Tree is at full power. It's like she regained a few centuries' worth of life. How's *that* possible?"

The Chief shook his head slowly. "No true faeries have come back to this realm since the war."

"How can you possibly know that?" I asked. "You can't watch all of Faerie from here, can you?"

In fact, if he'd been stuck here most of his life, the Chief and the other half-bloods were as clueless as the rest of us humans. Hell, *I'd* probably spent longer in Faerie than any half-blood in the city. *Hmm. I probably shouldn't tell them that.*

The Chief's eyes narrowed. "Don't presume to understand, Ivy Lane."

"She threatened to kill me if I didn't fulfil the vow. I'd say it's in my interests to figure out what makes her tick, don't you?"

"Then you should never have made a promise to a faerie. If you were half as intelligent as you think you are, you'd have found a way to avoid ensnaring yourself."

"A promise saved my life, you obstinate arsehole," I shot at him. "I won Lord Avalin's magic due to a vow we made, because the condition of our duel was that I'd get to come back home if I won. If a faerie vow hadn't worked out in my favour, I wouldn't be here."

His brows rose. "You won a Sidhe lord's power through a *vow?*"

"Because I killed him." A twinge of satisfaction arose when he flinched. "I was a weak human, only sixteen years old, when I poisoned Lord Avalin with iron and cut his throat with his own blade. Then the vow kicked in, and his magic transferred over to me. The reason I have the full magic of a Sidhe Lord, far more than you ever will, is because a promise is more powerful even than a lord of Faerie."

He drew his hands around his staff tight enough that his knuckles whitened. "His magic should have killed you."

"It didn't," I said. "If a human can steal magic, so can a pure fae like the Lady of the Tree. She's no Sidhe, but she was already more powerful than I was when she was exiled into this realm."

"Stealing magic from another faerie shouldn't be possible for a human," said the Chief. "Stealing a *talisman* isn't impossible, but handling a powerful source of magic is like speaking an Invocation. You will be judged, and if the magic finds you unworthy, it will destroy you."

"It didn't." I *had* claimed the magic. I'd spoken an Invocation, too, which was no doubt still a sore point with him, but I didn't care a bit for his hurt feelings. "If magic found *me* worthy, then it's not too big a leap to assume the Lady strode into the Grey Vale when the Ley Line was stirred up, picked up Velkas's blade, and was chosen as worthy of wielding its power. Is it?"

The fight drained out of Chieftain Taive with every word I spoke. His hands gripped the staff in a way that suggested he was using it to keep himself from sinking to the ground in despair. Or possibly holding himself back from hitting me over the head.

"This is ridiculous," he finally said. "There's nothing to prove the Lady of the Tree is behind these murders."

"Except she's the one who clued me in to the existence of the talisman in the first place," I pointed out. "Show me another faerie in town with as much power as she has. She's gathering energy from dead shifters to power this talisman like a giant magical battery, and if you ask me, she's stalling until she gets enough power to rip the veil open permanently this time. Are you going to sit here and let her do that?"

"I won't be threatened in my own territory," he snarled. "You just admitted you stole your magic from the place the true Sidhe send exiles. If ever you set foot in the Courts, you'd be executed as a common criminal."

"Thanks for the heads-up," I said. "I don't plan on ever going to the Courts, for the record, but you stand to get accused of murder at the very least, and she clearly has no intention of stopping unless someone challenges her. What can beat a talisman?"

"Another talisman of equal or greater strength."

"Don't suppose you've got one of those lying around?" My

heart sank in my chest. There weren't any, not in this realm. "Or contact with a faerie who does?"

He avoided my gaze. "Half-bloods are not welcome in either Summer or Winter."

"Looks like we have that much in common, then." I shook my head at him. "Get over yourself. A human wielding your magic isn't as big a deal as someone using it to commit murder. Have some sense."

"I won't risk my people's safety without proof, Ivy Lane," said the Chief. "I have a territory to protect, and if you're wrong, you'll cost us the freedom we've fought for as long as we've lived in this realm."

My hands curled into fists, more in helplessness than anger. Whether the Lady was the killer or not, her vow ensured I could never escape the consequences of our bond, and this guy outright refused to entertain the possibility of her guilt.

A buzzing sounded. My phone? No, not mine.

"Vance!" Drake's voice yelled from Vance's pocket. "The manor's garden is covered in thorns. They're attacking everyone."

I turned to Vance. "You didn't leave the thorn at the manor, did you?"

Vance swore under his breath. "Yes. I couldn't destroy it outright, so I assumed the iron wards would keep it contained."

"What on earth are you two talking about?" asked the Chief.

"You already said you didn't want to be involved." I was already typing frantically into my own phone to warn Isabel. I was pretty sure we'd removed every trace of thorn left in the road, but if the manor was under attack, the house was fair game. *Fuck. I can't be in two places at once.*

"I'll order every mage to return to the manor." Vance

nodded in the direction of the gate where he'd left the other mages.

"Don't forget it might be a diversion to take attention away from other potential targets," I warned. "Remember your cousin?"

His expression darkened. "I already have people watching my uncle's house. I'll go there again after we've dealt with the thorns."

"Thorns?" said the Chief. "What *are* you two doing?"

Ignoring him, Vance took my arm, and we both vanished.

15

The last thing I heard was the Chief yelling at Vance for using mage magic in half-blood territory, but we landed back at the manor before he could finish his tirade.

An expanse of thorns swept across the front lawn. Long tendrils splayed out, whipping at anyone who came near. Bursts of fire lit the air as Drake threw handfuls of flame at the plant, but his fire had little effect at slowing it down. Other mages gathered on the garden path, employing lightning and wind, water and ice, or if all else failed, hacking at the thorns with weapons. None made so much as a dent.

Vance waved a hand, and a large section of thorns vanished.

"Where'd you send those?" I lifted my sword to help. "They'll keep growing no matter where you put them."

"Seriously?" Drake brushed sweaty hair out of his eyes. "What the devil is this crap?"

"Faerie thorns." I jabbed at another oncoming tendril. "We need to use iron."

"Iron doesn't kill it!" shouted a terrified-looking apprentice. "This cursed stuff grows too fast."

"Iron is poison to all faeries." *It should be.* Dread coiled within my chest. Irene in hand, I slashed off a tendril before it could latch onto my wrist. Though the iron did effectively slice through the vines, the effect didn't spread to the rest of the plant, and the damn thing kept on growing.

I'd only ever seen thorns like these in Faerie, and a familiar deep-seated fear rose inside me, as though the thorny plants had taken root beneath my skin, tendrils unfurling through my veins.

"Backup's here," Vance said, at the sound of a car pulling up outside the gate.

A few more mages came running in, including Bailey and Rod, a mage couple comprised of an earth mage and an air mage. The instant they reached the garden, a long vine wrapped around Bailey's ankle and yanked the earth mage off his feet. His glasses fell off and shattered, and panic erupted among the newcomers. Rod glided upward off the ground—as an air mage, he couldn't fly, but he came pretty close—and he managed to snatch his boyfriend out of the thorns' grasp. Vance rescued a mage apprentice who'd also become entangled, but the thorns covered half the lawn by now.

"We can't let them get inside the manor," I hissed at Vance, who grunted in agreement. "The only way I can think of to stop this is to find whichever faerie is controlling the thorns and kill them."

Another swathe of thorns vanished at Vance's hand. "I'll transport the whole lot away at once, and we can deal with them somewhere else."

"Can you do that?" Displacing a plant with seemingly infinite regenerative powers before might be beyond even his mage talents.

Not that we had many other options. A second group of mages arrived and promptly found themselves overwhelmed, too. Whether they froze the thorns, burned them, or conjured up a lightning storm, the vines just kept on growing, and each slash of a weapon only seemed to aggravate the plant further. Many of them had suffered injuries, and cloaked mages helped their fallen companions limp out of harm's way.

I got in closer, hacking with my sword, intending to draw the attention of whichever faerie was behind this. A shudder raked through me as a vine tried to wrap around my neck, but I used magic to form a shield around myself, pushing the vine back so I could slice it to pieces.

With my shield in place, the plant could no longer grab me, but the same couldn't be said for the other mages. Drake yelled as a vine coiled around his ankle and dragged him along the lawn, towards the thick mass of plant in the lawn's centre. The mass resembled a giant mouth with thorns for teeth. *Oh, hell.*

I ran, throwing magic in wild bursts that slowed the thorns long enough for me to catch up and drive Irene down into the tendril holding Drake. He managed to pull himself free and scrambled to his feet.

"Whoever heard of a fireproof plant?" he demanded of the universe in general.

"Welcome to Faerie." I disentangled myself from the thorns, snagging my jacket in the process. "Logic need not apply."

Drake snorted. When another vine swiped at him, he retreated down the path towards the manor. At the entrance, Wanda stood alongside another young frost mage, both throwing handfuls of glittering frost magic. A coating of ice formed on the lawn, but the plant itself remained mostly untouched and its tendrils crept closer to the manor than ever.

"It's no use." Vance appeared at my side, hacking and slashing. "I'll have to displace the whole plant before the manor's safety is compromised."

I sliced off another vine. "If you're sure."

"I am." He spoke to the other mages. "Stand back, all of you."

The mages retreated, and a breeze kicked up around Vance. The swathe of thorns began to spin as though caught up in a tornado. The mouth-like formation snapped thorny teeth, but the tendrils whipped sideways, captured in Vance's power.

They vanished all at once, but as Vance took my hand, a familiar tugging sensation grabbed my limbs. "Vance, the vow—"

We vanished, and a nightmare greeted us on the other side. Straggly tendrils formed a gaping maw filled with protruding thorns. Brambles covered the rest of the huge face looming over us, and horror tightened its grip on me.

Thorns rising from a pit... rising to claim me.

I swung Irene, cutting thorns and memories both. The stabbing tendrils were thicker than before, and the thorns alone were as long as my fingers and sharp as knives. Soon bright-red blood beaded on my hands. Vance moved slower than usual, his eyes glazed with tiredness. It'd cost him a lot to transplant the thorns out of the manor, and if I had to guess, they'd been pulled straight to their source.

"Damn." I cut at a particularly thick branch, hacking three times before I severed it. "Where were you trying to send them?"

The vow no longer tugged at me, which all but confirmed whose territory we were on.

"Not here." Two blades materialised and slashed, severing thorny tendrils. "Another power intervened. I felt it."

"Yeah, so did I." In the form of the vow. The forested area around us grew more familiar with each strike of my blade. "We're in the Lady of the Tree's woods. Guess she heard us telling the Chief we suspected her. She didn't cover her traces very well, though, did she?"

"No." Vance spoke through gritted teeth as a half-dozen pieces of thorn exploded overhead. "But the thorns regenerate even when cut with iron. How is that possible?"

"I wish I knew." Another thorn flew sideways, severed by my blade. "I bet its creator is funnelling power into them. If we kill her, we stop the thorns."

"Right." Twin blades reappeared in his hands, and he looked into its open maw with deadly calmness. "I'll try displacing the air as I get closer. That ought to shield me from the thorns."

"You shouldn't…" *Overuse your abilities.* The words died on my tongue. I didn't need to give his limits away to the enemy, but damn, I hoped he'd be careful.

"I'll be fine."

My heart sank. The Lady of the Tree still, inexplicably, needed my help, but she wouldn't hesitate to take Vance down if necessary. *I have to finish her first.*

Vance pushed outward at the air, the twin swords slicing at any vine that came within range as he drew closer to the thorny beast's giant mouth. I called my magic into a shield and walked after him. Irene bit and slashed, sending bits of thorn flying everywhere, but our combined shields kept most of them away. Last time I'd become entrapped in a nest of magical thorns, I'd had no magic of my own. All the same, I held my breath as the thorny teeth snapped overhead, scraping at my shield. Similar thorns protruded around my feet, growing upward like stalactites, while the widening mouth resembled the entrance to a cave.

Common sense told me that crawling into a faerie's mouth would not end well, but the creature was nothing *but* mouth, and instinct told me this was where I needed to be. I overtook Vance, slicing down two protruding thorns, and the glow of my magic illuminated a wide space, in the centre of which stood a female figure. *There she is.*

The Lady wore a silken emerald-coloured dress, shimmering in the light of the magic pouring off every inch of her skin. She smiled at me with full lips, and the impact of her ethereal beauty slammed into me. Vance caught up and stiffened, eyes fixed on the being who looked for all the world like a pure Sidhe at home in Faerie. The blade in her hands, wreathed in green light, completed the picture.

"Damn," I said, my voice echoing off the cave walls. "Were you even trying to hide your traces? You were as subtle as a troll running full-tilt through a glass door."

"It was a deliberate move on my part," said the Lady of the Tree. "I needed your help, despite your propensity for sticking your too-human nose where it doesn't belong."

I lifted my sword. "Lady, meet Irene. I don't believe you've been introduced."

Vance's blade snapped at a thorny tendril attempting to creep over his shoulder. "Why did you force Ivy to hunt down an object you already have?"

"A valid question." I nodded to the Lady. "I have another: what's with this creepy place? Been taking decorating tips from the Princess of Thorns?"

"You've met." The Lady's mouth curved into a smile. "Yes... your time in the Grey Vale was somewhat eventful, wasn't it?"

"If you think I'm here for a chat, forget it. I'm not in the mood to talk. You murdered three people. With that." I indicated her sword. If not for its greenish sheen, it might have been a double of the one I'd held in my hands as I'd cut Avalin's throat. Unreadable glyphs flared up and down its length, and its aura made my own magic hum in resonance.

"They were necessary sacrifices."

"To power your talisman." The knowledge that I'd guessed right gave me no satisfaction. "Let me guess, you hopped over the veil to steal the talisman from Velkas's corpse when we were preoccupied with stopping the end of the world. I *knew* you lied about it being missing from Summer. The Sidhe nobles would never have let the likes of you retrieve one of their precious artefacts."

"You have more knowledge of Faerie than I gave you credit for," said the Lady. "Unfortunately, that won't help you now. I didn't lie when I said the talisman *was* stolen, though that was a very long time ago. In fact, I believe Velkas stole it himself during his exile from Summer. Sadly, I never had the chance to make him regret that decision before you killed him."

Jesus. I'd known she was old, but the way she talked suggested decades had passed, at least, and she'd been in this realm twenty years already. I was dealing with someone who had a century on me if not more.

"Clever of you not to specify where in Faerie you went," I added. "How long did it take to practise speaking the truth without saying anything of substance?"

What's her game? She couldn't have brought me here to kill me. Her plans were more calculated.

She smiled, waving a hand, and a dozen thorn-laden tendrils descended to strike at Vance. He snarled, severing half of them, but the rest swarmed him, snagging at his limbs.

"Cut it out." I stepped to his side and swiped upward, slicing through vine and thorn. "This is between you and me, not the mages."

"Your mage is a nuisance." She stepped towards me on feet as silent as the blade in her hands. She might as well have been made of air. "It's *your* magic I want to see, Ivy. Show me the power of Lord Avalin."

"My pleasure," I said, and threw magic at her.

The blue swirl of energy dissipated in front of her smiling face. "You can do better than that, Ivy Lane. I know you can. Haven't you noticed your power is getting stronger?"

I sliced upward at another vine, tightening my grip on Irene and ignoring her gloating tone.

"You must have," she went on. "Have you healed from any unexpected serious injuries recently? That did not used to be possible for you in this realm, did it?"

"You don't know my magic," I said automatically, although my heart sank. When those shifters had knocked me out the other day, Frank said I'd used a healing spell. And until recently, I'd only been able to use magic to heal myself when I was in the Vale. *Is she right?*

"I know your magic, Ivy Lane, because it shares a common source with mine." She bared her teeth in a wide smile. "The Vale calls to us both."

"Not interested." With the final vine severed, I leapt forward and swung Irene at her head.

She dodged, easily as light on her feet as a Sidhe warrior, and swung her own blade in retaliation. Irene shuddered at the hit, and I tightened my grip as I renewed my attack. *Holy hell, she's fast.* Within seconds, my arms ached under the strain of blocking her hits.

When we broke away from each other, I was panting, and she bore no sign of tiredness at all.

"You've been draining the life out of half-blood territory, too, haven't you?" I lifted my blade, my shoulders burning. "Your talisman's feeding on their magic."

She gave a delighted laugh, and her blade rose to meet

mine. I gritted my teeth, disarmed by her unexpected strength. Our blades pushed against one another, but she didn't give, though the iron ought to have some effect on her. We weren't even in Faerie, after all—but her blade was infused with the power of Summer itself. Not to mention three dead shifters, in addition to however many years Velkas had fed life into the talisman.

"I thought magic decayed in the Grey Vale," I gasped. "Isn't that why you need to keep adding fuel to your talisman?"

"Wrong." She bared her teeth. "In the Vale, the strong survive, and I earned this talisman when I killed the undeserving fool who stole the blade from Velkas's corpse. The magic judged me and found me worthy, and the same will happen when I take yours for myself."

Hell, no. "Not a chance." I kicked at the side of her leg but missed, my own magic-enhanced instincts barely compensating for her impossible speed. She drove forward in a strike that would have impaled my chest had I not lifted Irene to block her. Again, our blades clashed, and again, neither gave ground.

Life-drinker. Strong or not, she hadn't used the talisman to its full extent yet. If she wanted to, she could suck out my life force, dampen my magic… but she hadn't. Why?

"What the hell's the point in all this?" I yelled. "Why gain all this power? Is being one of the most powerful faeries in this realm not enough for you?"

"Summer itself will cleave to me," she hissed, her beautiful face positively inhuman. "I will not live in exile forever."

"Summer. Right." I parried her blow, sweat pouring down my back. "Revenge. The usual crap."

"Do not mock me, human." Her voice boomed out. "You have no idea of the pain of being stripped from your home and stranded in a world which is poisonous to your kind."

I laughed, lifting my blade. "Yeah, I do, Lady. I know *exactly* what it feels like. But I don't use it as an excuse to kill people and ruin lives."

"You slaughtered Velkas." She drove her blade at me, and I blocked, the hilt jolting in my hands. "He was *mine* to kill."

"Sure, I killed Avalin and Velkas, but I have this thing against melodramatic fuckheads who see humans as tools." I pushed back, driving my iron blade closer to her wrist. Iron *would* hurt her. No talisman would make her immune.

She vanished. I nearly overbalanced, stumbling into a wall of bristling thorns. I yelped and sprang back, Vance steadying me from behind. His face was a bloody mess where the thorns had scratched him, but his coat had kept off the worst of the damage.

"Where is she?" He swiped the blood away with one hand. "Blasted thorns."

"No clue." I swivelled on the spot, but I saw only thorny stalagmites and a cave that looked entirely too much like an open mouth. "You know… we should get out of here."

The Lady and I were far from finished, but being eaten by a thorny monster was not how I wanted to end my days.

Vance and I backed out of the thorn-lined cave. At the entrance, I called out, "Where are you hiding? Scared to face me after all?"

"*Follow me, Ivy Lane.*" The voice sang out, and I veered away from the thorns, looking for the source.

"Where the fuck are you?" My body lurched to the side as an invisible force latched onto me. "Dammit. She's calling me. Vance, don't—"

His hand closed over my arm as we vanished again. The tugging sensation dissipated as we landed in a clearing, flanked with enough trees for me to suspect we'd reappeared elsewhere in the forest. The Lady stood there, a smile on her lips.

"Come closer, little human," her voice crooned. "I invoke the vow. You agreed to find the talisman. You agreed to bring it to Faerie. With your help, and the talisman's strength at full power, I will claim your magic as mine."

"You *have* the talisman." It was obvious, though, that it didn't work to its full extent in this realm. She'd had to keep fuelling it with death, and now, with the veil back to normal, the only person in this realm capable of crossing over to Faerie… was me. "And I won't take you to Faerie."

Pain racked my body, stabbing like tiny needles underneath my skin. *Ow. Fuck.* If I fought the vow, I'd die, but there was a fairly good chance death awaited on the other side of the veil, too.

"Come on." She danced sideways with a childlike titter. "We shall meet at the Ley Line, human, and you shall fulfil the promise you owe me."

I gasped as the pain lifted, but not for long. When she beckoned, I dug my heels in, and another spasm shook my limbs. Drove deep into my skin, sharp as thorns.

"Don't fight it, Ivy," she crooned. "I'll even spare your mage, if you prefer… though I would dearly love to make use of that handy power of his."

"Stay away from him." I lurched in front of Vance, and she stepped up to meet me. Green light shone from her eyes, from the blade in her hands.

"Take us to the Ley Line." She addressed Vance, rather than me. "Or she dies."

I screamed. My grip on Irene trembled, threatening to break. A coppery taste filled my mouth, and my body spasmed as though trying to tear itself apart from the inside.

"Do it!" I gasped. "Vance—I'll kill her—there."

A snarl escaped his mouth. The Lady's hand curled around my arm, and her laughter tickled my ear. "Do as she says, Mage Lord."

The forest vanished. We landed on a hill crowned with trees. The distant shapes of crooked houses extended across the horizon. Ruined houses, with caved-in roofs and empty gardens, bordering a park that held a grim familiarity. Here, Avalin had taken me into Faerie, and more recently, Velkas's allies had almost ripped open the veil.

I broke away from Vance, gasping, and shook my arm. The Lady had already released me, but my skin burned with the impact of her touch, though the pain had gone. She'd kept her word.

We're on Faerie's doorstep. The veil was calm. Not a trace of the Ley Line was visible, but the Lady danced across the hillside, twirling, no longer paying us any attention.

"She's fucking unhinged," I breathed. "Vance—I meant it. I have to go to the Vale. She's stronger there, but so am I. It's the only place I can kill her."

A head-shake. "I won't let you fight her alone."

"Vance—" I broke off, staggering as another invisible tug seized my body and yanked me sideways. "She doesn't care if you die. She still needs me."

I highly doubted she and the other lords of the Vale were preparing a 'welcome home' party, but she'd kept me alive thus far. She needed me.

Yet my questions remained. Why come back here at all? What was her endgame? Revenge on Summer couldn't be the full story.

The Lady danced over to us, a manic grin on her lips. "Now, Ivy, you will take me to Faerie."

A fresh wave of pain accompanied her words; I doubled over, fighting to remain in the present.

"What do you want from me?" The words tore from my throat as the vow shredded my insides. "Why go to all this trouble? I can't do anything for your grudge against Summer. You know that."

She skipped behind me, whispering in my ear. "The god's power will be mine, Ivy Lane."

"The god." My heart gave a jolt, and through the haze of pain in my mind, the words of Frank the necromancer ghost replayed: *the Grey Vale... a piece of their world torn away by the magic of the ancient Sidhe when they exiled their gods.*

The life-drinker.

She wanted far more than a talisman.

"That's..." I coughed, tasting blood. "Is that why you had the shifters searching for that old tomb? The shifter ... came from the Vale?"

"Part of the god is contained within the mortal realm." She raised her voice, her breath tickling my ear. "The other part, in Death. But to access it, I need the power of Summer and Winter combined. The strength of a Lord of Summer and a Lord of Winter, offered willingly."

"You're dragging me to Faerie so you can kill me and claim my power in addition to your own?" Another set of needles jabbed underneath my skin, but my horror and anger prevailed. "No way. I'll send you to Death myself first."

I spun around, but Irene sliced through thin air. From behind, strong hands gripped my arms, squeezing hard. Blue light ignited from my skin, and my vision doubled as grey smoke thickened and rose to obscure the world.

Another hand seized mine. *Vance.* He was trying to pull me away, but if he got too close to that sword—

"Stop!" I screamed, driving forward, pushing my magic outward to break the Lady's grip on my arms. She hung on, tenacious, as the grey thickened and a tunnel of light bloomed in front of me.

No. We're here. We're already here...

"Get *off* me!" Magic flared from every inch of me, and I heard the Lady scream as her grip broke.

I slammed into solid earth, my elbows scraping against

fallen leaves. I lifted my head. Branches formed a canopy overhead, interlocking and reducing the sunlight to faint silvery beams. I pushed to my knees, wincing at the pain in my arms where the Lady's hands had gripped me. But she wasn't here.

Someone else lay beside me. Vance sat up slowly, brushing leaves from his coat, eyes wide open in shock.

"Shit," I whispered. "I'm sorry, Vance. I brought us to Faerie."

16

I remained on my knees for a moment, the echo of pain travelling across my skin. The Lady's vow had vanished along with her, now I'd kept my word.

Except for one slight issue.

Vance pushed to his knees. "Ivy?"

"Shit," I whispered again. "I didn't mean— Why did you have to grab me?"

The bloody fool had somehow hitched a ride through *Death.* He was lucky not to have been left behind. Recriminations choked my throat, vanishing when he lifted his hand and a half sword and studied the blade as though it was a foreign object. To my relief, my own sword had made it through, but I saw no signs of our enemy.

"This is… the Grey Vale?" Vance rose to his feet. "You're bleeding. Did you bring a healing spell?"

"Yes, but not enough for both of us." I pushed to my feet, my body protesting with a new array of aches. "Can't you displace objects from one realm to another?"

"No," he said quietly, sounding a little stunned. "I can't sense my ability at all."

Damn. I'd always known faerie and mage magic were incompatible, but to be rendered powerless was likely a foreign experience to him. Not that there was a damn thing I could do. "Did you see where the Lady of the Tree might have gone?"

He shook his head. I didn't know either, but she was in her element here. Her talisman was a thousand times stronger in the realm from which it originated—but then, my magic was equally potent. A faint blue glow shone around my skin, and when I consciously drew upon it, the aches in my body faded. My veins sang with fresh energy, banishing my exhaustion and dizziness.

Vance scanned the forested paths. "Do you recognise where we are?"

"Nope. No maps here." I grimaced. "I didn't know I could bring you with me. Pretty sure I'm not meant to do that."

He squinted at me. "Am I supposed to be able to see your magic? That blue glow…"

"It's stronger here." That gave no guarantee that he'd be able to see through anything else the Vale might see fit to unleash on us. "That's why I need to find her."

"And destroy her talisman."

"Not sure a talisman *can* be destroyed," I admitted. "If I kill her, I might be able to claim it for myself to prevent another faerie from stealing it, but frankly, I'd rather not have that thing in my house."

A skittering sound in the undergrowth made me lay a hand on Irene's hilt. Vance stiffened, too, but the wispy beings rising from the bushes didn't come any closer.

"Will o' the wisps," I warned. "They're tricky, but not overtly dangerous on their own. Just don't follow them off the path. That's usually a bad call."

Vance scowled. "Where is the Lady hiding? Doesn't time pass quicker in this realm than in ours? We might lose days."

"It does, sometimes," I acknowledged. "But I don't intend to stay here for long."

I hope not. The Vale was a poison to humans, and frankly, I wasn't sure I *could* get us both home when I didn't know how I'd brought us here in the first place. I'd never carried another person along for the ride before. But if I'd brought Vance here, I must be able to get us home, too. I refused to consider the alternative.

I took a few steps across the leaf-strewn ground. As I'd expected, the path was a mirror of the usual one I encountered in the Vale and contained no landmarks to speak of.

Vance moved in behind me, lifting his blade. "Do you know the way?"

"Nope, but it wouldn't matter if I did." I indicated the path ahead. "Supposedly, the realm shapes itself according to the desires of the person who owns the territory. This is neutral ground."

"And we can find the Lady of the Tree from here?"

"If she wants us to find her, we'll find her." I walked, and Vance kept pace with me. His narrowed eyes and tense shoulders indicated his mood, yet the lack of an accompanying breeze or thunderous crackle in the air really drove home how thoroughly this realm had dampened his powers. "You really can't use your abilities here?"

In answer, he extended his free hand. The blade vanished from his grip and reappeared in his outstretched hand; he must have lost the second one at some point during the fight with the Lady's thorns. "I thought so. I can only assume the realm itself is fuelled by magic that is incompatible with my own, and that I can't use my abilities on anything that belongs to Faerie."

"And our weapons don't count." At least he wasn't rendered entirely powerless, but this was a major complication in my plan to take out the Lady of the Tree without either of us getting hurt. "What about us? *We're* not part of Faerie."

"No, but I can't transport myself or anyone else to a place I haven't been to before."

"Ah." Probably for the best, but I hadn't reckoned on the Mage Lord's powers being totally cut off. Sure, my magic was at full power, but I resolved to stay right next to him until we found the Lady of the Tree. Or rather, the next Lady of the Grey Vale, if I didn't stop her first.

I pushed my shoulders back and walked with more confidence than I really felt, following a path strewn with leaves dappled silver by the light filtering through the canopy. I wasn't sure if this realm had a real sun or moon or if this whole setup was an elaborate illusion. Likely it didn't matter. Here, illusion and reality were one and the same.

Magic swirled around me, bright as starlight, humming through my bones. Like it or not, my power was tied to this place, and the blue glow haloed my entire body. The one exception was the area immediately above the hand in which I held Irene. My magic disliked iron, and when I'd killed Velkas, I'd had to let go of my blade to strike him down. The Lady had already demonstrated that her thorns were resilient even in the face of iron and steel, so I might have to employ a similar strategy here.

The scenery changed little as we walked. We might as well have been wandering in circles, with the only change being the occasional shifting shadow that passed behind the trees, indicating an unseen beast sensing interlopers on the path. Or potential humans to lure to their deaths. The sight of Irene was enough to deter them from coming near, but the same would not be true of other, deadlier beasts.

Finally, the path opened into a clearing. As soon as we entered, the trees closed in behind us, moving like they possessed a life of their own, and forming an unbroken barrier across the path. The only way out was ahead.

The clearing grew to the size of a football pitch. I looked at Vance, whose face remained impassive.

At least until the giant toad appeared.

The tell-tale shimmer of faerie glamour gave me a five-second warning before a giant wart-covered green body appeared in the middle of the clearing. Its squatting green legs were covered with hideous bumps bigger than my head, and its eyes were bright, bulbous and yellow. Vance's eyes widened, and so did mine.

"That's new," I said. When I was twelve, I'd unwisely watched *Pan's Labyrinth* with friends at a sleepover. This toad-like creature might have walked out of the nightmares we'd all had that night. Its warty mouth opened to reveal a tongue thicker than a man, pink and slimy. *Lovely.*

I skirted back, drawing my magic around myself in a shield, and lifted Irene. Whatever this new monstrosity was, all faeries were allergic to iron. The toad's tongue flicked out, attempting to lock around my ankle, but I sidestepped, my shield pushing it backwards. I spared a look for Vance, who looked mildly revolted by the whole performance. So was I, come to that.

"Neat trick," I said. "But we have an appointment to keep, so if you don't mind…"

The toad's wart-covered foot stomped, and the ground split in two. Without so much as a sound, the clearing divided down the middle with Vance on one side, me on the other.

"Hey!" I moved towards Vance, but the toad's giant tongue flicked between us. I veered back, my shield rippling.

Vance swung his blade and missed as his side of the clearing floated sideways. Wait, floated?

I blinked and the clearing became a giant pond, and we

stood on a lily pad that had split down the middle, sending Vance one way and me the other. The toad perched on another lily pad the size of a huge house, above murky water fringed by silver-leafed trees.

Bloody faerie glamour. Apparently even my Sight couldn't detect every oncoming trap, and Vance wouldn't have had a hope of seeing the trickery. He glared at the lily pad, gripping his sword in both hands.

The toad's huge tongue flicked at me, trying to lock around my legs. I swung my blade, and a spray of green-tinted blood hit the air. Green usually meant Summer magic. This creature had probably got itself exiled from the Seelie Court for eating someone important.

The toad stomped a foot and my lily pad tipped. I swore explosively. No magic would save me from being eaten alive or drowned, and I didn't have *time* for this bullshit with a far more dangerous enemy out there.

I met the toad's bulbous eyes and spoke with all the authority I could summon up. "You really don't want to pick a fight with me."

My magic echoed my words, the glow brightening, but the toad remained unmoved. It flicked its bleeding tongue at me, and I pivoted, gritting my teeth. The lily pad continued to move, drifting sideways, carrying me further away from Vance by the second. Too far for me to jump and reach him. I could swim, but Faerie's waters contained worse than sharks.

"What?"

The toad continued to watch me, its yellow eyes unblinking.

"What do you want?"

Pointless question. For most faeries here, the answer was 'tasty human flesh'. While it had picked me as a target and not Vance, that wasn't guaranteed to last. My sword couldn't reach the enemy from here, but using magic carried the risk of drawing my real foe into a place where I was literally out of my depth.

So be it.

Instinctively, I knew what to do. Sheathing Irene, I extended both hands. Light flared outward like I'd leaped into a blue-white flame. My magic drew its strength from pain and anger, and the Vale itself was built on suffering, haunted by the spectres of those who'd met their ends here. I let the magic pour through me and heard faint screams, perhaps those of previous unfortunates who'd been caught in this trap. A thin mist arose and faces shimmered before me, the dead loaning their strength to the magic flaring from my hands.

The blast hit the creature in its gaping mouth. A spray of water exploded outwards, spraying over my head, as the creature disappeared beneath the surface. Blinking wetness from my eyes, I looked for Vance and saw no signs of him. *Oh, shit.* For a heart-stopping moment, I thought he'd fallen into the water. Then I spied the other half of the lily pad closer to the shore. He must have climbed off, but the trees flanking the pond masked him from sight. My magic dulled to a faint buzz as I looked for a way off the lily pad. Swimming was out of the question. I'd need to find another way to reach him.

I took a step forward, and the scene changed. The pond vanished, to be replaced with the same clearing as earlier, minus the toad. Minus Vance, too. My hair was still wet, my clothes clinging to my skin, but no traces of the pond nor its owner remained.

"What the hell was that?" I demanded. "Was the whole thing an illusion?"

Cursing to myself, I stalked across the clearing. *Take me to Vance,* I thought, drawing upon the magic humming inside me. *Take me to him.* Avalin had used the same power to conjure up a castle from nowhere. I ought to be able to bend the Vale to my will and find Vance.

Except the Lady of the Tree likely shared in that power, now she held a talisman of her own. She might even have claimed a territory during her last visit, perhaps the remnants of whatever Velkas had left behind.

My steps took me out of the clearing and onto another silver-leafed path. No sign of Vance. My heart drummed with nervousness, not for myself, but for him. Mage Lord or not, humans were prey here. Even me.

Magic flared, a warning, and the ground fell away. I tumbled head over heels down a path that steepened into a slope, towards a huge hulking figure wreathed in thorns.

Thorns. I braced my feet against the leafy ground and regained my balance, staring up at a huge creature that held a thorny rope in each hand. Around ten feet tall and covered in green mottled skin, he definitely wasn't the Thorn Princess, unless she'd had a serious downgrade in style.

"Human." The ogre bared its dirt-stained teeth. "I caught a human."

"Big mistake, mate," I said. "You don't wanna mess with *this* human. Does the Lady of the Tree know you borrowed her magic? Or is it the Thorn Princess? I guess there's no reason for there to only be one faerie who wields creepy thorns."

If they were the sort that could override my free will as soon as they pierced my skin, though, I was in trouble. *Is this the Lady of the Tree's doing? Where is she?*

The ogre grinned down at me. "I won them in a game of wits."

"Someone's talking bollocks." This was one of the Lady's games, no doubt, but ogres packed some serious punch on their own without needing extra firepower.

I pushed upright and used my magic-enhanced instincts to

launch myself into the air, drawing Irene as I did so. I landed in front of the ogre and swept my blade across its neck, but a thorny rope grabbed the hilt of my sword, tightening, brushing against my skin. A shudder rose within me, and my grip broke as the thorny tendril wrenched the blade loose. Irene flew from my hands, spinning to a halt on the leafy ground.

"Nobody throws my sword and gets away with it, dickhead." I gathered magic in my palm and blasted the ogre in the chest.

More thorns blocked my path to the sword. I dodged, cursing my body for trembling and my mind for replaying whispers of the last time I'd fallen into a thorn-laden pit here in the Vale, reminding me that I hadn't been the same person when I'd emerged.

The ogre shook its head dazedly. "You aren't human."

"Oh, I'm human, all right." I threw another handful of magic at the beast, and then I lunged for my sword.

Another tendril wrapped around my ankle, but I whipped Irene into the air and severed the thorns, my heart racing in my chest. The blue light streaming around my non-weapon hand brightened, pulling in the lingering memories of the pain I'd suffered in the thorny pit.

Light exploded outward and sent the ogre flying back, ensnared within its own thorns. The beast roared, hands flailing, as the thorny vines tightened their grip. *Wait. Are they attacking their own wielder?*

I'd heard about faeries' attempts to steal one another's powers backfiring in a similar manner. If the thief couldn't handle the magic they stole, it'd eat them alive, and it was plain to see this dickhead had made a grave error in borrowing power from the Lady of the Tree.

My own magic surged and swirled around me, feeding on the ogre's pain as it flailed and panicked. I watched in sick fascination, unable to look away. The ogre gave one last spasm and lay still. A foul stench overwhelmed me as decaying magic and faerie blood as pungent as a week-old corpse dove up my nostrils and made my eyes water, yet my magic continued to swirl around me, drawing upon the lingering echoes of the ogre's pain.

Okay, that's fucked up. I took a step back, recoiling when the thorns began to creep along the ground. They'd killed the ogre, but there was still one target left. A thorny stem whipped at my ankle. I swiped back with my sword, holding my breath to avoid inhaling the decaying scent.

"You're mine, now, human," the Thorn Princess's voice whispered in my ear.

"No." Bright light streamed from my hands, blasted the thorns to pieces. "Fuck off. You're not here."

I slashed and struck, severing vine after vine. They kept coming, like layers of a faerie glamour peeling away one at a time, or like cutting the head off a hydra only for it to grow two more.

I needed to get out of here before I turned into a human pincushion... or worse, the Lady's willing servant. Like Wyatt.

"You wandered into my lair, and you'll die here. Pretty human. Pathetic human. Let me hear you cry out for help. Let me hear you sing."

"No. No, no, no. Please—"

Screaming, so tortured and high I could hardly believe the sound came out of my own mouth, while inhuman laughter resounded in my ears. Thorny vines wrapped tight around me, climbing up my legs. Driving into my skin, overriding my will, making it impossible to flee even if I'd had any way out...

I squeezed my eyes shut, my hands curled into fists so tight that the nails drew blood.

"Go back to the hell you came from." I raised my voice, trying to dispel the images beating at the doors. "Go *back*."

Magic ignited the air. I gathered a palm full of blue-white energy, dazzling enough to force my eyes open again. The ogre's corpse began to glow, too, as the echoing pain of its grisly demise fuelled my power, too.

A tidal wave of raging magic rose from me, exploding outward. Branches snapped, thorns shattered, and even the ancient trees shook to their roots as the wave of magic rippled through the thorns until nothing remained but fragments.

I stood surrounded by broken thorns, magic singing through my veins and humming in the air around me. No— not humming, but screaming, quiet enough to scarcely be audible. The collective cry of a thousand voices now reduced to silence. Faerie's last victims.

I dropped to my knees, the adrenaline draining away as quickly as it had arrived. Faerie was down one monster, but the realm had claimed so many lives already that even my magic would never let me forget.

I'd nearly been one of them. Fleeing Avalin's castle had led me straight into the Thorn Princess's lair, and I'd have died in that pit if not for Gerry coming after me. I owed the old man a debt I could never repay for risking his own neck to pull me out of the pit and remove the thorns buried in my flesh that had bound my will to the Thorn Princess.

I hadn't seen her since, but she'd haunted my nightmares almost as much as Avalin had. The faint screaming grew louder. I pressed my hands to my ears, as though if I pushed hard enough, I could remove the echo of their despairing voices.

"You left us here, Ivy Lane."
"You left us here to die."
"Now it's your turn."

"No," I moaned. "Stop…"

"You left us!" Helena's voice rose above the rest, insistent, accusing. My best friend, who'd died beneath the collapsing castle during my escape. Her cries scraped at my very soul.

A keening moan added to the cacophony. I was barely aware that the noise came from me, and that I'd curled up in a ball, until my head hit the leaf-clad earth. Leaves. No thorns.

There weren't any voices, either. Rationally, I knew that, but the screams sounded too real to be a mere illusion. My magic drew on the pain of everyone who'd ever suffered here. Who was to say that their ghosts weren't bound to me, too?

"Stop," I croaked. "I'll set you free. I…"

My own voice faded as the whispers grew louder, accusing, angry. Hitting me with the force of years' worth of rage and pain, driving into me like a thousand knives.

"You *left* me!" Helena's voice rose above the rest, loud enough that I flinched violently.

"I'm sorry!" I sobbed into my arms. "I'm so sorry."

"Ivy." Hands reached for mine. Not Helena. Vance's scent wrapped around me, and my fingers curled around his, grasping tight. The illusion fell away, the voices fading like a radio carried out of sight, and I opened my eyes.

The whole thing had been a trick, a conjuration of Faerie's magic. I squeezed my eyes shut again and clung to Vance's hand, stifling a whimper. "Fuck."

"I'm here." He drew me into his arms. "I'm here."

Vance hadn't got through Faerie unscathed. Blood stained my hands when I let go of him, and a shallow cut marked his face. Faerie had done a number on his smart suit, too. Whatever dirt-repelling spells he usually wore had probably been negated as soon as we'd travelled through the veil. Only his coat remained more or less intact. Blue-tinged faerie blood stained his arms, and his shirt had been torn in several places.

"None of that blood's yours, is it?" I figured the answer was no, but I touched my thumb to the cut on his cheek. "I knew you hadn't gone far. I thought… when you disappeared…"

"I'm here," he said. "And we're going on a date the instant this fiasco is over."

"Pretty sure any fancy restaurant would kick me out if I showed up like this."

He chuckled softly and drew me into his arms again. "I think they'd do the same to me."

I rested my forehead against his for a moment, listening to the sound of his quick breathing. "How'd you find me?"

"Your magic. A bright-blue flash lit up the whole forest."

"Lucky it was me." A howl sounded somewhere in the distance. "We'd better go before something nastier comes sniffing around that ogre's corpse."

"The thorns." Vance studied the dead ogre. "It wasn't the Lady who used them."

"Not this time." I shuddered. "Didn't work out so well for her minion either."

Past the ogre, silvery light shone on a path that now stretched into the distance again. Magic swirled to life around me, urging me forward.

Vance's steady hand rested on my waist, anchoring me in the present, as I walked towards our fate.

17

We walked for maybe five minutes, past nondescript scenery that seemed designed to irritate the crap out of me. Sneering faces peered from the trees only to vanish whenever I looked at them. Ominous noises echoed through the woods for no good reason. Snarls, random clicking, and horrible screeching sounds were par for the course. Sometimes they meant a nasty monster waited off the path. Sometimes Faerie was just screwing with us.

There was a good reason few of Avalin's prisoners fled from the castle, and those who did invariably showed up mutilated. The hundred hellhounds he had as security guards were enough of a deterrent.

"Bloody elusive old bitch," I muttered. "Where's she hiding?"

Despite my earlier confidence, losing an hour might mean losing half a day in the mortal world. We couldn't keep walking all day.

"She must have a hiding place," Vance said. "Perhaps from her previous visit. She came here, not Summer."

"That's her eventual end goal," I said. "Nobody can get to the Courts from here, as far as I know. They don't want their outcasts coming back and making trouble."

"I'm trying to make sense of her plan. She mentioned... gods."

"Yeah." Unease skittered down my spine. "The necromancer dude told me this realm was created when the Sidhe exiled their gods. Somehow this place is linked to Death, too, which is why I can get here..."

"...by walking through the veil." His expression remained calm, but I had the impression he was thinking hard. "She referred to a specific god, though, didn't she?"

"The life-drinker." I took in a breath. "What if the god the shifters believe in and the one the faeries exiled are the same?"

"Eraenar." His eyes flashed a lighter grey. "Yes. The shifters would never believe me, but I think it's certainly plausible that they're the same. Stories exist of godlike beings that walked between the realms thousands of years ago. Even the mages have similar tales."

"The witches have, too," I said slowly. "That means this realm and the mortal world have been connected way longer than the invasion. Centuries... or longer."

"The Sidhe already knew how to use the Ley Lines to cross realms when they invaded," he agreed. "They learned from somewhere, and most legends are based in truth."

"Then... *could* they have left the body of an ancient god behind?" I didn't know what to make of his entirely-too-accepting tone. "And the Lady of the Tree wants to steal his power?"

"I doubt she's a match for a god, if that is indeed what she seeks."

"I mean, yeah." A chill raised gooseflesh on my arms. "She

hinted that she needs *me* to help her, and it feels like I'm giving her exactly what she wants by seeking her out."

"Then you'll kill her." He looked into my eyes, his steady gaze grounding me. "Like Velkas, when she dies, she won't be coming back."

I swallowed and nodded. "Of course."

"Touching," said a light, feminine voice.

The Lady of the Tree stepped out from behind a nearby oak, wearing a fluttering emerald gown and a wide smile.

"You're right," she added. "This is exactly where I wanted you to be, Ivy Lane."

The path warped before my eyes, transforming into a hill strewn with leaves of tarnished silver. At the hill's peak stood a tree so tall that its peak pierced the canopy, branches extending out of sight.

"Did you intend for me to get eaten by a giant toad on the way here?" My heart thudded, my sweat-slicked hands gripping Irene's hilt. "Or killed by an ogre?"

"Oh, you had fun with my friend, did you?" She smiled broadly. "I always admire ambition, and it was quite the annoyance to carry the magic I won from the Thorn Princess in addition to my talisman. I was happy to let him borrow it for a while."

"So you did kill her, then." I'd figured as much. "Out of interest, why bother coming back to the mortal realm? You can't have wanted to kill the shifters badly enough to abandon your shot at building a little nightmare kingdom all of your own. And you didn't need my ability to cross realms if you were already here."

"I told you." She bared her teeth, slinking forwards. Her dress swirled around her like a living thing, the vibrant colour emphasising the unnatural gleam in her emerald eyes. Green light emanated from the sword, too, and from the

Lady herself as she circled Vance and me. "The god's power will be mine, but first I have to earn it, and to do so, I need the power of a Winter Sidhe to combine with my own."

"You don't get to steal my magic. It's mine." And I was through with faerie games. "Let's duel for it, under the laws of the Seelie and Unseelie courts. If I win, I get your talisman and your magic. I lose, and you get mine."

The metallic sound of Vance's blade added extra punctuation to the end of my speech.

"The Mage Lord stays out of it," she said. "I'll duel you alone, Ivy Lane. You'll lose, and you will give me your power."

"I think you have enough already."

"Wrong." Her voice dropped to a whisper. "Your realm poisoned me, stole decades of my life, cut me off from my home. I'll never forgive any of you. That power you wield never should have been yours in the first place."

"I won't let you screw over our realm for the sake of petty revenge." I raised my blade, magic flickering around me like lightning. "This ends now."

"Not the iron sword," she said. "You'll fight me with your magic, or not at all."

"We already made the vow," I said. "You didn't specify that I couldn't use other weapons." Sure, my magic was strong, but I wouldn't leave Irene out of our fight if I could avoid it, and I'd witnessed enough of her wordplay to want to employ some of my own.

The Lady unsheathed her own sword in a waterfall of green light. "You'll regret mocking me, Ivy Lane."

"I'd dramatically add your name to the end of every sentence, too, except I don't know what it is." I talked fast to cover the dread crawling up my spine. This was it. I was committed to fighting her alone, without Vance's help. If I lost, he'd have to watch me die. "Unless you really are called 'Tree Lady'—"

She brought her sword down in a slashing motion, sending a whipcord-like thread of neon-green magic at me. I jumped to the side, gathered magic in my weapon-free hand and hurled a handful of bright-blue energy at her.

The Lady blurred, then reappeared several feet closer. A grin lit her face, her dress streaming around her in a way that should have impeded her ability to move but didn't. Silvery leaves flew into the air as roots burst from below the ground, burrowing towards me.

I jumped, my magic-enhanced speed carrying me ten feet into the air, and landed behind her—but the Lady had gone, and the roots changed direction and aimed at Vance.

"Hey! Cut it out."

I ran towards him and hit solid air. A thread of magic tightened around my wrist, tugging me backwards, helpless to intervene as the roots formed a cage around Vance. Locking him out of the fight.

"If you hurt him, I'll rip you to shreds," I growled under my breath.

The cord of vibrant green magic pulled on my wrist, tightening around my free hand. I'd have to sheathe my weapon to pry it off, which was no doubt her plan. "How're you immune to iron?"

"Iron is a weakness only to those who are already weak." The Lady hovered next to my shoulder, holding the other end of the whipcord in her hands. Bloody faerie glamours. "Our talismans are more ancient and far stronger."

I spun and kicked. Had she been a normal human, the kick would have connected with the side of her knee and likely broken her leg, but she twirled in a circle, the whipcord dragging me after her into an undignified stumbling dance. I swung my blade, and the Lady vanished before I met my target.

"I'm not impressed." I turned my head, but the cord of light pulled me the other way. There, the Lady reappeared, swinging her own blade at my neck.

I raised my sword to counter her, but the cord dragged me sideways, propelling me into the path of her swing. I called on magic, and shimmering light blocked her weapon, humming in my veins, lifting me up on its wings.

The Lady smiled at me with her perfect teeth. "Give me that beautiful power, human."

"Not a chance in hell." I pushed outward, willing my shield to drive her weapon back, and green and blue light intermingled as each of us fought to gain the edge.

Velkas's blade shone brighter than ever, its glow matched only by mine, and the light dazzling my eyes prevented me from seeing the second cord close around my sword hand. Digging into my wrist until the circulation cut off. My eyes watered with pain, and a gasp escaped. Blood blossomed on the surface.

"Release the iron, Ivy," she said, "or lose your hand."

I got the message. *Sorry, Irene.*

The instant I let go, the green tendril encasing my wrist jerked free and snatched Irene's hilt out of the air. The second thread of light released me, too, but she had my sword caught in her energy stream.

"Hey!" I ran at her, halting mid-lunge when Irene spun in the air and flew straight at my chest.

I dropped to my front. The blade whistled over my head, propelled by the unnatural speed of faerie magic, and I lifted my head to find the tip of her sword pointed at my throat.

At once, the renewed buzz drained from my body, my limbs weakening. *Oh, shit.* With a single touch, Velkas's blade —the life-drinker—drained my life force. I jerked back, and

Vance shouted a warning from within the cage of thorns. A sideways lunge spared me from being speared through the back by Irene, still airborne, pointing at my spine. Trapping me between two blades.

I called on my magic, willing it to restore my flagging energy, and to my relief, my body straightened upright as my strength returned and my tiredness vanished.

Then I swayed, the energy rush draining as quickly as it had arrived as the blue light dimmed.

"Did you forget, Ivy?" crooned the Lady.

Comprehension dawned. I'd forgotten Velkas had been able to dampen my magic as well as draining away my energy, and without magic, I had no defence against either blade. Moving out of the way of her sword would land me right in the path of my own.

Behind me, Vance roared.

If I had to pick one weapon to impale myself on, one choice remained. I used the last of my energy to pivot away from the talisman and into the path of the spinning iron blade. Irene sank to the hilt in my shoulder. My arm instantly went limp, dull pain thumping through my body without magic to heal the wound. My other hand closed around the hilt, and I twisted to face the Lady. She held her sword in the same position where it had been touching my throat and wore an oddly strained expression on her face.

What's with her? Power radiated from the blade, yet she didn't move, her hands gripping the talisman as though unable to let go. Her words from earlier rang through my mind— *it was quite the annoyance to carry the magic I won from the Thorn Princess in addition to my talisman.*

Annoying… or impossible. She'd claimed a Sidhe's talisman, and that came with the need to prove herself its equal. She stood rigid, both hands clenched around the sword, her beautiful face stretched in a grimace.

I called my magic again and it rushed over me, healing the wound in my shoulder. As I lifted Irene, the Lady still didn't budge, tremors running through her body in an attempt to wrest control of the power in her hands.

"You aren't strong enough to wield it." I walked closer, skirting around the outstretched blade in her hand. Her shoulders bunched, straining to move, but the tremors held her still. The sword was vibrating hard enough to make her teeth chatter. Disbelief mingled with satisfaction as I lifted my own weapon.

"I'd apologise for such an undignified death," I said, "but you murdered people. You hurt little kids. That's not something I can ever forgive."

I angled Irene to pierce underneath her ribcage and stabbed.

Magic exploded out from her body in a shockwave that took me off my feet. I slammed into earthy ground and rolled sideways, dazzled by the sudden glow emanating from the Lady of the Tree. Had she regained control?

I gritted my teeth, pulled on all the magic I could gather into me, and leapt at her. My fingers locked around her dominant weapon hand, mimicking her own strategy, while my other held Irene. Our blades ground together, and panic lapped against me, mingling with the pain in my sword hand. I held my grip, blue light streaming from my palm. Her blade dropped an inch. Two. My body hummed all over, the world shrinking into a bubble, consumed by the struggle of Winter against Summer. Human against faerie.

The Lady's wrist snapped beneath my fingers. She cried out, yet her sword remained suspended in the air, pushing against mine until the iron creaked and my palm blistered with the effort of keeping hold of the hilt. Irene wasn't strong enough.

The magic might be too much for the Lady to control, but

it obeyed her enough to drive her weapon against mine, to leach the energy from my skin, and to dampen the glow around my hand until I released her broken wrist.

I tried to pull my sword free, but now I was the one who couldn't move. The iron gave way, and with a wrenching crack, Irene shattered into fragments.

My hand remained in place, frozen in shock. The Lady, too, stood with her injured wrist held outward towards the blade that moved as though propelled by a force beyond its wielder. The magic itself held sway, and her blade was intact where mine was nothing but ash.

Irene.

Without the iron, magic returned in a rush, but my power bled into hers, a twisted combination of blue and green merging above the blade. If she claimed my power, it'd be the final catalyst. The veil would break open, Faerie would over-whelm Earth, and nobody would remain to stand in her way.

I let my hands drop. I wouldn't be giving her any more of my magic. "You win."

"Then give me your magic, human, and wither to dust like your blade."

"I don't think so." I reached for the last loophole, the last possibility I'd counted upon when I'd sworn the vow. "You already got some of my magic. That's what we agreed upon. You've taken plenty already."

"That was not the vow we swore." Her voice was more of a croak, her body trembling, and though one of her wrists wasn't broken, she hadn't moved to pick up the floating blade.

"Actually, it was," I said. "You win, you get my power. You should have specified how much. You're not the only one who can screw around with words. The vow we made never said you could take *all* of my magic."

The Lady screamed and reached for her blade. I dodged,

tackling her from the side. She hadn't expected the direct assault, and we both crashed to the ground in a heap. I let my mercenary instincts take over, punching every inch of her I could reach. My knuckles broke against her jaw, healing instantly. She might have the sword, but I was physically stronger, and I'd more than happily beat her into submission until she conceded.

Dull pain pierced my back, so faint that it didn't hit me that I'd been stabbed until the point of Velkas's blade came out of my chest. I stopped mid-punch, a gasp on my lips.

The Lady uttered a manic laugh. "The power still serves me, human!"

The blade withdrew. I screamed aloud, my chest afire, blood spurting. Stumbling back, I hit a wall of bristling thorns.

Huh? Confusion filtered through the haze of pain. My thoughts slipped over one another, old fear warring with new pain, and the Lady's laughter intensified. *The thorns...* they were real, or sure felt like it, and the path was no longer a path, but a familiar pit.

No. It's a trick. An illusion. Impossible...

But here, in Faerie, the impossible could become real. A mere illusion could reach out a hand and rip out your still-beating heart.

"Goodbye, Ivy." The Lady's voice resounded, echoing down from above. Above the pit. Fuck. I was really... here.

My chest burned, dripping blood. Thorns encircled me. They coated every side of the pit, bristling spikes poised to strike me. The Thorn Princess had made an art of it, wanting the torture to last as long as possible, and the thorns had been layered to draw out the pain without inflicting a fatal blow. While I was already bleeding out, I wouldn't be able to stop them. I'd die here.

I gathered magic in my hands, but the blue light felt weak,

insubstantial. She'd taken too much from me and dampened the rest.

So much for my bravado.

I wouldn't cry. I wouldn't close my eyes. I'd stare death in the face, and I wouldn't look up at the cage poised on the pit's edge, nor listen to the faint roar of despair from within. I refused to give her the satisfaction.

A breeze hit me from behind, and I staggered, my head spinning as someone caught my arm—and then I was gone, and I lay on my back on a bed of leaves. Not thorns. Bright-blue magic ignited the air, and I gasped as the pain in my chest disappeared. Tears ran down my cheeks, even as my breaths came easier and my body registered that I was no longer in danger of imminent death. My mind remained a tempest of confusion. I'd been in the pit, on the brink of being stabbed by a thousand thorns, and now I wasn't.

I lifted my gaze. Branches arced over my head. I was in a cage, but made of tree roots, not thorns.

The cage Vance had been trapped in.

No. He didn't. Please tell me he didn't.

I lurched to my feet. Magic shot from my hands before I was consciously aware of it, shattering the arcing tree roots and revealing the slope leading into the pit. Below, the thorns converged on the spot where I'd been standing, ready to die.

Oh, god. He didn't.

I screamed, like I was the one who'd been stabbed, and leaped into the pit. Magic held me, steadied my fall, and burst from my palms as I crashed down on top of the thorns, not caring when the skin of my hands tore and repaired itself as quickly. I tore my way through layers of thorns, screaming his name over and over. *Vance.*

Beneath the last layer of thorns lay the Mage Lord. Unconscious or dead, I didn't know. Didn't dare imagine.

"Vance."

He'd displaced me out of the pit without a care for whether he got stabbed in my place. He'd thrown his arms over his head to protect himself, but the thorns were lodged in his chest like darts. My hands gripped the front of his blood-soaked coat, scrabbling to find a heartbeat. It was there—unsteady, but there. His wrist was slick with blood, but I found a pulse, and I bit my lip to keep from collapsing into relieved sobs.

The wounds weren't deep enough for him to bleed out, but there were too many of them, and it was impossible for me to single-handedly haul Vance's dead weight out of the pit.

I'd joked that I'd rescue him next time. Didn't seem quite so funny now. If we stayed in here much longer, he'd die… but carrying him through the veil might be equally fatal.

"Vance." I shook him. "Don't do this to me. God, Vance. No. Please."

Magic danced around me, brightening. I pushed it away. "Don't you fucking dare feed on him. Heal him instead."

No. My magic could only heal me, not others, and if I had any healing spells, they might not even work.

I dug frantically in my pockets. I had one healing spell left that wasn't soaked to uselessness thanks to the water from the giant toad's trap. The band was slightly damp, but when I turned it on, faint blue light mingled with the magic flowing from my hands.

"Heal him. Come on. Please—"

Blue light formed a film over my vision, blurring with my tears. The spell had worked, but we weren't out yet, and the only way to leave this realm was to pass through Death.

Better hope Frank was in a generous mood.

I gritted my teeth, held onto Vance, and imagined the grey haze through which we'd entered. Magic swirled around me, forming a thickening layer of blue smoke. *Yes. Get me out.*

Blue smoke became grey, from which translucent faces stared at me. My bodily sensations disappeared, and I could no longer feel Vance in my arms.

"Ivy Lane," bellowed a voice. "What the devil do you think you're doing?"

I hadn't been yelled at like that—in a schoolteacher disciplinary way—since my parents had been alive. I stared at Frank in shock as he waved a hand and sent all the nearby spirits scurrying out of sight.

"What—?"

Frank's transparent form flickered in anger. "You brought a mortal with you."

"Vance." I looked around into the grey, my hands grasping thin air. "Where is he? Please—I didn't mean to bring him. The Lady of the Tree tricked me with a faerie vow."

"The Lady of the Tree?"

Hell. This wasn't any time for explanations. If Vance hung around in Death for too long, he wouldn't make it home.

"She's trying to do what Calder did and open the veil, but —worse. I'll explain later, but I need to get home. I can't tell you anything until Vance is safe."

"You brought a mortal into Death."

"And I'll push you *out* of Death if you don't let me take him home," I retaliated. "I don't need a lecture from you. If you don't let us through, I'm gonna haunt you for the rest of your unearthly existence, and trust me, it'll be a damn long time."

The necromancer's almost transparent face twisted in a scowl. "You're violating the guild's rules so thoroughly that you'll be locked up for the rest of *your* earthly existence if the necromancers find out what you did."

"Guess you'll have to keep your mouth shut, then," I told

him. "Who knows, maybe this time they'll send me flowers and cake when I save all their arses."

Frank sighed. "Someday, the necromancers are going to notice all the transgressions I've overlooked on your part."

"And I'll gladly pay the consequences if necessary. I never chose this, you know."

"Not all of us choose the paths we walk." A hint of contemplation entered his voice, which faded along with his body, and then so did I.

18

Ten minutes. That was how long it took the mages to reach Vance and me. I counted the seconds as I waited, having been forced to call the Mage Lord's number myself because he didn't have his own phone with him. Drake had picked up right away, because apparently Vance often left his phone lying in his office at the manor. What he didn't often do, however, was disappear for a full day without contact. The council was up in arms, ready to storm into the manor and demand answers.

I didn't care. If it meant more people to save Vance's life, I'd reveal my faerie magic to the whole council if necessary.

We'd come out of Faerie on the same hill from which we'd left, except the sky had darkened to indigo, tinged with pink from the newly set sun. According to Isabel, Vance and I had been gone eight hours in human time. With George to babysit, Isabel couldn't leave the flat.

"I'm sorry," I whispered to her through the phone. "I failed. The Lady's still alive, and anyone associated with me might be in danger."

"Don't worry about me," said Isabel. "You scared the shit

out of me, I won't lie, but you're okay and that's what matters. Just focus on taking care of Vance."

"I will."

I'd taken to obsessively checking his pulse while I waited. He'd lost so much blood that his face was pale as death by this point. He was breathing, but erratically. Not just from the blood loss, but he'd expended a ton of power by displacing both of us while in Faerie, and he'd already been exhausted.

I ended the call and resumed pulling Vance across the grass. I had no weapon if anything attacked us while we were out in the open. Irene's loss was another ache I didn't want to confront. The sword I'd carried ever since I'd returned from Faerie had broken in my hand. Ten years we'd fought together and I'd lost her to a fucking tree.

Headlights appeared on the road. Seconds later, several cloaked figures ran towards us. Mages. I sagged with relief, giving Vance a shake.

"They're here. C'mon. We're going home."

His eyes opened a little. "Ivy."

"You okay?" Not the smartest question. The grass was dark with blood, and my arms were numb from dragging him.

"You—Ivy." His head dropped forward on his chest.

"Yeah?" My heart thumped. "Don't die on me now, Vance. We're almost there. Hey!" I waved frantically at the mages.

Drake reached us first. Vance groaned when his second-in-command pulled him upright and draped Vance's arm over his shoulder. A second mage joined him on the other side, while a third waited behind. Bailey, his face anxious, held out a healing spell.

"Reckon we'll need a few of those," said the fire mage, his own face as pale as Vance's. "Damn faeries. They did this to him?"

I nodded once, not daring to speak in case I shattered like my blade. The mages hauled Vance into the back seat of the car while I sat in the front with Drake. His driving was more dangerous than ever, and when we nearly collided with a tree, he raised a hand and reduced it to cinders.

"Stop that!" Bailey yelled from the back. "It's impossible to apply a healing salve with you trying to turn us upside-down."

"How is he?" I asked, trying to see through the mirror.

"He's alive," Bailey answered. "What did he *do?*"

"Displaced himself." And me. He'd said transporting people cost more energy. Moving two people at once, and in a realm where his magic didn't function as well as it did here… *dammit, Vance, what were you thinking?*

Fifteen minutes later, I sat in the corner of the room into which they'd brought Vance, picking at my bloodstained fingernails. The space resembled a cross between an ordinary living space and a public meeting room, with one side dominated by a large table and the other containing a sofa and chairs grouped around a fireplace. Shelves lined the walls, mostly filled with books and boxes of spells. Soon half their contents were piled on the table, courtesy of Bailey, who Drake informed me was something of an expert on spellwork despite not being a witch, including healing spells. The problem was that none of the mages had ever had to heal a wound inflicted in the faeries' realm before. Vance was still bleeding, his face slack and unconscious.

All I could do was sit in the corner, watch the flashes of light that accompanied each healing spell, and count the books of healing remedies that Bailey had stacked on the table to stop myself curling up in a ball and sobbing.

"Ivy!" Wanda's panicked voice made me jump to my feet. "Do you need a healing spell?"

I looked down, belatedly realising my shirt was stained

with enough blood to have come from a fatal wound. "I'm fine. It's—not my blood." I'd explain my healing ability after this was over. Because then I'd have to get into what we'd been in Faerie for in the first place, and the last thing I needed was to send everyone into a panic while their leader was incapacitated. I swallowed, my eyes stinging. "Is he going to be all right?"

"If he stops bleeding." She glanced over at him, worry pinching her face. "It's like something's blocking the healing spell."

"Did you get the thorns out?"

"Thorns?"

My mouth dropped open. "Shit. They must be glamoured."

Her eyes widened. "Drake, Ivy says there are thorns."

"I'll do it." I ran to Vance's side. His shirt was torn, thorns embedded in the fabric stuck to his chest. *Fuck. Please tell me they won't give her control over him. Not that.*

"Ivy," he rasped suddenly, eyes flickering open.

I jumped. "Vance. Don't move."

His gaze darted around the room, landing on Drake. "Get on the phone to the council," he said, his voice rough. "There's a faerie—"

"Wait till I've got those thorns out first," I said. "Sorry. This is going to hurt."

His grey eyes pierced me, surprisingly alert. "Aren't you a sight for sore eyes."

"Speak for yourself." I didn't manage a smile, though if he could make jokes, the healing spells must have had some effect. In order to heal fully, he'd need to be rid of those thorns. As I pulled out one of the smaller ones, a faint breeze stirred.

"If you even think about using your ability, *I'll* knock you out."

The corner of his mouth lifted. I heard Drake snickering behind me.

Gritting my teeth, I yanked another thorn out. His coat had protected him from the worst of the damage, but I'd never figured the first time I'd be undressing Vance Colton would involve so much blood. My stomach knotted at the sight of the deep wounds beneath the sharp points, but I continued my work.

"Send out a warning to every mage in the region," Vance rasped to the other mages. "Make sure the witches and necromancers know, too. The faerie has Sidhe-level magic —" He cut off in a hiss of pain.

"If you want the mages to still have a leader when the Lady comes back and attacks us," I said, yanking another thorn out, "you'll keep still."

"She can't cross between—" He snarled when I pulled out another thorn. "Realms."

"Never underestimate a faerie." My hands were shaking, but I managed to remove the worst of the thorns without looking too hard at the damage. My hands were slick with blood, and despite holding a conversation, I knew Vance was covering up how much it really hurt. When I got to the second last thorn, claws shot from his hands so quickly they'd have impaled me if I'd been in the way. Hardened dark scales spread up both arms. *Shit.* He was shifting.

The window rattled. Icy air swept through the room, the curtains billowing, paintings rattling in their frames.

Drake swore and ran over to help. I wiped my bloody hands on my jeans and grabbed the last thorn. Vance's hands lifted, entirely covered in scales, which had spread up to his elbows. As Drake seized his shoulders, I shouted, "Someone get a healing spell!"

The thorn came out in a spray of blood. Vance's hands jerked, and I seized them, not caring when they crushed mine. A series of crashes sounded from across the room, a breeze whipped my hair back, but I had eyes only for Vance. A healing spell ignited, his wounds began closing, and the rough grip on my hands loosened but didn't go away altogether. Our hands were locked, my face inches from his.

"You," I said, "are the biggest fool I've ever met."

Drake cleared his throat loudly. I looked over my shoulder and spied the other mages setting the bookcase upright. Vance had knocked over half the furniture, by the look of things.

Vance released my hands and sat up, ignoring my protests. "Get my phone," he growled at Drake. "Tell the council we've a potential war to prepare for."

19

While Vance was on the phone, I took the tray on which the mages had piled the bloody thorns outside. Drake objected to my leaving the manor, but my graphic description of the thorns' blood-control powers effectively shut him up. Once I was on the street outside, I unleashed a blast of magic that obliterated the wooden tray as well as the thorns.

"Fuck me," Drake breathed, watching from behind the front gate. "That magic of yours is something else."

"Wasn't enough." I kicked the ashy remnants of the thorns off my feet. "Did we definitely get them all?"

"Yes, we did. Stop being bloody paranoid." At the pointed look I gave him, he shut up and slunk back into the house.

Vance was pacing the main room, barking orders into his phone. Even with the thorns gone, I couldn't be certain that the Lady hadn't hitched a ride back into this realm when we'd returned. I was in no position to face her again without a weapon. Quentin lurked at the side, offering blood-replenishing spells, but Vance ignored his suggestion to rest and continued to shout instructions into the phone. The third time he almost shifted in a rage, Drake all but dragged his boss out of the meeting room into the hall.

"You've lost entirely too much blood to be walking around giving orders," he said. "Quentin, make sure the Mage Lord stays put. Have either of you eaten anything since before you left?"

"No." I stepped out of the room and laid a gentle hand on Vance's arm. "He's right, you know. You don't have to take charge of everyone."

"I'm having considerable difficulty convincing the council of the urgency of the threat."

"Probably because you're ranting like an enraged poltergeist trapped in a summoning circle," Drake said. "Go eat. I'll talk to Lady Granville, and I might even refrain from insulting her."

"That'll be the day." But the tension had seeped out of him a little, and when I released his arm, he beckoned me through another door into a kitchen equipped with modern furnishings and filled with the smell of delicious cooking. "Let's humour them. You look like death warmed over."

"Er, hello?" Admittedly, he'd used a cleansing spell to get rid of the blood and put on a clean shirt, while I'd prioritised getting any remaining thorns out of my hair over changing out of my bloodied clothes. But he was the one who'd been close enough to death that it seemed a miracle that we were both standing here.

Quentin gave me a nudge towards a chair at the small table on one side of the room. "Sit down, both of you. I take it that isn't your blood, otherwise you wouldn't be walking."

I glanced down at my wrecked clothes. "Long story."

"Starting from the part where you walked into your own sword," growled Vance, though he took the seat opposite me at a warning look from Drake. If it wasn't for the knot of worry inside me after the close call we'd had, I'd have been amused at the number of people who'd taken it upon themselves to order the Mage Lord around.

"You saw the fight." I sat back as the brownie placed two water glasses and two plates of homemade pasta on the table in front of us and then dissolved into the shadows like a ghost. Talk about efficient household staff. "I was outgunned. It was get hit by Irene or get hit by her super-powered sword. I knew I could heal myself, but she—she destroyed my sword." I rested my head in my hand, an ache in my chest. I'd always assumed my sword was my one solid, dependable defence against the faeries.

Vance's hand curled around my wrist. "It wasn't your fault."

"I didn't say—"

"I know what you're thinking." He entwined my fingers with his, leaning across the table. I lifted my head, noting that his hand had the same callouses mine did, marks from years fighting with a sword.

"Sure you do." I gave an empty laugh. "I failed. She didn't die. Instead, *you* nearly did, and she went off god-knows-where with half my magic to add to her own. For all I knew, she stole enough from me to be able to cross realms without my help next time."

His hand squeezed mine. "Like I said. Not your fault."

I exhaled. "Please don't ever do anything so reckless again."

"I'll make no promises." He loosened his hold on my hand. "Eat. You'll stay here tonight. It's not safe to go back alone."

You'll stay here tonight. I dropped my gaze, my cheeks burning, and ate quickly, trying to restore my energy. I could feel Vance's eyes on me, but he didn't say anything until we'd both finished eating.

"I meant it," he said. "You ought to call—"

"Isabel." I dug out my phone and found the battery was

almost dead, but I had enough left for a quick call. I ran out into the corridor.

"Ivy." She gasped out my name. "You're okay? Is—"

"Vance is fine, but my phone's about to die and I'll have to stay here at the manor tonight. Vance can't use his ability—no, you *can't*," I added, seeing his scowl. "You haven't seen any—thorns?"

"No, and I haven't heard anything new from the shifters either."

I expect not, since their killer was occupied. "Good. When the Lady finds out I'm not dead, she'll be pissed off, and..." A wail in the background reminded me of who accompanied her. "Is George okay?"

"He's throwing a tantrum, but I've got it under control," she said. "Be careful—both of you."

"You, too. I'll call you first thing in the morning." I ended the call and pocketed my phone.

Vance had gone back into the meeting room, and Wanda hovered near the door.

"Ivy?" Wanda peered at me. "Are you sure you don't need a healing spell? That's a *lot* of blood."

"No. The blood's mine, but..." I chewed on my lip, debating, then said, "I have faerie magic. I can heal when I'm in their realm."

Her eyes grew round. "Really? You can heal?"

"Only in Faerie," I said, though that wasn't strictly true anymore. "I—it's my fault we were there in the first place."

"No, it isn't. He told me." Wanda stepped into the hallway. "You can shower in the guest room. I'll see if I can find some spare clothes."

"Oh. Thanks." I hadn't even thought about clothes. My top was a lost cause, my jacket soaked in blood. My hand found Irene's empty sheath at my side, and a lump grew in my throat. "Is Vance speaking to the council again?"

"He is," she confirmed. "He told them that the Lady of the Tree is a top-grade threat. The manor's warded against all intruders, if that's what you're worried about."

Not if she uses those thorns again. "I'm banking on her not realising I survived. She disappeared as soon as she—as soon as Vance—"

"Ivy." Wanda hugged me. "You'll both be fine."

I hugged her back, then remembered the blood. "Sorry."

"Don't worry. We're swimming in cleansing spells here. Quentin always keeps the supplies topped up."

I wiped my eyes with one hand. "I should have been able to kill her. If I didn't hate those fucking thorns so much…"

"It's not your fault." She glanced behind her at the partly open door to the meeting room. "Vance has always tried to shield me from the faeries, but I know they get in your head and make you doubt yourself."

"I don't need the faeries to doubt myself." Not when I'd fucked up so royally that I might have doomed everyone in this manor. "The magic I use… it's stolen. From a Sidhe. I don't know how much Vance told you—"

"Not that." Her eyes rounded. "He said that he wanted to respect your privacy, but—a *Sidhe*?"

"Don't be too impressed." My nails bit into my palms, my mind conjuring images of the blue light streaming into the Lady's blade. She might not have full control over her own power, but could I really say the same of mine? It'd tried to feed on Vance's pain, and the notion sickened me. "The Lady of the Tree is on the same level, and unlike me, she's willing to hurt people to get what she wants. My power… it's violent, angry, and it feeds on death and misery. I thought I could make the magic my own, but maybe it's too late to turn something that twisted into an advantage."

Wanda was silent, and the echo of voices behind the door reminded me we weren't alone. A flush crept up my neck at my own outburst. "Ignore me. I'm talking crap and we've a war to win."

"You aren't talking crap," said Wanda. "It's a valid fear, but I don't believe for a minute your magic can make you do anything you don't want it to. My grandmother says magic is never stronger than you are. She was talking about mages, of course, but from what Vance told me, it sounds like the faerie magic has been testing you in the same way."

"I… I don't know. It seems to have a mind of its own these days." But it hadn't destroyed me the way those thorns destroyed the ogre, which meant I must be strong enough to handle the power despite my aversion to its source. *The magic judged me and found me worthy*, the Lady had said, and unlike her, I'd never been rendered immobile by my own power. I'd always remained in control.

"Anyway, I'll leave some spare clothes in the guest room," said Wanda, beckoning me to the stairs. On the upper level lay an unknown number of bedrooms, each with an ensuite bathroom.

I gladly stepped into the warm shower. Even with the abundance of soap, it seemed to take an age to scrub the blood from my body. I couldn't even tell how much was mine and how much was Vance's. We should both by rights be dead. Faerie had saved my life. Luck had saved Vance's.

Wrapping my hair in a towel, I left the bathroom and found Wanda's spare clothes on the guest room bed. She was taller, but I was more muscular, her T-shirt straining across my shoulders. At least my jacket had survived. She'd used a spell to clean the blood off and another to repair the scrapes and slices the thorns had inflicted. Good as new, but nothing in my pockets had made it out. Including my daggers. And Irene…

I closed my eyes, angry with myself. *It was just a sword.*

They can be replaced. I'd almost lost something far, far more important.

I left the guest room and found Vance waiting in the corridor outside. "Did you talk to Isabel?" he asked.

"Yeah. You're supposed to be sitting down."

"I finished talking to the council," he said. "They'll likely want to ask some questions in the morning, but they won't bother us tonight. I wanted to invite you to have a drink with me."

"What, a date? Now? Here?"

He smiled. "You aren't going anywhere, are you?"

"No." He still managed to look good even after nearly dying at Faerie's hands, his hair damp like he'd showered, too. "One drink. I need to stay sharp."

I assumed the Lady would have already shown her face if she'd followed us home, but when she learned I'd survived, she'd be here in a heartbeat. She'd got a taste for killing, and nothing would satisfy her more than hurting me again.

I shut the thoughts off. *Not tonight.*

Vance's eyes darkened like he'd guessed my thoughts. He reached out and took my hand. "Come with me."

His room was as extravagant as I'd imagined. Easily the size of my entire flat, it contained a huge four-poster in the room's centre and fitted furniture along the walls. There was even a fireplace, its embers casting warm light onto the thick white carpets.

"You're going to make a performance out of this, aren't you?"

Oh, dear god. This was too much. I'd lie down and put my head on the floor, but the plush carpet was probably worth more than a year's rent. The polished furniture gleamed, while a bottle of wine and two glasses lay out on a desk, circled by low-burning candles reflected in the gold-framed mirror that covered part of one wall.

"No performance." He poured two glasses and handed one to me.

I took it with a shaking hand. I needed all the courage I could get.

The wine went straight to my head after two sips. I put the glass down. "You probably shouldn't be drinking alcohol after losing so much blood."

"I'm fine," he said. "Witch healing spells work on almost anything."

"Not death," I murmured. "I have to fight her tomorrow. I won't watch her hurt you again. I can't lose you." My voice came out quiet, and my eyes burned.

He pulled me close to him. "I'm not going anywhere."

I pressed my head against his fast-beating heart. He was so warm, so close, so *alive*. The warmth chased away the memories of his limp body in my arms, of the grief I'd carried for so long that it had woven into my very skin.

No. I'd spent too many years living in fear, afraid that the faeries would take away the people I loved. Terrified to expose my own scars. Vance had seen them already, and nothing was worth being too afraid to live, to love, to hope.

Vance's hand trailed through my damp hair, his other hand circling my waist. He kissed me softly at first, then dived in, fierce, demanding. By the time I came up for air, he'd removed my top and his own shirt was unbuttoned. I had zero recollection of moving, but I could hardly draw breath to protest at him using his ability again. Also, the view was thoroughly distracting. My hands explored the contours of his chest, tracing soft skin over hard muscle. He inhaled sharply and lifted me, wrapping my legs around his waist, and carried me to the bed.

I held my breath when his fingers brushed the worst scars underneath my ribcage, but his mouth found mine, sending warm, liquid heat straight to my core and blanking out every self-conscious thought in my head. He unhooked my bra with one hand and began trailing kisses from my neck to my abdomen. White-hot lust blazed through me, my blood turning to fire.

"Vance," I breathed.

He looked up at me, eyes dark. "Do you want me to—?"

I just nodded. Vigorously.

His hands worked my jeans off, my own palms braced against his shoulders. His skin was warm, his touch feather-light until his fingers found what they were looking for. I gasped aloud at the sensation. Oh *god.* At this rate he'd make me come before he'd even removed all his clothes.

"Vance," I gasped. "I don't have protection with me. Do you?"

He lifted a hand and a foil packet appeared. I arched an eyebrow. "I told you not to use your power—"

The rest of his clothes vanished, swept away in a faint breeze that tingled against my bare skin. My protests died. Oh, holy hell.

He smirked. "Lost your voice?"

I reached to poke him, and he caught my arm, pulling me tight against him. My lips grazed his ear. "Damn you."

"You already did." His thumbs circled my nipples. "Tell me you want me, Ivy. Scream my name."

When he had the condom on and thrust into me, I did. My fingers dug into his shoulders as he moved against me. I tried to take it slow at first for the sake of his injuries, but Vance was having none of it. In seconds we were locked in a fast rhythm. Heat pulsed through my veins, pushing away the darkness that had pursued me ever since we'd left Faerie behind.

I clung to the heat, chasing the ache deep in my core until I came apart, shattering against him.

Vance held onto me tightly afterwards like he was afraid

I'd break if he let go. His hands traced patterns on my flushed skin, and I tensed when his fingers brushed against my scars.

"Is something wrong?"

I indicated the marks where the thorn wounds had healed over, an ugly raised pattern extending from my shoulder, down my chest and stomach to my hipbones. "There were no healing spells in Faerie." I managed to keep the tremor out of my voice, but he heard it all the same.

"You think I care about scars?" He kissed me lightly. "Before you tell me faerie thorns are an occupational hazard of a relationship with you, I'm not buying it."

He'd read my thoughts, damn him. "Not just thorns. Soul-sucking death stealers, trolls, ogres, banshees…"

"Tedious council meetings. Paperwork. You'll have to stand by my side at those fancy parties you hate so much."

"That's *not* the same as nearly dying, Vance."

"You might change your mind after an hour in the same room as the mage council."

"Can't be as bad as the necromancers, can it?"

"Hmm." He trailed a hand through my hair, his eyes as grey as soft clouds on an autumn morning. "Don't die on me again."

"Same to you."

It was easy, now, to promise never to cross the veil again. Easy to pretend I had a choice, and that I wouldn't need to use my magic to its full extent to defeat the Lady of the Tree and the talisman she wielded. No one else would suffer at her hands. Especially not Vance.

I snuggled closer to him. "Tomorrow can do whatever the hell it likes. We have one night."

He pressed his lips to my neck and began a new trail of kisses across my collarbone. "I can work with that."

20

I blinked awake to find Vance sitting up in bed, his eyes wide open and his expression alert.

"Nothing happened, did it?"

He shook his head. "No. I keep expecting a call, or the emergency alarms to go off."

"Me, too," I said, leaning over to check the clock on the bedside table. "It's six in the morning. The shifters will be back in human form within an hour, if they aren't already."

"They will." He passed me my phone.

"How… you grabbed my charger from my flat, didn't you?" I poked him in the chest—now totally wound-free. "I told you not to—"

Clothes appeared on the bed. To be precise, *my* clothes, and not the bloodstained ones I'd worn the previous day or the outfit I'd borrowed from Wanda.

"Vance."

"I'm fine," he said. "Besides, you can't pretend you didn't enjoy last night."

No. Definitely not, especially faced with his incredibly tempting naked body. His mouth quirked and his hand trailed down the side of my jawline, to my neck. His other hand reached to pull me closer to him.

Someone rapped on the door. Vance swore under his breath.

"Who is it?"

"Quentin, sir. The council are calling for you."

Vance swore again and let go of me. "Is it an emergency?"

"No."

"Give me ten minutes." He walked to the en-suite bathroom, stark naked. Not fair. "I'm going to shower. Want to join me?"

"Ten minutes?" I raised an eyebrow.

He smirked. "We don't have ten hours. Coming?"

"Hell, yes."

Ten minutes ended up being twenty. I suspected Vance would have left the door locked all morning if not for the growing sound of raised voices from below the pounding water. He switched off the shower, kissed me once more, and walked out, the water dissipating in an instant. Insta-drying spell, I guessed. Handy. The pleasant tingling sensation running all over my skin didn't vanish along with the water, but by now, it sounded like half the mages were congregating in the corridor outside.

"They sound pissed off." I walked out of the ensuite bathroom and jumped when my clothes reappeared in my arms. "Vance!"

He grinned. "I imagine the mages would appreciate it if we joined them as soon as possible."

Once I was dressed, I shrugged on my jacket and went to find Irene. And then I remembered.

"Ivy?" Vance walked to me. "Something up?"

"My sword." I didn't need to say more.

"I'm sorry. You can take anything from our weapons room downstairs. Just tell me which you like."

I swallowed. "I know it's ridiculous, but Irene was special. I don't know—"

"Vance Colton!" Drake's voice roared. "Ivy Lane! Stop boning and come and talk to the council."

That wrung a smile out of me. "The entire mage council knows about us now."

"Good," he said, picking up the bloodstained clothes I'd worn yesterday. They disappeared before I could grab them.

"Hey—"

Vance opened the bedroom door. Drake stood outside, mercifully alone.

"I managed to shove them downstairs," Drake said in explanation. "Three angry Mage Lords in the house and I haven't even had coffee yet. Nobody should have to deal with Lady Granville at this hour in the morning."

Vance's eyes narrowed. "I told them to contact me only if it's urgent."

"Nobody else died, did they?" I asked quickly.

"No," said Drake, "but something weird showed up on shifter territory."

Vance and I exchanged looks. "Show me," he said.

———

A new hole in the ground had formed in the field near Wyatt's farmhouse, as though a giant had passed by in the night and had pulled a huge chunk out of the earth. Bands of metal were scattered around, twisted and ruined, again like something massive had ripped them apart. Not a human. Hell, not even a shifter at full power could have torn through solid iron.

Iron. Holy crap.

Vance's uncle stood next to Rita and Anabel, and more

shifters had gathered around them, staring into the gaping hole as though expecting an explanation to leap out of it.

"How did we not hear anyone digging last night?" Wyatt gave Vance an accusing look. "Who was here?"

"Don't look at us." Uh-oh. Hadn't Vance put a sound-proofing spell outside their house? Not only was there a massive hole on their doorstep, but the ground had cracked all the way along the fence bordering their house. If it had spread much further, they might have woken up to find themselves buried.

Around the pit, the earth had formed a sheer edge, like a cliff, but from this high up, I couldn't see what lay at the bottom.

"Is this really the tomb?" My feet caught on a chunk of metal. "This is iron, right?"

More pieces of metal were littered throughout the field like the aftermath of an explosion, but I doubted any earthly substance had been responsible. I'd seen witch spells detonate near the shifters' fence and barely leave a scratch. Faerie magic, it went without saying, couldn't even touch iron. But that talisman...

"It might have been a warding circle." Vance surveyed the scattered bits of metal. "Or a cage."

Alarm flooded me. Now I looked closely, some of the iron shards that remained intact did resemble bars that might belong to a cage. A *massive* one. Had the Lady of the Tree been behind this? She must know we were both alive, if she'd gone back to the thorn pit later to check her enemy was dead and found us gone, but if she'd somehow made it into this realm, there was no reason for her not to have shown her face.

Unless she'd been busy with something else. Something... godly.

"This is her work," I murmured. "Has to be. She used the talisman."

Vance's eyes widened. "Did she remove whatever lies inside that pit?"

"I don't know." Transporting ourselves into a hole that potentially contained a sleeping god was a recipe for a grisly fate, but there was no other way to find out what lay within. What had been imprisoned.

I couldn't begin to imagine how anyone had made these iron bonds in the first place. Surely not the Sidhe. They couldn't handle iron without dying, whether they carried a talisman or otherwise.

"What the hell are you doing here?" demanded a voice.

Two shifters marched over, or rather limped. The thuggish guys who'd kidnapped me before, looking somewhat worse for wear, but both upright and glaring daggers at both of us.

"Looking into the giant hole." I gestured ahead of us. "I can give you a close-up view, if you like."

One gave me the finger, and the other spat at Vance. "You, Mage Lord, are gonna pay for what you did to us."

Vance moved at the same time as I did. His blade appeared in his hand as fur exploded along their skin. One of them was behind me in a blink. Hot breath blew against my neck. My elbow shot back, catching him in the throat. The impact jarred through my arm but gave me the chance to grab for the sword I'd brought. I'd picked two, neither of which felt like Irene, but they'd get the job done.

I swung the blade at the shifter's head, but he ducked and tackled me head-on. The combination of my own speed and the shifter's unnatural strength sent us both flying backwards. I rolled over and kicked him off me before he could pin me down, driving my blade into his flank. He landed heavily beside me, roaring in anger as blood sprayed the ground. His paw swiped, and I rolled, loose soil shifting beneath me.

Oh, boy. I'd rolled too close to the pit's edge, and with the shifter bearing down on me, I had nowhere to run. I came upright and drove my blade at my attacker. He veered away, paws slamming into the unstable earth. Too unstable. The edge fell away, and my hands scrabbled to gain purchase on ground that was rapidly shifting, sending me tumbling into the pit.

Light flared up around me, forming a shield that I sincerely hoped would spare me from a bone-crunching end.

My back hit solid earth. I gasped for breath, the wind knocked out of me, but the shield had held off the worst of the damage.

The sound of shifters fighting drifted into the pit, but the gap above my head showed nothing but overcast sky. I'd dropped my sword during the fall. I pushed upright, wincing as sharp metal dug into my legs. Iron shards, sticking out of the walls, and...

And around the monster curled on the floor of the pit.

I scrambled to my feet. Pressed a hand to my mouth to stifle a scream that came out as a hoarse squeak. 'Monster' was an inadequate word for the huge, scaled beast, but it was all I had. Its vast body covered an area the size of my flat, or bigger. It lay curled up, its clawed feet pulled up to its chest. Wings lay slack behind its huge, muscled back like leathery tents.

Dragon... I tested the word in my head, yet even that felt inadequate to describe the sheer *size* of the creature before me. A god. It could only be a god.

The sound of a sword being pulled from a sheath wrenched my gaze away from the beast. Layers of faerie glamour peeled away, revealing the beautiful form of the Lady of the Tree, standing right beside the creature's head.

Don't. The futile plea died on my tongue. What in hell was she doing?

"Give me what's left of your power, Ivy Lane," the Lady of the Tree called to me. "Or l shall wake Eraenar."

"You can't wake up a *god*." I managed to speak this time, my voice a choked whisper. "That talisman has finally gone to your head. You've lost it."

"The god's power has diminished during his imprisonment," said the Lady. "However, I have to admit that there might be some unfortunate side effects to his rising, at least for the shifters who live close to his abode… from what I witnessed, his exposure alone was enough to have a significant effect."

Holy shit. The shifters had started to lose their grip when the god had first been found. What would happen if he awakened? *Best not to think about that.*

"Why the hell would you even *try* to provoke a god?" I hissed at her, trying to keep my voice low. "I thought you wanted to go back to Summer."

"I cannot open the way into Summer without the combined strength of both Summer and Winter. I need *all* your magic, human. What you gave me was enough to come back to this realm, but not enough."

Guilt mingled with the horror brewing inside me. Because of me, she'd been able to come back. Because I'd let her take my magic, she'd shattered the bonds keeping the god contained.

"I'm not convinced." I held my breath when the beast's claw shifted a fraction, and a breeze lifted the hair from my scalp. Primal power simmered in the air, carrying a metallic taste not unlike the mages' depository… but it was something else entirely that the aura reminded me of. Something that made me abruptly certain that if the god's eyes snapped open, they'd be as grey and arresting as the person who shared his blood.

I filed that thought away to deal with later. "If all you wanted was my magic, you might have challenged me directly without dragging the shifters into it. Or their god."

"Yes," she said, "but two talismans alone cannot challenge the Courts. A god, however…"

"That's assuming the god will help you." Her decision would backfire on her, no doubt, but the rest of us would be caught in the backlash, too. "Seriously. I don't think you realise what you're messing with. You aren't even Sidhe."

"I have the life-drinker," she said. "I am more than a Sidhe."

She lunged. I dropped to a crouch, hands scrabbling to pick up the sword I'd dropped, and raised my weapon to block her. Her blade cleaved mine in two like a knife through butter, and the two halves fell to join the shards of metal already littering the ground.

"I won't do this here." I backed away from her, and away from the sleeping beast. "This is no place for a duel. We're too close to the Ley Line."

The pit was vast enough that it might even overlap with the Ley Line at some point, but the aura of power emanating around the sleeping beast suggested that we didn't need to be standing on the brink of the realms to set off a chain effect that would make Zombie Night look like a quiet day at the zoo.

"Isn't that the perfect place?" Her sword sang with bright-green magic, tendrils swirling around her. A similar glow arose from the sleeping creature. *Life-drinker.* Damn. I had to get her away from that beast.

"I beg to differ." How close were we to the Ley Line? Might I be able to take us there? She might have taken some of my power, but most of it still resided with me. And without it, she couldn't wake the beast. Whatever threats she made, she needed both of us, and if I rose to her bait, the combined clash of our magic would be enough to fulfil her goal.

I tapped into my magic and launched into a sprint, leaping high enough to soar straight past the sleeping god. I held my breath as I passed over those sharp reptilian claws, but the god didn't stir. The Lady's frustrated cry pursued me as I landed, kicked off, and jumped again. The pit had expanded wide enough to form a deep crevasse that zigzagged northeast, towards the area where Wyatt had initially been digging. The Ley Line.

The thin ribbon of light expanded as I neared the original pit. A familiar shimmering overlaid my vision, my eyes showing me two visions at once. Both the pit, and a path wreathed in silver light. I could cross into the Vale... but how could I guarantee I wouldn't wake the monster in the process?

It's that or let her wake him herself.

The Lady's scream of rage caught up to me, and a blaze of green light announced her presence. "You cannot run, Ivy Lane!"

"Oh, I'm not running." I focused on the greyness doubling my vision, my magic flooding the air and mingling with the fog rapidly closing in around me. Sensation disappeared, briefly, but I didn't linger. I aimed for the path unravelling before me and landed on my feet.

The Lady's arrival was less dignified. She appeared as though blown in by a gale, staggering, her usual composure absent. *Not used to my magic, is she?*

I waved a hand. "Bye."

And I was gone, back into the grey, past screaming spirits and out of Death. The Lady's enraged scream followed me back to the land of the living, where I crashed backwards into something solid. Not giant-god solid, but muscular-human solid. Vance. He must have transported himself into the pit.

"Ivy." He steadied me against him, eyeing the hulking beast that was just visible from this end of the pit. "What the devil is *that?*"

I almost said, *your ancestor.* That would not be wise. The giant beast slept on, but no trace of the Lady remained. "I've won us time, but not much. The Lady is trying to wake up that creature. I stalled her by pushing her into the Vale, but she'll be back. She stole enough of my power to cross realms." We had a few minutes at most. I turned around and kissed him fiercely, cupping his face in my hand. "You need to get everyone as far away from here as possible, unless you have a way to contain an enraged shifter god."

His shoulders stiffened. "That... no. You can't stay here, Ivy."

"I'm not." I spoke quickly. "I'm going to kill her before she wakes up that beast, but I wanted to make sure you knew what we're up against. She needs my magic to complete her plan. She didn't steal enough, but I'm still no match for her as I am now."

"Then what?" His gaze searched my face, desperate. "You can't give up your life."

"No." I took in a breath. "There's only one way to win this. I need a talisman of my own."

21

Vance went very still.

"We don't have time to argue," I said. "She might get back before I do. She'll be looking for me, and I need to get into the Grey Vale and claim a talisman before she finds me. I know what to do. I—I understand now." *I think.*

He nodded. Once. Not daring to look back in case I lost my nerve, I closed my eyes and let the veil pull me into its embrace.

This time, the crossing was so smooth, it was like falling asleep. The hazy uncertainty of being weightless lasted only seconds, and then I stood on a familiar silver-leafed path. Ahead lay a clearing, where a magnificent castle waited for me.

An illusion. I'd seen Avalin's castle fall apart, had brought it crashing down myself. Faerie was screwing with my head again, but I'd bet everything I owned that what I needed was inside the giant imitation of a castle.

Illusion or not, every detail was the same. You could have fit three copies of Vance's manor in the space it covered. Its turrets and towers extended as high as the canopy. Sheer walls of alabaster stone gleamed with a blue sheen, reflecting the magic that sustained the castle and everything inside it.

It's not real. Avalin's magic was mine now. I hadn't conjured this place, but Faerie's gift for irony was unmatched, and in a way, everything had started here.

I'd died. I'd lived. I'd been reborn.

I took a few deep breaths and approached the castle. Arched doors invited me inside, swung open without me lifting a finger.

The hall looked the same as ever. High ceiling. Stone walls. A long balcony extending above a staircase that had been a ruin of crumbled stone the last time I'd seen it. I stared for a moment, tasting both the fear and triumph of my past self. I could pinpoint the exact spot on the cracked stone floor where I'd dealt the killing blow.

Magic flared from my palms, swirling around me in an incomprehensible dance. A reminder. Where to look?

I started with the weapons room. Swords, knives, and every other type of weapon imaginable hung from the walls, and a voice whispered behind me.

"You picked the dagger last time."

"You're not him." The words came out automatically, my body rotating. Somehow it wasn't a surprise to see Avalin leaning casually against the door, as solid as the day he'd died. Six feet tall, slender and inhumanly attractive, clothed in his usual black-and-silver armour. Silken black hair flowed to his armoured shoulders, and a blue-tinted silver blade gleamed in his right hand.

That's what I need.

I wasn't a weak sixteen-year-old prisoner anymore. I didn't have to resort to trickery. This time, I could fight Avalin as an equal. More than an equal. Whatever this creature imitating Avalin might be, it didn't have a drop of his magic.

I moved closer to the rows of weapons. At the end, a sword caught my eye, a shimmer reflecting on the metal sheen of a blade. Iron, polished to perfection, but with the same dents on the hilt as Irene had.

A pang shook my heart. Faerie had created an exact image of my sword, as detailed as the castle in which we stood. The message was plain. I was to fight the thing that looked like Avalin with the sword I'd never get to wield in real life again.

An image wasn't the reality. This Irene was nothing but a mockery, but if Faerie wanted to play this game, I'd oblige. My hand closed around Irene's hilt. "If I win this fight, I get to keep your sword."

"Very well." He sounded exactly like Avalin, every melodic inflection tapping on my spine like piano keys. "If I win, Ivy Lane, I will claim your magic back."

"Won't happen," I said. "You aren't him, and the magic wasn't yours to begin with."

The imitation of Avalin glided back into the hall, to the place where we'd fought last time. Memories played out in distracting echoes in the corner of my mind, but I brushed them away. The echo of my old fear persisted even now, but this situation didn't even compare. During our first duel, I'd had nothing to fight for but my own survival.

This time, I had a world—more than one world— counting on my victory.

I made the first attack. Long-honed instincts fuelled by the magic surging in my veins knocked Avalin's imitation onto the defensive immediately. His sword clashed against mine, and I parried the blow and swiped at his wrist. This version of Irene wasn't made of iron—it couldn't be, if Faerie had created it—so cutting him wouldn't be enough to sap his strength in a heartbeat, but that was fine. I was far more skilled than last time, and coupled with my enhanced speed, I'd be on an equal level with this bastard if not higher. But our duel had a purpose: to win me a talisman. To prove I was worthy of the magic, I needed to use it to beat him.

I parried another blow and lifted my free hand, hurling a torrent of vibrant blue energy at him. Not-Avalin swept aside, eyes narrowing, and launched into a fresh assault on me. I stood my ground, blocking his every swipe, throwing magic left and right between clashes. One attack hit, and my blade slid through his defences, slicing down a gap in his armoured side.

I whipped the sword free, but no blood flowed from the wound. Instead, his entire body went transparent, incorporeal, save for the blade gleaming in his hand.

I stepped back. "Gonna show your real face now?"

"This is my real face." Avalin's voice sounded the same, but his body had faded into a ghostlike shape no longer cloaked in armour. His eyes, though, remained as vibrant blue as the day I'd killed him.

The word *wraith* drifted through my mind. Wraiths were powerful beings that haunted the Vale, capable of imitating the form of someone who'd perished here, but there was no such thing as a true ghost. This being was nothing close to Avalin.

"I know what you're thinking, Ivy," whispered the ghost.

"Sure you do."

I raised a hand and focused on pulling as much magic as possible towards me. *This is what I have to do, right? I have to prove myself worthy of mastery over this power.* My shield grew into a shimmering haze, as though I stood in a pure white flame.

Then a familiar screaming rose in my ears as all the pain and anger locked in the castle flooded me, fed into the light streaming from my hands and body.

My legs trembled under the sudden assault, my head pounding. The thing that looked like Avalin smiled at me, his eyes as vibrant as the energy pouring around me, through me.

"Take it all, Ivy Lane, and let it consume you."

No. I already have the power. Don't I? I'd taken Avalin's magic, yet the being in front of me shone with a similar light, and the blazing pain in my body threatened to overwhelm me. My body shook all over, my teeth rattling in my skull. An image came to mind, of the Lady of the Tree struggling to keep her grip on the talisman she'd claimed, her hands locked around the sword, her body unable to move.

I hadn't taken all the power. Some had remained, had formed this ghostly creature that haunted the Vale where Avalin had perished. That was the true nature of a wraith. Not a spirit, but pure magic contained within an incorporeal form that had survived its owner's death.

As I struggled, more ghostly forms appeared before my eyes, with faces I knew as well as my own. Faces who'd haunted my dreams for the past decade.

"Not again," I gasped out.

This wasn't the first time I'd seen those faces, but now, within the very castle where they'd met their end, it was harder to convince myself they weren't real. The room wavered around me, the walls shimmering as though to mimic the day they'd collapsed and crushed everyone beneath them. Everyone but me.

"You held the magic yourself," whispered a voice. "You could have stopped it. You could have saved us."

The voice came from Avalin, but it sounded like someone else. Helena. Of all those I'd left behind, I regretted losing her the most. I'd told her to meet me at the back of the castle. Told her we'd escape together. She'd trusted me and had suffered the same end as the other prisoners. She'd dreamed of sunlight and had died in the darkness without ever seeing the mortal realm again.

Avalin's face warped into hers, each detail stark, down to the scar on her face from one of Avalin's fits of temper and the soulful eyes brimming with emotion.

"That's right, Ivy," she whispered. "You must destroy me, as you did before, to claim this power."

"I didn't destroy you." The words tasted like ash in my mouth. "I didn't do any of this on purpose. *His* power did. The magic destroyed the castle…"

But was that true? I'd hated this place. Hated every inch of the walls, every stone in the dungeons, every corridor that echoed with the screams of tortured humans. That hate, that pain, had been ready to explode out of me, and the power I'd claimed had been all too willing to oblige.

I'd run from that truth. Like every other truth I'd avoided facing in the years since I'd returned. Yes, I'd been terrified of and resentful towards the magic as often as I'd relied upon it to save my own life and the lives of those I cared about. But in the end, what I'd feared the most was what might await me when I tapped into its full potential. My fear had told me that I'd see Avalin waiting at the end of the path I walked, and that becoming one with the magic would make me one with the man who'd tortured all of us.

Helena's face flickered, becoming Avalin's again. Wavering between one and then the other. My closest friend and my bitterest enemy.

The true face of the one I sought to destroy, though, wasn't either of those individuals.

The ghost's features changed to those of someone I'd seen in the mirror. Or flashes of her. My own face, twisted into a grimace of fear that reflected not a Sidhe's abject terror of death, of the oblivion that awaited on the other side of immortality, but my own bone-deep dread that the power I wielded would destroy those I loved again.

"I didn't destroy them," I said to the illusion, and to myself. "You did."

I drove the blade forward, into my own heart.

Irene collapsed into shimmering light that reformed into a blade-like shape, not of iron but of pure magic. As the blade's edge pierced the figure that had been Avalin and then Helena and now myself, its ghostly face shifted again and its mouth twisted into a hideous scream. Bright-blue pits shone where its eyes used to be, no longer remotely human. The beast was pure magic, death energy concentrated into one form and bolstered by the spirits of those lost within the castle's walls. Their anger and pain lingered, their rage and despair added fuel to the fire, but in the end…

In the end, I'd accept their anger, their pain, their rage. I would never forget them, but neither would I cling to the guilt. A sigh escaped my lips as the wraith collapsed. Blue light shot upward in a pillar, sending me staggering back. The pillar of light shrank down, coalescing into a shining blade. It lay upon a bed of leaves, a clearing as empty as though no castle had ever stood there at all.

Not quite empty. A sole ghost crouched beside the blade, small and slight and dressed in the rags she'd died in. Helena lifted her gaze to mine, and the grief arose, as fresh as the day I'd left her.

"Helena." My tongue felt heavy in my mouth. "I'm sorry."

She held out her hands, indicating the blade that lay on the ground at her feet. I dropped to a crouch, too, my hands moving to grasp the hilt. The sword gave a sudden tremor, light gleaming down its length, and my veins hummed with a sense of abject *rightness*. The magic and the sword were one, and now they were mine.

My gaze slipped to Helena again. She stared up at me, not with resentment, but pride.

An idea occurred to me. My power gave me the ability to pass through realms, and I'd already proven I could bring someone living along for the ride. A ghost should be no different.

I released the blade with one hand and extended the other towards her. "Come with me."

Her hand was cold, her touch feather-light, but I held on all the same. A glow extended from my palm to hers, carrying us into the fog, into mortal Death. A place that while gloomy, wasn't endless, not like the Grey Vale. Here, the pain didn't last forever.

Helena's hand slipped from mine. Her mouth formed a smile. Her wide eyes said, *I forgive you.*

Then Death's grey wings carried her away.

<h1 style="text-align:center">22</h1>

I flew out of Death and straight into the middle of a ferocious wind current. The gust sent my body hurtling back. I landed, sprawling, the weight of my new sword digging painfully into my leg. Ow.

The sword. My new weapon had made it out. Here, the blade didn't shine quite as brightly, but the silvery sheen held no resemblance to any metal in this realm, and the blue edge mirrored the flicker of magic dancing up my arms.

Roaring sounded behind me. Two wolves grappled with teeth and claws, blood spraying onto the grass. Huge cats and other beasts ripped at one another, the horrific clamour grating against the hum of magic in the air.

They'd all reverted into their animal forms, and the entire area beside the rift in the ground had become a battleground. *Damn.* Vance better have got out of the pit, but I didn't see him among the brawling mass of snarling, fighting shifters. Nor the two dickheads who'd captured me. How much time had I lost in Faerie?

Two grappling shifters veered into my path. I raised a hand and sent a jet of magic at them. I didn't put a great deal of force behind it, but the blast flung their bodies aside with no resistance. My sword hummed, feeding a current of energy to my hands. Whoa. Was this how a Sidhe felt at the height of their power?

Mine, sang the magic, rolling through my veins. The pain and shock of the fighters poured into me, into the shimmering blade in my hand, and I blasted another shifter off their feet as I neared the pit. I didn't see any movement within, and I bloody well hoped that giant dragon hadn't woken up. The air was already thick with magic, a smoky haze that warned me the veil was thinning, and the shifters paid no more attention to me than they did anyone else. They were too far gone, jaws snapping, claws tearing at anything that moved.

Not just each other. When I turned away from the pit, I spied flashes of light that could only belong to the mages. Vance would have ordered them not to inflict any fatal wounds, but the shifters held no such inhibitions.

Someone has to stop this.

I advanced through the fighting, magic blazing from both sides of my blade and knocking down shifters and mages alike. I kept my eyes open for Vance, whose power was distinctive enough that I ought to be able to see it even amid the melee, but still—nothing.

My heart lurched when I tripped over the first body. A cloaked mage lay face-down in the dirt, while an enormous wolf lifted another limp body between sharp teeth. *Wait. That's—*

Wanda dangled from the wolf's jaws, seemingly unconscious.

"No!" My scream drew another shifter's attention, but I hit my attacker with a current of magic without breaking stride. As I caught up to Wanda, I swung my blade through the shifter's neck. Magic burst outward; Wanda slid out of the shifter's jaws as the momentum took the wolf's head clean off. *Whoa.*

I crouched beside Wanda, lifting her hand. A pulse fluttered. "Dammit. We need to get out of here. Where in hell is Vance?"

"He went after her." Drake moved in, his red hair wildly askew, blood streaming from one ear. "She took Anabel."

I swore explosively. "Where?"

He pointed into the shimmering haze that now smothered the Ley Line. "No clue. Somewhere in there."

Not Faerie again. "On it. Is Wanda—?"

"I'll take care of her."

Adrenaline and magic both poured through my veins as I launched into a run, my feet skimming the ground. Not a single shifter that crossed my path made contact. I blasted them all aside without slowing.

The smoke thickened as I neared the Ley Line, and I swore my feet left the ground altogether. Had I taken flight after all? Or gone into Death? No—I could still feel my body, and the sword's heavy weight in my hands, but I could no longer feel grass beneath my feet nor see the brawling mass of shifters around me.

Then a platform appeared underneath my feet, and the smoke cleared, revealing a staircase that spiralled upward into the air.

Is this her work? The faeries could warp reality, and we were so close to the Ley Line that it wouldn't surprise me if she'd brought part of Faerie with her right here to the mortal realm.

The stairs felt solid enough, so I climbed. If the Lady was at the top, I'd gladly knock her off her pedestal.

The stairs ended at a bridge that stretched into the distance. A cloud drifted past... no, that wasn't a cloud but another platform like the one I'd arrived on. Several people stood on a narrow space suspended over empty air, including Vance. He'd shifted almost entirely, his eyes flat and inhuman and unseeing. Bars enclosed a cage barely big enough to contain him, and outside the cage stood a few smaller figures. *Children.* Anabel and George were among them.

"You fucker," I growled under my breath. The platform was too far from the bridge to reach without jumping, and it looked unsteady enough that I wouldn't have been surprised if the Lady intended for it to sink the instant I jumped.

Damn. How to get those kids out of here? And Vance… *don't look at him,* I told myself. *He'll be fine when you get him out of here. When she's dead.*

I walked along the bridge. My blade hummed, its glow bright enough the Lady would have been able to see me half a mile away.

"Seems a pity to expend so much effort on an illusion," I said loudly. "I thought you needed your magic for more important purposes than playing games with a human. Or have you given up on waking the god after all?"

A layer of glamour peeled away, revealing her standing on the bridge less than ten feet from me. *There she is.*

I raised my blade in greeting. "I knew you were here somewhere."

"Ivy." She twirled in a flurry of green leaves, her own blade aglow. "You got away from me before. That was a mistake, and so was leaving me alone with your mage."

My heart sank through the bridge under my feet. *I'll kill your mage first,* whispered Calder's voice in my ear.

"*Your* biggest error was being an arrogant, conniving old hag," I said.

Her teeth peeled back from her lips, no longer beautiful but feral. In a swift movement, she leaped, and I did, too. This time, the clash of sword on sword didn't hurt. Magical energy surged through me, giving me strength enough to meet her strikes as an equal.

"You found a talisman," she said, her beautiful singsong voice grating against me.

"I earned it." I swiped her sword aside and dealt a glancing blow to her left arm. Green-tinged faerie blood spurted, but bluish light immediately encased her skin. Instant healing. Had she stolen that from me, too? "Unlike you."

I got close enough to kick at her, but a solid barrier of green light formed around her body and my foot glanced off. *Fine.* I released the sword's hilt with one hand and hurled a blast of energy at her, forcing her to jump high to avoid being struck. She landed and returned the favour, and our deadly dance took us across the platform, trading blows that ought by rights to have knocked at least one of us over the edge.

"I earned my magic," she snarled. "*You* didn't. You should never have been allowed to claim that talisman."

"I don't make the rules and neither do you."

Her blade sliced open my arm, but the cut sealed itself before the blood could fall. No wound she inflicted left a mark, and even falling off the bridge might not be fatal, but the same couldn't be said for those kids trapped on the platform. Or Vance.

"Impressive, Ivy Lane." Her blade met mine, locking my sword in place. "You've learned some new tricks."

"Got the hang of your new weapon yet?" I broke away, returning another strike that she blocked. "I'm not convinced you're strong enough to handle it."

Her eyes glowed green. "I'm strong enough."

"We'll see." I feinted to the left, then stabbed to the right, sending a pulse of power through my blade.

My strike missed. The magic didn't. Blue energy struck

her full in the chest, sending her flying straight over the edge of the bridge. She caught her balance midfall and sprang, not at the bridge but at the platform on which the children huddled.

Landing beside George, she grabbed him by the scruff of his neck. *Don't you dare hurt him.*

I jumped, sailing across the gap, and my feet slammed down onto the platform's edge. It wobbled but didn't fall. The other children formed a terrified huddle while Vance watched with unseeing eyes from the cage.

"Wake up!" I'd have tried to knock some sense into him, but I wasn't sure my new weapon was capable of dealing a non-fatal blow and the same went for the magic roaring in my veins. My human instincts to save George fought with the primal urge to strike the Lady down and let my newfound magic take her apart. She held George out, his feet nudging against the pit's edge.

"Let him go," I growled.

"Such a lovely mortal child." She grinned. "Would you give up his life to save the others?"

No. She knew I wouldn't, but if I angled myself so that I caught George during the fall, I had confidence my magic would catch me.

As I lunged, a tugging sensation halted my steps. The vow.

"Stop that." I willed my limbs to move, to shake off the unspoken command. "I think we both know the promise you forced me to make was total bullshit, like everything else you've ever said. You already have your talisman."

"I never specified *which* talisman."

Fucking faerie word games. "You only asked me to *find* the talisman, not to give it to you. And you never said it was a talisman at all."

"I dictate the terms of the vow, human."

"Not quite." Energy surged along my blade and my sword ignited in blue fire. A hint of uncertainty slid into her eyes and vanished so swiftly that I might have imagined it.

"You're human." She held George off the ground so that his legs dangled above the endless fall.

"Not since I slit Avalin's throat with his own sword." I readied myself to jump. "And certainly not now I've claimed his sword as mine."

A crooked smile twisted her mouth.

"What's so funny?"

In answer, she let go of George.

I lunged forward, my blade arcing into her chest. The Lady screamed, more of an animal noise than a human one. I was already leaning over the edge, catching George in midair. I seized him around the middle, lifting him one-handed and setting his feet on the platform.

The Lady stood suspended, impaled on my sword. Blood streamed out, and wisps of bright-green magic floated around her, drifting away amongst the clouds.

"You lose." I held the sword's hilt, the tip still lodged in her chest. "I win."

She gave a coughing laugh. "Do you want to know which favour I offered to Calder, Ivy Lane?"

"Not really." A lie, but I didn't care what taunt she chose to unleash with her last words. I had to get the kids to safety and open that cage. Away from the Ley Line, Vance would come to his senses. He had to.

"He wanted revenge on humans, and he'll have it. You've already lost." She coughed again. More blood spurted. Magic flared from my blade, and her body burst apart in a shower of green light.

Several children screamed. Underneath my feet, the platform dipped alarmingly. As though her magic had been holding us upright.

"Shit. Shit. Vance, get us out of here." I turned to the cage. "She's dead. She can't control you."

He shook his head. The scales on his hands didn't recede, but the alien light in his eyes dimmed to light grey. From behind his neck, something fell to the floor. A thorn.

Sudden fury flashed in his eyes. Vance swiped out, claws slicing through the cage bars. As he climbed out, Anabel flung her arms around him.

"Come here," he called to the other children. "I'll get us away."

Are you sure? I knew what using his ability on that level would cost him, but there didn't seem to be another way to get off the platform before this place fell apart.

"Be careful," I called to him. "I'll be right behind you."

Vance's expression told me how little he cared to leave me behind, but transporting multiple people at once would run the risk of utterly exhausting him right before he ran into an army of shifters. I wouldn't take the risk.

All the same, my heart twisted in my chest as Vance and the children vanished, and I was left on the platform with nothing but the Lady's sword, lying where she'd dropped it.

I wouldn't make the mistake of leaving it behind again.

I crouched beside the blade, the life-drinker. Its luminous green glow persisted beyond its wielder's death. I'd won it, according to the terms of our duel, but one super-powered talisman was quite enough to handle. What choice did I have, though?

The platform gave a warning tremble. My fingers brushed the blade's hilt, then I quickly scooped it up. Now to get out of—

A roar sounded. Not an enraged shifter's roar, but like an industrial machine mixed with a series of thunderclaps. I twisted around, a sword in each hand.

My feet locked into place as a spasm of fear shook my

entire body, turning my bones to juice and my skin to goose-flesh. Underneath the bridge, a vast shape moved. The size of a house, dark as pitch, with wings as wide as the cage which once imprisoned it.

The shifters' god had woken up.

23

A bone-shaking tremor rattled the swords in my hands, and the platform dipped, threatening to tip me over. Instinct took over, carried me in a leap from the platform to the bridge. Below, the clouds cleared enough to reveal the monster, its huge, scaly body ending in a forked tail. As it rose higher, the undercurrent rippled through the air and threatened to sweep me off the bridge.

I ran. Fast. Either my fear had shaken off my superhuman speed or even a Sidhe couldn't outrace a god, but the beast remained below me no matter how quickly I sprinted. Gasping for breath, I willed myself to return to reality.

Finally the air shimmered, and I burst through the illusion onto solid ground.

Right in front of the oncoming dragon rising from the pit.

Now I understood why shifters could stand up to fear-spells and faerie mind tricks. This creature was fear incarnate—primeval, deadly, and merciless. There was no comparison. Not to anything in this realm or any other.

We were all going to die. Probably everyone in the whole

city, too. Who knew what the god would do? If I were in its place, I'd be royally pissed off at whoever had put me to sleep and chained me in iron.

Pity I can't do the same. I had to do *something,* though, and the two talismans I carried offered the combined strength of both Summer and Winter. That was likely what had woken the beast in the first place, as the Lady had intended, but surely—

I'd scarcely raised the two swords into the air—one wrought in green light, the other in blue—when air buffeted me, knocking me flat onto my back. I managed to keep my grip on both swords, but the impact jolted through my shoulders doubly hard with the combined weight of the weapons.

Looking up at the sky, I was greeted by the sight of the dragon-like beast flying overhead, without so much as a glance at me. I'd confronted it with the power of both Summer and Winter, and the creature had swatted me aside like a fly. It didn't care.

"Ow." I got to my feet, wincing. I was pretty sure I'd dislocated at least one shoulder. Now my shock had worn off a little, I was kind of insulted. "Dickhead. You could have at least *looked* at me first."

A burst of fire flared up. Not high enough to reach the dragon, but enough for me to pinpoint Drake somewhere amid the people staring up at the sky. Both shifters and mages alike had ceased their battle to gawp at the spectacle.

The beast didn't seem to notice them. Maybe it wasn't going to kill everyone after all, but could I take that chance? The shifters might have temporarily stopped fighting, but most were still in animal form, beyond reason, caught in the creature's thrall.

The beast turned, mid-flight, wings billowing. Coming this way.

Oh, hell.

I looked wildly around. The broken remains of the iron cage lay scattered on the hill, but I couldn't even begin to figure out how to put the thing back together, and whether I had one badass sword or two, nobody could put down a beast of that size. It drew closer, wings gusting air at the field. Like a spell had broken, the shifters fled, scattering before the oncoming monster.

"Get over here!" I raised both swords to the sky again, sending a jolt of magic through my new blade that arced into the clouds.

Again the beast ignored me, soaring over the field, over the mages hurling attacks up at its scaly hide. None made contact. Nothing could touch the god.

Except me.

Poking a sleeping dragon was unwise. Blasting an enraged dragon in flight was suicide, I knew, but I could think of no other way to get its attention. I put on a burst of speed and ran forward, and then jumped, firing a blast of magic straight up at its beating wings.

Dazzling blue light filled the sky, and its body jerked to a halt in midair. *Holy shit, I actually hit it.*

Then those huge wings wheeled around, and its eyes locked onto a new target. Not me. Vance stood apart from the mages on a raised hill. The air above his head crackled with energy, a tempest brewing—and I knew the fool would throw himself between me and the beast without a second's thought, even if it meant his death.

And it would. No magic could kill the beast. That blast I'd sent would have taken a person apart but had barely tickled the giant god. But what—

My other hand vibrated, reminding me of the second blade… the life-drinker. I'd had no practise. Hadn't even checked the blade would do my bidding and not fight against me like it had the Lady of the Tree. But the sword and the dragon shared the same title for a reason. *Life-drinker.* It had to be the key.

The dragon plummeted, wings outstretched, and swooped towards Vance. No time for second-guessing. I focused on my left hand this time, on drawing upon the green light simmering within the second blade I'd claimed. I was rewarded by a flash of green that mirrored the blue glow in my other hand.

The beast didn't even slow down.

"Get over here, you scaly bastard." I launched into a run, blown sideways by the currents of air disturbed by its wing-beats. Vance stood with his hands braced, and I knew it took every ounce of power he possessed to keep on his feet.

"Over here!" I screamed again, and this time sent a bolt of magic through both swords at once.

The twin attacks smacked into the dragon's scaly hide, and its flight path finally veered towards me. Vance too, turned my way, shouting my name. Begging me to stop.

I held up both swords. No iron cage remained, and even two talismans couldn't conjure up a miracle, but dammit, I couldn't let it hurt Vance.

I kept backing away, the glow from my swords rising like twin pillars reflected in its huge eyes. Now all its attention was fixed on me, as I backed into the grey haze where this realm overlapped with the Ley Line. My vision doubled, revealing the illusory bridge the Lady had conjured up.

I took in a deep breath and stepped into the faerie realm.

The monster's enraged roar reverberated through my head as my body fell backwards, through the grey, and straight into the silvery light of the Vale. I'd barely been in Death a half-second before I stood rigid on the Grey Vale's path. *Please let this work.*

With the veil almost transparent, the god had seen exactly

where its prey had disappeared to. I held the swords high and willed them to ignite. Blue and green streams of light flared up, piercing the canopy. Over the humming of magic, the roaring grew louder. *Yes. Come here.*

The dragon's huge form appeared above the interlocking branches, moving closer, drawn to the magic radiating off me like a beacon. The combined might of two talismans rippled through the Vale itself, and I felt the realm itself respond to me. Recognising me. Shaping itself to my thoughts. In the same way that Avalin had built a castle from nothing, I'd build a prison.

The sound of beating wings filled my ears. I stepped backwards, my enhanced speed fuelling my retreat from the beast's approach. It neared the canopy, seconds from crashing through and ending me in one grisly bite.

I closed my eyes. Willed the realm to shift according to my will. The ground hardened underfoot as earth became stone. I imagined the trees on either side becoming solid walls, enclosing the descending beast. And then a ceiling slamming down on its head.

A crash jolted through me. My eyes opened as the dragon's body smacked against the ceiling that had materialised above our heads. *Holy shit, it worked.*

The beast's huge head shook, as if dazed. Its wings beat, unable to extend and fly. Its eyes lowered to me, grey and intelligent and reproachful.

I licked my dry lips. "Can you speak?"

The beast roared, a deafening sound that echoed in the enclosed space. *I'll take that as a no, then.* Hands pressed to my ears, I waited for the reverberations to pass.

"I'm gonna have to leave you here until you can promise not to hurt any more humans. Or anyone else, come to that." Some of the beasts of the Vale deserved its wrath, true, but its mere presence had affected the shifters so badly that I couldn't allow it to return to our world.

The dragon let out another roar, stirring a current of air that crashed into the shield I conjured half-consciously. The prison I'd built trembled to its foundations. The blue-tinted blade in my hands glowed bright and angry, feeding on my fear.

"Don't look at me like that." To my own surprise, my voice came out relatively calm. "If you threaten my friends, you'll get no mercy. I created this place. I can dream up a worse prison."

Despite the bone-deep primal terror stirred by the beast's presence, a torrent of power rolled through me, stirred by the twin blades in my hands. Summer and Winter. I'd felt the same sensation once before, when I'd read the words of the Invocation, and sealed the veil.

Here, in Faerie, my words had even more power.

Glyphs shone upon the blades, sliding to the hilts, and words nudged at my tongue, as though they'd been waiting for me to say them.

I obliged and opened my mouth. The language I spoke felt foreign and familiar at once, and the Vale itself picked up its echo, singing my words back at me. Threads of green and blue streamed from each sword, swirling around the beast's magnificent head. Each word was infused with power strong enough to rattle the ground under my feet, to raise the ceiling and touch the stars. The faeries hadn't been screwing around when they'd made their language. This time, it didn't feel like the words were tearing loose from my lungs. More like a choir had started to sing, and my own mouth had opened to join in the chorus.

The dragon landed on four clawed feet, and its eyelids closed. Its head fell, slowly, to rest on its front claw, its huge body relaxing into sleep.

The flow of words ceased. The glyphs faded from the twin blades and my trembling hands dropped to my sides. The beast lay quite still. Harmless.

I waited a minute. The beast didn't move. Neither did I. I didn't know for sure, but I was fairly sure I'd spoken an Invocation, and without ripping myself out of my body this time.

I might have stayed there for hours, if not for the whisper of the spirits stirring around me, as though to remind me that I couldn't stay here. Despite the power I'd harnessed, I didn't belong in this realm.

I belonged at home. With Vance.

Closing my eyes, I exhaled, and willed myself to leave Faerie.

The veil welcomed me into its embrace. Being disembodied shook away some of the symptoms of shock, but not all of them.

"Ivy Lane." A familiar transparent figure floated beside me. "Did you hear nothing of my warnings?"

"Sorry, Frank," I said to the necromancer. "I didn't have any other options."

"I explicitly told you not to bring any other humans through the veil. Instead, you brought a—"

"God," I finished. "I had to imprison it somewhere outside of our realm, so Faerie was the only option."

His eyes popped out, but I didn't care. After what I'd been through today already, Calder could stride past and I'd give him the middle finger. I was done. I just wanted to go home.

"You'd better have locked it up tightly," the necromancer finally said. "The whole of Death is stirred up thanks to the problems you've unleashed, Ivy Lane."

"I don't create problems, I solve them." I paused. "Okay, maybe a bit of both. Can I go?"

"You may, but you'll tell Lord Evander exactly what you

did. It's time the living necromancers accept what they're up against."

"I look forward to it." They couldn't do anything more to hurt me. Every time I went up against Faerie, it made me stronger, and putting a giant god to sleep had pretty much ensured I'd never be scared of a living person again. Lord Evander could suck it. "The veil will go back to normal, right?"

"If you're capable of leaving it alone for five minutes," said Frank.

"Can't make any promises." And I wouldn't. Recent events had been enough of a reminder that words held power, whether uttered by a human or faerie.

Death faded. Seconds later, I stood near the edge of the pit. My body ached like I'd gone one-to-one against a shifter at full power, and my shoulders burned, reminding me of the two heavy swords I carried. I needed a healing spell and a nap. I needed…

Vance. My heart lifted at the sight of him stalking towards me, though he didn't look happy. Oh, boy.

Vance didn't say a word. He just walked up to me and hugged me, arms wrapping around my shoulders. No claws or scales. The Ley Line was quiet. Still.

I said nothing. Just hugged him back.

Vance released me. "The beast. What did you do?"

"Sealed it in a prison in the Grey Vale. I'll tell you about it later, but we need to get this talisman somewhere safe before anyone realises what it is."

"The council can wait." His eyes narrowed as he took in the green-tinged sword in my hand. "Yes… that needs to be secured. I'll put it in our storeroom." In response to my raised eyebrow, he said, "I know undead attacked us at the doors, but it's not possible for anyone except a Mage Lord to enter the main chamber. It's the most secure place in the city."

Likely true, and I had to admit I'd rather not take the sword into the manor. I'd won its allegiance, but after the incident with the thorns, it'd be a while before I trusted anything Summer had touched.

"The others." I swallowed, remembering. "Wanda. Did she make it?"

"Drake told me she's alive."

I released a breath. "Thank god. It looked bad."

"We'll check on her once the talisman's sealed. I'd prefer that the shifters didn't see it."

"Good point." The shifters themselves had retreated, fleeing from the dragon, and the pair of us stood alone by the pit. "Let's go."

Vance transported us directly inside the mages' depository, where the Invocations and various other dangerous magical objects were sealed. I was all too happy to let go of the talisman when Vance took it from me, though his gaze lingered on the other sword in my hand.

"I can take care of this one." I hadn't had a chance to look closely at the details, but the edges were engraved with glyphs and so was the hilt. I couldn't read the meanings from a distance, but I had little doubt that if I wanted to speak another Invocation, the sword would oblige.

"Of course." Vance pressed a hand to the door, and a shimmering curtain folded over the air before it opened, recognising him.

I studied my new blade. "I suppose I should think of a name. I'll ask…" Crap. "Isabel."

I scrambled for my phone and skimmed through a dozen frantic messages from Isabel. The first: *George is missing, Ivy. What's happening?*

Ivy???

Are you alive???

You'd better call me, Ivy.

The last message said, *oh god I saw a dragon. Tell me you're not with it.*

I sent her a quick message: *I'm okay. George is, too. Are you?*

IVY. Tell me everything. I've had three phone calls telling me you and the mages were fighting that dragon but it's gone now. CALL ME.

I exhaled, leaning against the wall. *Wait at home. I'll tell you everything. Have to deal with something urgent first.*

"Isabel's okay," I called to Vance inside the room. "Where's George?"

"With his family." He left the chamber, the door sealing itself behind him. "We should head back."

In a flash, we landed next to the pit, where the cracked ground spread from the field all the way to Wyatt Colton's doorstep. The shifters were back, and at least fifty of them gathered around a small group of cloaked mages. Others were scattered throughout the field, and my heart plummeted at the sight of at least twenty unmoving bodies lined up in a row.

Vance swept towards a pale woman lying at the end of the row. "Wanda."

"She's alive." Drake crouched over her. Wanda was covered in blood, but her wounds had sealed, and I sagged in relief.

"Good," Vance said. "Take her back to the manor."

He moved to the next body, also a mage. They'd acted fast enough with healing spells to prevent any permanent damage, but the same couldn't be said for the shifters. I watched the mages carry away their injured, while Vance supervised, making sure everyone got the attention they needed.

"Three mages seriously injured," he muttered to himself.

"Sixteen shifter deaths, all caused by other shifters. No doubt they'll try to blame the mages either way."

"The two who attacked me…"

"Dead," said Vance. "Deservedly so."

"Yeah." The Lady was dead, too, and even that was of little comfort to me. Another battle had claimed lives and ruined others. "I hope she'll be okay. Wanda, I mean."

"So do I." Vance stood still, hands clenched at his sides. "I'm glad the shifter curse can't be passed on through biting. This isn't something anyone else should have to suffer."

"Are you… are you feeling okay?" He'd returned to normal, without a claw in sight, but the grimness in his expression told me he wouldn't forget the cost the shifters had paid for our victory. "Wait, did you say curse? You aren't cursed."

"You saw the creature that shares my blood," he said. "Some legends say the Sidhe unleashed it on humans as a punishment."

"Who says that? The mages?" I crossed my arms. "Please. If shifters are cursed, then so's every half-blood. Every faerie. Hell, even the necromancers. I mean, being able to see the dead is a curse in itself."

"There is that," he said. "Speaking of the latter…"

"I know." I heaved a sigh. "I need to talk to Lord Evander, but he'll start hosting parties in the crypt before he forgives me."

"Yes." His gaze travelled over the field. "In fact… I think he might have finally noticed the disturbance."

I squinted. Several cars belonging to the mages were parked at the field's edge, but nearby were a few smaller vehicles, and the individuals clustering around them certainly weren't mages. *Oh boy.*

"All right." I took a resigned step towards the newcomers. "Let's get this over with."

24

We were halfway to the necromancers when Vance was called away to intervene in an argument between the mages and the shifters, which left me with the pleasant task of explaining the day's events to Lord Evander. Throughout, his eyes remained glued to the sword in my hands, to the point where I wondered if he'd taken in a single word I'd said.

"I'd introduce you, but I haven't named her yet." I hefted the blade, waving farewell to my brief resolution to play nice with him. It was impossible to look at the short, scowling man in his faded suit and feel anything other than contempt.

His eyes narrowed. "I'd have thought your recent brushes with death would have taught you some humility."

"I trapped a god," I said. "This is as humble as I get, especially when I'm dealing with people who didn't lift a finger to help."

"You..." He trailed off. "I don't have to take a lecture from the person who nearly damaged the veil beyond repair."

"I'm not the person who woke up a god and set it loose in the city," I retaliated. "Forgive me for wanting to repair that damage. Even Lord Frank Sydney agreed with me. Remember him?"

Lord Evander's face paled. "What?"

"Frank. Your old buddy. We're friends. This isn't the first time he's helped me out while you looked the other way instead." *He also doesn't like you much.*

Hands shaking with fury, Lord Evander turned his back. "I won't listen to any more of this."

"You'll meet with us later," said Vance from behind me. "And we'll discuss the future of your arrangement with the Mage Guild."

"I won't be ordered—"

I pointed my sword at him. "Listen to me, if you won't listen to the Mage Lord. I'll remind you I recently locked a god up in a dungeon, and I'm not above taking *you* for a tour of the Vale if it gets you to shut the fuck up."

He flinched. I lowered the weapon and watched him slink away, fighting a smile. Damn, that was satisfying.

"He'd better keep his appointment," Vance muttered. "I suspect the necromancers had a hand in that god's burial."

"The *necromancers?*" I echoed. "What would give you that idea?"

"It used to be standard practise to use iron to bind the dead," he said. "The god wasn't dead, only sleeping, but the same rule applies."

"Whoa." Lord Evander *had* said the guild's headquarters was sealed in iron because of an old superstition, but had they truly once been involved with the Sidhe and their gods? How had they fallen so low in the centuries that had elapsed since?

"That's why I wanted to repair our arrangement with them," said Vance. "Lord Evander might be a fool, but his guild contains power we might need for our survival."

"Yeah," I murmured. "No kidding. Wow. What happened to them?"

"The invasion happened." A hint of bleakness entered his expression again. "I imagine we'll be grappling with the consequences for many years to come."

I figured he was referring to the battle, too. The shifters were livid that so many of their own had died, and while the mages had offered an apology for their own actions in the battle, it was plain that the shifters once again blamed the Mage Lords for not being able to prevent their kin from attacking one another. Others blamed the half-bloods, but Vance cut in and said they weren't at fault for what the Lady had done.

The necromancers hung around being creepy for a bit, then sloped off back to the guild. After the mages dispersed, Vance set his attention on his uncle. Wyatt had returned to the farmhouse with his wife and daughter, but they hadn't gone inside. With the giant hole on the doorstep, I suspected they'd have to find new accommodation, and I also suspected that Vance was the one who'd have to take on the responsibility.

"You." Wyatt watched our approach through narrowed grey eyes. "I warned you, and once again, you endangered my family."

"That's funny," I said. "I remember someone digging a hole in the ground while under the influence of a magical thorn, and it sure as hell wasn't Vance."

Wyatt's eyes swung around to my sword, which I hadn't sheathed yet. It was a handy way to end most arguments before they started. "I was being manipulated," he growled. "So was Anabel."

"Welcome to the club," I said. "All of us were manipulated. You're lucky to be alive."

"No thanks to you." He directed this at both Vance and me. "Your position as Mage Lord makes me a target."

"So does living on top of the Ley Line," I retaliated. "Word of advice: pick somewhere a little less unstable next time."

"I will *not* be driven from my home." His eyes flashed a dangerous grey colour, reminiscent of both Vance and of the beast that gave him his blood. I wondered if shouting an Invocation in his face would put *him* into an endless sleep.

"She's right," said Vance. "The Mage Guild would be happy to provide you with new accommodation in a location of your choosing, warded against faeries and all other dangers."

"I won't bow to the Mage Lords."

"We're trying to save your daughter's life," I said. "They targeted her, too, you selfish bastard. This isn't your choice to make."

Rita, who'd been silent the whole time, said, "We'll accept your offer."

Wyatt turned to her. "Absolutely not. It's my decision."

"Then you can stay behind." I gave him my sweetest smile, letting the tiniest bit of magic ignite the blade in my hands.

He managed not to flinch, I'd give him that.

"I'll choose where we live," he said through clenched teeth, and stalked off towards the farmhouse.

Vance shook his head. "The fool. He'll come around, grudgingly accept the offer, then blame us for something else in a month."

"Dickhead."

I turned away from the house and spied more shifters returning home. Henry and Disha were among them, George curled up in his mother's arms.

"Let me speak to them."

Henry's eyes narrowed at the Mage Lord, though Vance

stopped several feet back, allowing me to talk to them privately.

"Sorry." The word wasn't enough, and the glare that Disha shot me confirmed she would never forgive me for endangering her son.

"We're moving," said Henry. "I think it's best we don't live upstairs anymore."

"Oh. Okay." After that shifter's dead body had showed up on the lawn, that came as no surprise. "It's your choice."

"Are you mocking me?"

"Not in the slightest." I was too tired for that, but I also wanted to make it quite clear that I wouldn't allow the shifters to send any more threatening mobs to the half-faeries' doorstep. "Were you aware that the first shifters likely came from Faerie?"

"What?" Shock flashed across his face. "No."

"Well, they probably did," I amended. "Maybe pass that on to the others, in case anyone is considering stirring up trouble on half-blood territory again."

He took a step towards me, and a blue glare from my blade halted him in his steps. He cast a protective glance at his wife and son and then walked away without another word.

"Just wanted to make sure they didn't take any heat for what the Lady did," I muttered. "Though I guess the mages will take more of the blame, given that they were here."

"We offered compensation. That's all we can do," Vance said. "I notice Chieftain Taive hasn't deigned to show his face."

"Figures. We'll talk to him later." I gave an eye-roll. "He'll be thrilled to know I claimed two talismans."

"I bet," he said. "What will you do now?"

I shrugged. "Go home. Talk to Isabel. Figure out how

we're going to get new neighbours without mentioning the corpse on the lawn in our ad. Or that time a massive thorny bush materialised in the road. Or…"

"Or you could turn the upstairs flat into an office," said Vance. "For your freelance business."

"Where in hell would I get the cash to… no. Absolutely not." I gave him a pointed glare.

"Why not?"

"Because I owe you entirely too much already."

"You don't owe me anything," said Vance.

"Hello? You got me a job, you're the reason I'm not out on the streets…"

"You did most of it yourself. As well as saving the world as we know it." He half-smiled. "I'll let you think about it first."

"I'll see what the landlord says," I relented. "I'm not exactly a model tenant with *one* flat, let alone two. I haven't actually told him about the thorns yet."

"Speaking of which," said Vance, "is she dead for sure?"

"Positively dead," I said. "She was a pure faerie. No cheating death."

"Good." He leaned in and brushed his lips over mine. "Tonight, we'll have our date. And I can promise I won't bring roses."

I grinned. "No bloody roses."

———

"Impossible," said the Chief.

I'd been hearing that a lot lately.

"Nope." I lifted my sword, 'accidentally' brushing the front of his armoured coat. "This is the real deal. According to your rules, I'm equal to a Sidhe now."

"You're a human, and yet you have the audacity to make demands of me?" The Chief's staff hit the ground with a thump. We'd met in the forest near his home, and he'd taken to me a clearing that contained a wooden throne with the same level of authenticity as his staff. In other words, it looked as though he'd plucked a normal chair out of a rubbish heap and spruced it up a little.

"I'm not demanding anything except the right not to get attacked here in your territory," I said. "Also, it'd be nice if you listened to my warnings next time. The Lady was the villain. People died, a god nearly got loose in town, and once again, you ignored everything I told you."

His mouth opened and closed a couple of times.

"I'm not asking for compensation," I added. "But it'd be nice to have a little cooperation. If you get so much as a hint that anyone in your territory is working against humans in any way, or might be in league with the Grey Vale, report them immediately to me. Or to Vance. This isn't a game, Chief. It's the third time someone has tried to break the veil in the space of a month, and I refuse to let there be a fourth."

The Vale had stepped up its game. Yes, the Lady had acted alone, but she wasn't the first to set her sights on Earth and she wouldn't be the last. We needed every defence we could get. I didn't know the long-term consequences of that god's awakening either, but there were bound to be many. Both in the Vale and at home.

"Fine," he said. "There's no need to resort to threats."

"No threats, Chief," I said. "Just a reminder of who holds the power."

A flush darkened his face, but he said nothing, and I left the clearing without looking back.

Vance waited for me outside. "Ready?"

"As I'll ever be." We'd seen almost every supernatural in a

position of power in the city within the last day, and now only one was left on the list. "Let's go."

Lord Evander waited for us outside the necromancers' headquarters along with three other black-clad figures. One of them was Colby, who eyed me with visible terror in his expression. *Ah, now he recognises me.*

"You guys might want to consider adding some colour to your ensemble," I informed Lord Evander. "It's a little dull."

"Ivy Lane," he said. "You're permitted *one* meeting with the dead. Only one."

"One per week as necessary." I hoped I wouldn't need to come here *that* often, but undeniably, the best way to meet with Frank without wandering over the veil was to come directly to the necromancers. They'd permitted me to use their private outdoor crypt. Thoughtful of them.

The iron-bound door of the small mausoleum opened on a single square room. At first, its dark corners appeared empty, until the pinpricks of white candlelight brightened to reveal a summoning circle.

A transparent figure floated within the grey smoke rising within the candles. "Ivy. You came."

"Frank," I said. "I thought we should formally meet in front of your living counterpart."

Lord Evander glared at his predecessor. "You neglected to tell us of your previous encounters with Ivy, Lord Sydney."

"Because I rightly predicted you'd raise hell, figuratively speaking," said Frank. "Ivy might be an anomaly, but her ability grants her right of access to your guild, including all supplies. It's the law."

"Absolutely not," Lord Evander snapped. "I'd *never* let her create a summoning circle."

"As if I'd ever want to," I countered. "No thanks. I get enough creepy in my everyday life already. Now the introductions are out of the way, you can go. We have something important to discuss."

"If you're going to continue to come here to the guild, you will show me the proper respect."

"Leave, Evander," said Frank. "I will speak to Ivy myself."

With a final glare at me, the necromancers' leader stalked out of the mausoleum and left me alone with Frank.

"You, Ivy, are going to end up in trouble one of these days."

I arched an eyebrow at him. "Trouble? Me? Never." When he sighed, I ploughed on. "I have a question about that god. Was it originally the necromancers who bound it in iron, however long ago that was?"

"I cannot tell you," he said. "If it's true, it was far, far before my time—before the guild itself existed, in all likelihood."

"I thought so. People would have noticed a dragon buried under their feet." I was surprised the shifters hadn't, but then again, it had been buried on the Ley Line. They might live closer to its boundaries than was wise, but the Line hadn't always been as volatile as its current state. That, like most of our current problems, was due to the invasion. "Luring it into Faerie *didn't* damage the veil, did it? I couldn't think of any other way to deal with the issue."

"The veil is resilient, believe it or not. The beast caused a ripple, but not lasting damage."

"You were acting like the whole thing would come crashing down on our heads." Not that I blamed him, considering. "You mentioned the Grey Vale was originally created when the Sidhe exiled their gods… right?"

"Yes." His voice was quiet, his eyes bleak. "A long, long time ago. I cannot pretend to know the details of how, exactly, the Sidhe bound their gods, nor why the Vale was tied to our realm in the process."

"And the gods… were linked to the shifters," I said. "Right?"

His mouth pressed together. "Again, that's long before my time, and few records exist. That said, it's believed that the gods once passed back and forth between realms as they desired, and it's possible that there was some… intermingling."

Damn. "Gods and humans? Really?"

"It's no less likely than humans and Sidhe."

"No, but *they* only came here during the invasion."

"Navigating realms is hardly a new innovation," said Frank. "The necromancers are living proof, in a manner of speaking."

"Ha." He had a point. Maybe all the realms had once been closer, a very long time ago. "Question. If ghosts can wander through the veil into Faerie by accident, can they hide there to avoid moving on to the afterlife?"

"Conceivably? Yes. Likely… no. It's rare."

"As likely as a god waking up and taking flight?" Calder's warning lurked in my mind even now, and while I assumed that I would have already encountered his spirit if he'd slipped into the Vale, the knowledge that ghosts *could* thwart death was not a welcome one. "That's not reassuring."

"It isn't meant to be," he said. "Ivy, I have to underline the consequences of meddling with the veil. Every time you cross causes a ripple, and while what you did appears to have had no lasting effect, that doesn't mean you should make a habit of it."

"I'd be worried if someone made a habit of ferrying gods between realms." I shook my head. "And for the record, I have no intention of taking Vance anywhere near that place again either."

"Good," he said. "I shall let you know if there is anything

else worthy of your notice, and I'll do my best to keep you updated."

"Thanks," I said genuinely. "You know, I think you're the only supernatural associate I've spoken to who's actually been amenable."

"And I'm dead," said Frank.

"There might be hope for the living yet." Vance entered the room behind me, eyeing the necromancer. "So this is Lord Sydney."

"You're the Mage Lord," said Frank. "I see the resemblance. You're the spitting image of your grandfather."

Vance stilled. "You knew him."

"For a time." Frank's gaze slid past him. "I would prefer not to interact with my living counterpart, so I'll say goodbye now. I'm sure we'll speak again."

"Yeah," I said. "Thanks again."

The candles sputtered out and the smoke faded along with the ghost.

I turned to Vance. "I don't want to talk to Lord Evander again either. Let's go."

Vance took my hand, and we reappeared in front of my flat.

"I'm impressed. Five meetings and no arguments." His eyes gleamed with amusement.

"The huge glowing sword helps." I swivelled to the garden, spying a dishevelled and decidedly human figure hovering behind the new layer of tripwire spells, talking to Isabel. "That'd be the landlord. Care to help me explain we're converting upstairs into an office for dealing with supernatural problems?"

"I think you and your new sword will do fine on your own."

"Sure we will." I kissed him, then went to meet Isabel.

Once we had the landlord's permission, we'd begin

setting up our new office. I was pretty sure she'd already started drawing up floor plans and decorating schemes.

When they spotted me, I waved, the sunlight reflecting off the glowing sword in my hand. "I'm sure Isabel has already told you all about our plans to expand our business and purchase a new office," I called to the landlord. "So… what do you think?"

ABOUT THE AUTHOR

Emma is the New York Times and USA Today Bestselling author of the Changeling Chronicles urban fantasy series.

Emma spent her childhood creating imaginary worlds to compensate for a disappointingly average reality, so it was probably inevitable that she ended up writing fantasy novels. When she's not immersed in her own fictional universes, Emma can be found with her head in a book or wandering around the world in search of adventure.

Find out more about Emma's books at www. emmaladams.com.

www.ingramcontent.com/pod-product-compliance
Lightning Source LLC
Chambersburg PA
CBHW020748190726
48285CB00006B/1936